HIDDEN SPRIN... ...ES

— 3 —

MURDER Is NO ACCIDENT

A. H. GABHART

Revell

a division of Baker Publishing Group
Grand Rapids, Michigan

© 2017 by Ann H. Gabhart

Published by Revell
a division of Baker Publishing Group
P.O. Box 6287, Grand Rapids, MI 49516-6287
www.revellbooks.com

Printed in the United States of America

Library of Congress Cataloging-in-Publication Data
Names: Gabhart, Ann H., 1947– author.
Title: Murder is no accident / A.H. Gabhart.
Description: Grand Rapids, MI : Revell, a division of Baker Publishing Group,
    [2017] | Series: Hidden Springs mysteries ; #3
Identifiers: LCCN 2016047551| ISBN 9780800727109 (softcover) | ISBN
    9780800728595 (print on demand)
Subjects: | GSAFD: Christian fiction. | Mystery fiction.
Classification: LCC PS3607.A23 M876 2017 | DDC 813/.6—dc23
LC record available at https://lccn.loc.gov/2016047551

Scripture quotations are from the King James Version of the Bible.

Published in association with the Books & Such Literary Agency.

17 18 19 20 21 22 23   7 6 5 4 3 2 1

MURDER *Is*
NO ACCIDENT

Books by A. H. Gabhart

Murder at the Courthouse
Murder Comes by Mail
Murder Is No Accident

Books by Ann Gabhart

The Outsider
The Believer
The Seeker
The Blessed
The Gifted
The Innocent

Words Spoken True

Angel Sister
Small Town Girl
Love Comes Home

Christmas at Harmony Hill

THE HEART OF HOLLYHILL

Scent of Lilacs
Orchard of Hope
Summer of Joy

To my family, with love

1

When Maggie Greene heard a noise in the big old house below her, she sucked in her breath to listen. She couldn't get caught up in the tower room at Miss Fonda's house. That would not be good. It didn't matter that Miss Fonda had told Maggie she could come here whenever she wanted. The old lady's face had lit up when she remembered being fifteen like Maggie and hiding out here to write in her diary.

The tower room was the perfect place to write. But Maggie's mother wouldn't think Maggie had any business anywhere inside the house unless they were cleaning it for Miss Fonda. So Maggie kept her visits to the tower room a secret.

After Miss Fonda had to go to the Gentle Care Home, Maggie's mother did say Maggie could come feed Miss Fonda's calico cat, Miss Marble, who lived out in the garden shed. But the cat excuse wouldn't help if Maggie got caught inside the house. She'd be in trouble.

The thing was not to get caught. So she stayed very still and listened for what she'd heard. Or thought she heard. No sounds now. Old houses could creak and groan for no reason.

Maggie crept over to the window and felt better when

the circular drive down below was empty. She rubbed a spot clean on the glass with a corner of her sweater. No telling how long since these windows had been washed. The years of grime didn't let in much of the October sunshine.

She shivered and pulled her sweater tighter around her. But it wasn't a feeling-cold shiver. More that kind of shiver that made old-timey people like Miss Fonda say somebody must have walked over their grave.

As Maggie started to turn away from the window, a car did pull into the driveway. She took a step back, but she could still see the red-and-white sign shaped like a house on the car's door. She knew who drove that car. Geraldine Harper.

Everybody in Hidden Springs knew the realtor. They said she could talk a bulldog into selling his doghouse. Maggie had heard her sales pitch back when her parents had hoped to move out of the trailer park and buy a house. That was before Maggie's father lost his job. Since then, there wasn't any talk about new houses, just worries about paying the lot rent in the trailer park.

That didn't keep Mrs. Harper from calling about this or that perfect house. Calls that nearly always led to arguments between Maggie's parents. A couple of weeks ago the woman stopped by the trailer where Maggie's father told her in no uncertain terms to stop bothering them about houses. Mrs. Harper gave him back as good as she got and then kicked their little dog when he sidled up to her, his tail wagging friendly as anything.

She'd probably kick Miss Marble too if she spotted the cat, but maybe the cat would stay hidden. Like Maggie. If Mrs. Harper caught Maggie in Miss Fonda's house, things were going to be bad. Really bad. Surely Mrs. Harper wouldn't climb up to the tower room. She had on a skirt and shoes with a little heel. A woman had to dress for success, she'd told Maggie's class last year on career day. But she definitely wasn't dressed for climbing the rickety ladder up to the tower room.

All Maggie had to do was stay quiet. Very quiet. And hope the woman left soon. She needed to be home before her mother came in from her job at the Fast Serve. The "doing homework at the library" excuse didn't work past closing time.

The woman pulled her briefcase and purse out of the car and headed toward the front steps. She must have a key. Maggie couldn't believe Miss Fonda wanted to sell her house. She loved this house. She was always begging to go home whenever Maggie went to visit her.

Maggie couldn't see Mrs. Harper after she stepped up on the porch. She couldn't hear her either. The tower room was a long way from the front door.

But what about the back door? That was how Maggie had come in. If Mrs. Harper found it unlocked, she might blame Maggie's mother. Say she was careless. They might fire her mother.

Maggie's heart was already beating too hard before she heard somebody coming up the steps to the third floor. Too soon for Mrs. Harper. She would just be coming in the front hall where the grand staircase rose up to the second floor. But somebody was in the hall below. A board creaked. The one in front of the room that had the trap door to the tower. Maggie always stepped over it, but whoever was there now didn't.

Mrs. Harper must have heard the board creak too. Her voice came up the stairway. "Hello?"

Nobody answered. Certainly not Maggie. And not who-ever had just stepped on the squeaky floorboard. Maggie wasn't sure she could have answered if she'd wanted to. Her throat was too tight.

The door opened in the room below Maggie and something crashed to the floor. Probably the lamp on that table beside the door. It sounded like a bomb going off in the silent house.

"Who's there?" Mrs. Harper's feet pounded on the steps.

Maggie desperately hoped whoever it was wouldn't decide to hide in the tower room. Her heart banged against her ribs, and she put a hand over her mouth to keep her breathing from sounding so loud.

Relief rushed through her when the door creaked open and the floorboard squeaked again. Where earlier the steps had sounded furtive, now they were hurried. Mrs. Harper's heels clattered on the wooden stairs up to the third floor. Those steps were narrow and steep, nothing like the sweep-ing, broad staircase from the first to the second floor.

Maggie slipped over to the trapdoor into the tower and eased it up a few inches. She couldn't see anything, but maybe she could hear what was happening.

"What are you doing here?" Mrs. Harper's voice was stri-dent.

The other person must not have found a place to hide. Whoever it was mumbled something, but Maggie couldn't make out any words.

"Stealing is more like it." Mrs. Harper sounded angry. "I'll not let you get away with it."

Maggie did hear the other person then. Panicked sound-ing. Maybe a woman's voice. Maybe not. "I can explain."

"You can explain it to the sheriff."

"Wait!"

Mrs. Harper didn't wait. Her heels clicked purposely on the floorboards as she moved away. The other person rushed after her.

A shriek. Thumps. The whole upstairs seemed to shake as the bumps kept on. Then it was quiet. Too quiet.

Maggie lowered the trapdoor and scooted away from it. She waited. Down below, a door opened and shut. Not on the third floor. On the first floor. Somebody leaving the house. Maggie counted to one hundred slowly. Once. Twice. Everything was quiet. Maggie peeked out the window. Mrs. Harper's car sat in the same place in the driveway.

What if the woman was hurt? She might have fallen. Something had made all that noise. Maggie couldn't just stay hidden and not help her. It didn't matter whether she liked Mrs. Harper or not.

She took a deep breath and squeezed her hands into fists to keep her fingers from trembling.

You're fifteen, Maggie. Stop acting like a scared three-year-old.

The trapdoor creaked when she lifted it. Maggie froze for a few seconds, but nobody shouted. She put her foot on the first rung of the ladder, but then climbed back into the tower room to hide the notebook full of her stories. She'd never worried about that before, but nobody had ever come into the house while she was there until today.

She spotted a crack between the wallboards and stuck the notebook in it. When she turned it loose, it sank out of sight. Well hidden. With a big breath for courage, she climbed down into the room. She stood still. All she could hear was her own breathing.

With her foot, she scooted aside the broken lamp and went out into the hallway. She made sure to step over the squeaky board.

The silence pounded against her ears. She'd never been afraid in the house, even though people said it was haunted. People had died there. Miss Fonda told her that, but that didn't mean they were hanging around now. Maggie didn't believe in ghosts. She really didn't, but right that moment, she was having trouble being absolutely sure.

"Mrs. Harper, are you all right?" Her voice, not much more than a whisper, sounded loud in Maggie's ears. She shouldn't have said anything. If Mrs. Harper had followed the other person outside, Maggie might sneak out of the house without being seen.

A little hope took wing inside her as she reached the top of the stairs. Hope that sank as fast as it rose.

Mrs. Harper was on her back at the bottom of the steps. She wasn't moving. At all. Maggie grabbed the railing and half stumbled, half slid down to stoop by the woman.

"Mrs. Harper?" Again her voice was barely audible, but that didn't matter. The woman stared up at Maggie with fixed eyes.

Maggie had never seen a dead person out of a casket. She wanted to scream but that wouldn't help. Nothing was going to help.

She should tell somebody, but how? She didn't have a cell phone. Not with her family struggling to buy groceries. Maybe the other person did. The one who had chased after Mrs. Harper to keep her from calling the sheriff.

But that person must have walked past Mrs. Harper and on out the door without doing anything. Maybe worried like Maggie about getting in trouble. Afraid like Maggie.

Maggie stood up. It wasn't like she could do anything for Mrs. Harper. The woman was dead. A shiver shook through Maggie, and she rubbed her hands up and down her arms. She could leave and nobody would be the wiser.

A chill followed her down the stairs. Her feet got heavier with every step. Whether she got in trouble or not, she couldn't leave without telling somebody. When Maggie spotted the white cell phone in an outside pocket of Mrs. Harper's handbag at the bottom of the stairs, it seemed the perfect answer. She didn't even have to unzip anything. She gingerly picked it up and punched in 911. The beeps sounded deafening in the silent house.

"What's your emergency?"

The woman's voice made Maggie jump. She must have hit the speaker button. She didn't want to say anything. She thought they just came when you dialed 911.

The woman on the other end of the line repeated her question. "Respond if you can."

Maggie held the phone close to her mouth. "She can't. She's dead."

"Who's speaking? What's your location?" The woman sounded matter-of-fact, as though she heard about people being dead every day.

Maggie didn't answer. Instead she clicked the call off so she couldn't hear the questions. She started to put the phone down, but then she remembered those police shows on television. She pulled her sweater sleeve down to hold the phone while she wiped it off on her shirt. Her fingerprints were all over the house, but nobody would be suspicious of that since she helped her mother clean there. The 911 voice didn't have to know who Maggie was.

Maggie propped the phone against Mrs. Harper's purse. The police surely had ways of tracking cell phones, so they could find Mrs. Harper easy enough. But Maggie didn't want them to find her too.

She slipped through the house and outside. Her hands shook so much that she had to try three times to get the key in the slot to lock the back door.

When she turned away from the house and looked around, she didn't see anybody. Not even Miss Marble. She ran across the yard and ducked through the opening in the shrubs.

She didn't think about whether anybody saw her.

2

Michael Keane didn't know whether to be sorry or glad the old window in the sheriff's office was too dirty to let in the October sunshine. The thought of the sun on the lake down by his log house made him wish he was fishing instead of stuck at his desk doing paperwork.

Across the room, Betty Jean Atkins peered over her computer monitor at him. "If you'd learn to use a computer, you could do that faster."

"I know how to use a computer."

"Yeah. That's why there's dust on your keyboard." Betty Jean fastened her eyes back on her monitor, clicking the keys without a glance down. "Technology doesn't bite, you know."

"Somebody has to keep the ink pen factories going. Last I heard people weren't even writing checks anymore." Michael stared down at the form on his desk. "Looks like if that was true, we wouldn't have all these cold check reports."

"People without money are the ones still writing checks. Those cash cards block you out if you don't have money in your account." She shifted some papers on her desk. "You should take a computer class this winter. I'll get Uncle Al to pay the fee. Somebody besides me needs to be computer literate in here."

Sheriff Potter was Betty Jean's uncle, but related or not, she more than earned her salary keeping the office in order.

Michael didn't bother answering her as he looked at the sheriff's desk in the back of the room. "Where is the sheriff? I haven't seen him all day."

"He's on vacation, remember? He and Aunt Edna are taking a cruise to celebrate their anniversary. Thirty-five, I think. Or maybe thirty-six. Thirty something."

"I thought he was leaving on Monday." Michael frowned down at his desk calendar.

"Vacations can start on Friday if you're the boss." Betty Jean shrugged. "Hope that's not messing up any big date plans you had tonight. If so, romance will have to wait." She flashed a smile over at him.

Betty Jean was the one forever chasing romance, but it kept outrunning her. She was nice enough looking, with light brown eyes and curly hair she tried to keep from curling. She wasn't slim, but not exactly fat either. Plump fit her, but plump wasn't a word that would ever cross Michael's lips to describe her. She was continually going on this or that diet, but the extra pounds weren't what kept her from finding a fellow.

She was too picky, but when Michael told her that, she let him know in no uncertain terms she wasn't about to settle for any Tom, Dick, or Harry. She was holding out for a Prince Charming, like in those romance novels she read.

Michael shoved the finished report into a folder. "The

only big date I have is with some nightcrawlers and a few unwary fish."

She raised her eyebrows at him. "You better stay on the part of the lake where you get a signal on your radio then. In case something happens."

"Nothing's going to happen. This is Hidden Springs. Weekends take care of themselves."

"You wish."

He did wish that. While everything wasn't always peaceful in Hidden Springs, that's how Michael wanted it. He grew up in this little town. One of his ancestors actually founded the town, and now his aunt, Malinda Keane, was ready to stand at the town's figurative gateway to keep out anything or anybody threatening the small town.

Aunt Lindy said Hidden Springs didn't need box stores. They needed hometown businesses and people who took care of one another. So far Aunt Lindy was winning. Main Street still had a few stores, along with the lawyers' offices, the *Hidden Springs Gazette* office, and the Grill. In September a couple of newcomers had actually opened up shops on Main Street in hopes of pulling a few tourists into town from out on Eagle Lake. He didn't know how the new stores would make out when snow started flying and the tourists went home.

As if Betty Jean were reading his mind, she asked, "Have you stopped by that new tea shop? Waverly Tea and Books."

"I went in last week to meet the owner. Not exactly the kind of place you'd expect in Hidden Springs." Lana Waverly, with her sleek appearance and sophisticated air, came across as big city all the way. Not someone who would want to live in Hidden Springs.

"Cindy up at the Grill isn't happy about her opening up. That's for sure." Betty Jean clicked a few keys and the printer across from her desk began humming. "She let me know the Grill had tea. Decaf and regular. No need for any fancy tea shops on Main."

"Cindy doesn't have anything to worry about. Folks will still want her pie and coffee."

"Maybe so. But Lana Waverly has muffins along with her tea. The kind you put on a plate with a doily. And her plates aren't paper or plastic either. They're vintage china."

"Doilies? I thought those went out with the forties."

"Not at all." Betty Jean gave him a look as she got her letter off the printer. "Ladies like muffins on doilies. Makes eating them feel fancy. Not so fattening. Plus, Lana's a writer. That's why she plans to stock books along with serving tea."

"What's she write?"

"She's not published yet, but she wants to write mysteries. Like Agatha Christie."

"Sounds like she's aiming high." Michael put his archaic pens back in his desk drawer. Maybe he should ask this Waverly woman if she still used ink pens to write, like Agatha Christie, but then he'd once seen a photo of Agatha Christie with a typewriter. So maybe she eschewed pens even back then.

"What's wrong with aiming high?"

Betty Jean didn't expect an answer and he didn't give one. After working with her for almost three years, he had learned when to talk and when to listen. With Betty Jean, it was a lot of listening.

"If you're dreaming, you might as well dream for bestsellers." Betty Jean scanned her letter before she went on. "She plans to invite authors in for book signings. Eventually start a book club or a theater group. Bring a little culture to Hidden Springs."

"That couldn't hurt." He doubted Lana Waverly would make it through the winter before she searched out more fertile ground for culture. The other new business had more chance. Bygone Treasures billed its merchandise antiques, but some of it looked more like junk to Michael. The owner, Vernon Trent, claimed people liked finding diamonds in the rough in a place like his.

The man had hit up Aunt Lindy to sell some of her family heirlooms, but he was barking up the wrong tree there. She intended to pass along every bit of her Keane heritage to Michael as soon as he married and started up the next generation of Keanes.

The thought of Aunt Lindy's expectations brought Alex Sheridan to mind. The two of them danced back and forth but never found a song they both could agree on. She was a high-profile lawyer in Washington, DC. He was a small-time deputy sheriff in Hidden Springs. No halfway points for either of them. Lately they'd had some close encounters. But not close enough. She was back in Washington and he was still here in Hidden Springs.

To keep from thinking about the impossible, he teased Betty Jean a little. Vernon Trent was single and not bad looking in spite of a bit too much salesman polish for Michael. Ready to smile about anything. Still, the age range worked.

"I saw you going in Bygone Treasures yesterday. Find anything interesting?" Michael sat back in his chair and smiled at Betty Jean.

"I was looking for a butter dish. I broke mine." She dropped the letter on her desk, grabbed her coffee cup, and filled it at the coffeemaker behind her desk.

Michael was surprised by the color that flashed in her cheeks before she turned away. Obviously, Vernon Trent wasn't just any Tom, Dick, or Harry.

"He sell you anything? Hank says Vernon Trent could sell a comb to a bald man." Hank Leland, the editor of the local paper, had already run an article about Trent's new business.

"What's Hank know?" Betty Jean's voice was a little stiff.

"Why do I get the feeling you don't want to talk about Mr. Trent?"

"I have no idea what you mean." With her back to Michael, she stirred a packet of sweetener in her coffee and then opened another one to spill into her cup.

"I thought you liked your coffee black. No sugar."

"It's good to try something different now and again."

"Like shopping for a butter dish at an antique store?"

"Right." She turned to glare at him, her cheeks still pink. "Like doing something besides fishing all weekend."

"I like fishing," Michael said.

"And I like looking at antique dishes."

"And maybe the guy selling them?" Michael raised his eyebrows at Betty Jean.

The phone rang and Betty Jean grabbed it like a lifeline. Obviously the new antique dealer in town had caught her eye. Maybe Michael should check out Vernon Trent. Make sure this guy was on the up-and-up before Betty Jean got too involved.

"Sheriff's office." After she listened a moment, she spoke

in a calm voice as she shot a look over at Michael. "Yes, I understand, Mrs. Gibson. Don't worry. Michael will find her."

"Miss Fonda make an escape again?" Michael stood up.

"Again." Betty Jean put down the phone. "Poor old lady. She just wants to go home. Mrs. Gibson said she settled Miss Fonda in the sitting room in front of the television while she did some laundry. One of her other ladies promised to yell if she went for the door, but when she came back, Mrs. Stamper was asleep and Miss Fonda gone."

"At least it's not raining the way it was last time she made a run for it." Michael smoothed back his light brown hair to put on his hat.

"Some of these days she's going to forget the way to her house and no telling where she'll end up. Mrs. Gibson says her memory is going downhill fast."

Most of the time Miss Fonda was fine at Mrs. Gibson's, but now and again she decided to go home. So far the little woman had made the walk between the Gentle Care Home and her old house without problem. She avoided the road, so maybe her memory wasn't all bad. She generally cut through the graveyard between Mrs. Gibson's house and the Chandler mansion.

Heading home put a skip in her step as though she could forget her arthritis, the same as she could forget how old she was. As yet, the dementia hadn't stolen her long-ago memories, so she knew how to be her young self. It was the old woman she no longer knew.

The nearest to a relative Miss Fonda had was the wife of her late husband's brother. A widow herself, Ellen Elwood took care of Miss Fonda's business, but she was getting older too. Ellen had a son, but Miss Fonda didn't have much use for him. So Michael generally tracked down Miss Fonda himself.

She never gave him any trouble as long as he let her go on to the house and try the locked door. Then when she couldn't find a house key in her pocket, she would agree to climb in his cruiser to go back to Mrs. Gibson's to get her key.

Michael didn't know what he'd do if she ever sat down in one of the chairs on the porch to wait for her parents to show up. Once in the car, things seemed to clear up a little for her, and by the time she got back to the Gentle Care Home, she remembered living there. It helped that Mrs. Gibson always had a glass of tea and something sweet ready for her. Within five or ten minutes, Miss Fonda forgot she'd even made an escape.

But one of these days, she was going to trip on a root or a footstone in the graveyard. Or as Betty Jean said, finally forget the way and wander who knew where. Maybe into trouble.

After Michael passed the Gentle Care Home, he turned into the cemetery. He usually spotted the old lady before he made it back to the second gate, but not this time. Miss Fonda must have been gone longer than Mrs. Gibson thought or had gone a different way. Michael turned back out on the highway.

The Chandler house sat on a large lot beside the cemetery. Quiet neighbors, Miss Fonda said. Through the trees, Michael could see the tower room that rose above the roof of the old house and gave it a distinctive air.

The Chandlers made a fortune in distilling before Prohibition put them out of business in the thirties. The house was built long before that. And while they lost much of their wealth during the Great Depression, they somehow held on to the house. Perhaps by finding and cashing in some of the treasure reputed to be hidden in the house by a long-ago Chandler.

Miss Fonda laughed at the rumors. She told anyone who would listen that the Chandlers' treasure was simply the house.

Michael pulled up into the driveway. A car was already there. Geraldine Harper's. That didn't bode well. Sonny Elwood must have coerced his mother into letting Geraldine list the place for sale. If Miss Fonda found that out, she'd be devastated.

Michael's radio crackled as he stepped up on the wide porch. He keyed it on.

Betty Jean didn't waste words. "Dispatcher called. They got what might be a crank call from Geraldine Harper's phone. Said somebody was dead. You need to track Geraldine down and see what's going on after you take Miss Fonda back."

"That won't be hard. Geraldine Harper's car is here at Miss Fonda's house."

"What's she doing there?"

"What's Geraldine do? She sells houses."

"Not Miss Fonda's!" Betty Jean sounded concerned. "You can't let her do that."

"Not police business," Michael said, even though he felt the same way.

"I guess you're right. But a stolen cell phone is. Better check to see if Geraldine's lost hers."

The front door was ajar. When he rapped on it, the door creaked open. Nobody was in sight, but a purse and briefcase were on the floor at the bottom of the winding stairway.

Propped beside the purse, as though placed there with care, was a white cell phone.

"Are you still there, Michael?" Betty Jean's voice crackled through the radio.

"Something's not right here," Michael said.

"Not if Geraldine is selling Miss Fonda's house. That's not right for sure."

"Hold on." Michael pushed the off button. He needed to listen.

He called Miss Fonda's name. No answer. Then he tried Geraldine's name. Still nothing. He made a quick circle of the bottom floor. Everything was just as Miss Fonda must have left it the day Ellen packed her out to the Gentle Care Home. The last newspaper was still on the breakfast table. Nobody was there.

He went back to the wide staircase. He could imagine ladies sweeping down them in their fancy dresses to make a dramatic entrance.

"Miss Fonda, are you here?"

This time a keening sound answered him. Surely Geraldine Harper hadn't been so cruel as to tell Miss Fonda she was going to sell her house.

"Geraldine?" he called.

The keening sound got louder. Michael took the steps two at a time.

All the way at the end of the hall, Miss Fonda was crouched beside something. Not something. Someone. The cries were coming from the old lady. The other person made no sound at all.

Geraldine Harper lay in a tangle at the bottom of the narrow stairs leading to the third floor. One shoe was missing and her eyes stared up at nothing. Miss Fonda held Geraldine's hand up to her cheek as she rocked back and forth and wept.

"Miss Fonda." Michael touched her shoulder.

Miss Fonda finally seemed to hear him. The keening stopped as she looked up at Michael with sorrowful eyes. "It was him. She's dead because of him."

3

"Who?" Michael looked up the steep stairs. Nobody was there.

"Bradley." Miss Fonda's voice quavered. "And don't tell me I'm wrong."

Michael stooped down to take Geraldine's hand away from Miss Fonda. Not long dead. While Geraldine Harper wasn't his favorite person, it was sad seeing her broken like this.

"Everybody said she was so lucky to marry Bradley, but now look." She stroked Geraldine's arm. "Oh, dear Audrey. You should have never married him. Never."

"Audrey?" Michael frowned, then realized Miss Fonda's mind had wandered back to a different time. He needed to get her away from the body and her bad memories. He put his arm around her trembling shoulders. "Come on, dear."

"I can't leave her." Miss Fonda looked at him, her eyes vague.

Michael wondered who she might think he was. He hoped not the Bradley she was blaming for this Audrey's death.

"We've got to go tell someone." He hesitated but sometimes it was better to go along with Miss Fonda when her dementia confused her thinking. "About Audrey."

"If we must. We do need to find little Brad. Make sure he doesn't see this." Miss Fonda tried to stand up. A surprised look crossed her face. "I don't think I can get up."

"Here, let me help you." Michael lifted her up easily. Under her bulky sweater, she was a mere wisp of a woman.

He kept his arm around her and turned her away from the body. Her breathing sounded labored as Michael helped her down the stairs, but she wasn't crying now. At the bottom of the stairs, he dared a question. "Who's Audrey?"

She gave his arm a little shake. "What's the matter with you? You know Audrey. My sister." She said the last two words with extra emphasis. A frown deepened the wrinkles on her face.

"Audrey, of course." Miss Fonda obviously thought he was somebody who knew her at whatever age she had settled into. "Let's go get a drink. You're probably thirsty after your walk."

She gave him a puzzled look. "I am thirsty. But I don't think I've been for a walk, have I?"

Michael avoided answering. "Let's get that drink. Then I have to make some calls." He turned her away from Geraldine Harper's purse and bulging briefcase at the bottom of the stairs and guided her toward the kitchen.

"Telephones." Miss Fonda gave a disgusted snort. "I suppose they're all right in their place, but a person shouldn't have her ear forever attached to a telephone receiver like Audrey. Dear heavens, if she'd pay half that much attention to little Brad, he wouldn't need to be with me all the time. Not that I mind. Not one bit. I love him like he's my own." Another frown crossed her face. "I'm almost sure I need to tell him something, but I can't remember what. Do you know?"

"We'll figure it out after you rest a minute." Michael pulled a ladder-back chair out from the table.

"I am tired, but I can't imagine why. I haven't done a thing all day." Miss Fonda lowered herself down in the chair. She took a sip of the water Michael got for her. A smile crossed her face. "Little Brad is such a sweet child. Not at all like his father. Or Audrey either, as far as that goes. More like Father. Good-natured. And so curious about everything. That boy can ask a question a minute." Miss Fonda laughed. "I tell him he might be president some day."

"How old is he?"

"Nine." She looked around. "I can't imagine where he's got to."

"It's a school day, Miss Fonda." Past school time, but that wouldn't matter to Miss Fonda.

"Of course." She laughed a little. "How silly of me."

She seemed to have forgotten the body upstairs. That was good, but he couldn't forget it. Another unexpected Hidden Springs death. He kept his ears open for any sound that might indicate somebody else in the house. He couldn't put any dependence on what Miss Fonda said about another person there since she hadn't known it was Geraldine. But Geraldine had fallen down the stairs. And somebody else knew that, besides Miss Fonda. Somebody had called 911 on Geraldine's phone.

He needed to make sure that person or anyone else wasn't in the house now, but he couldn't leave Miss Fonda alone. She might wander away. And he couldn't leave Geraldine

Harper's body untended while he took Miss Fonda to the Gentle Care Home.

He moved behind Miss Fonda and called the office.

Betty Jean's voice exploded out of the phone. "Don't you turn me off like that before you let me know what's happened, Michael Keane. I was ready to hit the panic button."

"You don't have a panic button." Michael pressed the phone tight against his ear and kept his voice low. Miss Fonda didn't appear to hear him. In fact, her head drooped a little, as though she might be dozing off.

"With all that's happened lately, that's changing." Betty Jean pulled in a deep breath and blew it out in his ear. "So what's going on?"

"It wasn't a crank call. She is dead."

"Who? Miss Fonda?"

"No, Geraldine Harper. Looks like she fell down a flight of stairs."

"The Chandler mansion ghosts must have seen her realtor signs and pushed her." Betty Jean rushed on. "That's awful. I shouldn't have said that. Geraldine is really dead?"

"Broken neck, looks like."

"So who called?"

"I don't know. No sign of anybody here except Miss Fonda. And Geraldine's phone is propped beside her purse by the front door."

"Propped, as in somebody set it there?"

"Right."

"Maybe you better look around."

"Good thinking." Michael almost kept the sarcasm out of his voice. "Except I need to keep an eye on Miss Fonda."

29

"She okay?"

"Not really." Michael looked to be sure the old lady was asleep. "She found the body and thought Geraldine was her sister. She was distraught but looks like she's already forgotten now."

"I guess that's good. Funny how dementia works on people. Letting them remember things that happened back whenever, while they have no memory of things now. Aunt Sadie was like that before she died."

"So you think Miss Fonda might be remembering something that really happened?"

"Maybe." Betty Jean sounded thoughtful. "My mother used to talk about an accident there at that house a long time ago."

"We can dredge up that story later." Michael looked out the kitchen window where a calico cat streaked across the backyard. "Better concentrate on Geraldine right now."

"So what do you need?" Betty Jean's voice changed as she got down to business.

"Justin." That was the coroner. "Ellen to come get Miss Fonda."

Betty Jean interrupted him. "Ellen's in Phoenix visiting her daughter."

Michael let out a sigh. "Then I guess you better call Sonny." That wasn't going to make Miss Fonda happy, but what else could he do? The other deputy in the office might be an option, except it was almost time for school to let out. Nothing short of a national disaster could make Lester Stucker desert his post in front of Hidden Springs Elementary at school crossing time.

"You want me to ask him to send Felicia Peterson? She

sits with Miss Fonda sometimes, and I hear she and Sonny have been keeping company."

"She'd be better than Sonny. Maybe." Felicia Peterson was one of those people who never seemed to fit anywhere. Cindy hired her at the Grill but let her go when she gave up on Felicia ever getting an order right. Then Felicia worked at the drugstore until some pills went missing. They didn't have proof she was the culprit, but once she was gone, no more pills disappeared. Felicia seemed to stumble through life without ever tripping up completely.

She and Sonny Elwood would be a pair. But Michael couldn't worry about that. Not now. "Whoever. If you can't locate Sonny or Felicia, call Mrs. Gibson. Miss Fonda is her responsibility."

"I'll get somebody there pronto," Betty Jean said. "Anything else?"

"Yeah. Guess you'd better call Geraldine's family."

"I don't know of any family except her son." Betty Jean sounded doubtful. "He moved to Florida years ago."

"No nieces or nephews?" Didn't everybody in Hidden Springs have family here?

"None I know about. She moved here from Tennessee years ago after her husband died. Her son was a couple years ahead of me in school. He was cute in a nerdy kind of way."

"See if you can find his number and I'll call him later. And get that 911 call so we can listen to it. Maybe we'll recognize the voice."

"Sure, but I can't stay late today. It is Friday, you know, and I've got plans."

"A date?"

"You take care of business there and I'll take care of my business."

Betty Jean clicked off the line before Michael could ask if her business had anything to do with antiques. It didn't matter. He had his hands full without worrying about Vernon Trent and Betty Jean.

Miss Fonda's eyes flickered open and she smiled. Not her fretful smile, but her comfortable, old-lady smile. She was back in place, at least temporarily. "Michael. What are you doing here?"

Michael pushed an answering smile across his face. "I came with you for a visit to the home place. To make sure everything was okay."

She looked around. "And is it?"

"Looks like it, doesn't it?"

"I guess." She rubbed her hand over the tabletop. "Except the house feels so empty. Like everybody left and forgot to tell me where they went." Then she sighed. "And now I just have to wait. But they won't let me wait here, will they?"

"Mrs. Gibson is expecting you for dinner." Michael pulled another chair out and sat in front of her.

"Is she?" Miss Fonda sighed again. Then she brightened a bit. "Do you think she'll have pie?"

"She might. Something sweet anyway."

"I like sweets. Audrey tells me I'm going to get fat. She eats like a bird. So afraid of losing her figure." The puzzled look settled on Miss Fonda's face again. "Where is she? Isn't she here?"

"Not right now." Michael kept his smile easy.

"She's probably off in Eagleton at one of her social events.

That girl is always on the go. Guess I'd better be on the go too." She pushed down on the table to stand up.

Michael didn't try to stop her. By the time they walked outside, somebody might be there to get her. He took her arm. "Let me help you."

"Thank you." She patted his arm. "Such a nice young man."

The front door opened and Sonny Elwood called, "What's going on here?"

A tremble went through Miss Fonda. "Oh dear. He sounds angry. He won't like me being here. He never did."

4

"It's okay, Miss Fonda. You know Sonny. He's your nephew."

"Not mine." Miss Fonda's voice was low, almost fierce. "Gilbert may have to claim him, but I don't."

"Who called the sheriff?" Sonny demanded as he came toward the kitchen. His steps were loud on the hardwood floor. "It's nobody's business except ours if we want to sell this monstrosity. Fonda will never—"

He stopped in midsentence when he stepped into the kitchen and saw Miss Fonda. "Aunt Fonnie. Did Mrs. Gibson let you get away again?" He raised his voice and gave the old lady a supercilious smile.

"I am not deaf, young man." Miss Fonda stretched up to her full five foot height and glared at Sonny. "And my name is Fonda. Fonda Joyce Chandler Elwood."

Sonny's smile didn't change. "I know your name. The question is, do you know mine?" He flicked his glance over at Michael as if including him in on a joke.

Michael didn't smile. "Miss Fonda needs a ride back to Mrs. Gibson's."

He'd never liked Sonny much and right now he liked him

less by the minute. The man was all surface looks, from his blond hair combed back without a strand out of place to his button-down collars. No substance underneath. The man had to be well into his thirties and still living with his mother.

"Then why don't you take her?" Sonny's smile disappeared. "No need bothering me. You're the public servant."

"Didn't Betty Jean call you?"

"Betty Jean? No, but I do have an appointment to meet Geraldine here. She's doing an appraisal. Not that it's any of your business." Sonny looked down the hall toward the front door. "Where is Geraldine anyway?"

"Have we seen Geraldine?" Miss Fonda's puzzled look was back. "Maybe she went somewhere with Audrey."

Sonny blew out a disgusted breath and rolled his eyes. "Deliver me from crazy old women." His muttered words were loud enough for Miss Fonda to hear.

Michael considered forgetting about being that public servant and punching the man in the nose. But he restrained himself. "There have been some complications. After you take Miss Fonda back to Mrs. Gibson's, I'll explain it all to you. In detail." He'd like to tell the man some other things in detail.

Sonny folded his arms across his chest. "You take her. I've got an appointment with Geraldine Harper." He looked like a spoiled five-year-old.

"Geraldine isn't going to be able to keep that appointment. Not today. Not ever." Michael didn't want to talk about the woman being dead in front of Miss Fonda. Not and bring back her keening grief.

Right on cue, a knock sounded on the front door. Justin

Thatcher called back through the house. "Michael, are you in here? Where's the body?"

"Body?" The color drained from Sonny's face.

"I hope you've been paying the insurance premiums." Michael gave Sonny a hard look as he eased Miss Fonda past him toward the front door. "Come on, Miss Fonda. I'll walk you to the car."

"Geraldine?" Sonny said.

"There's been an accident." Michael looked over his shoulder at Sonny.

"It wasn't an accident." Miss Fonda's voice quavered. "I know that's what people said, but I know better."

"What's she talking about?" Sonny asked.

"Something that happened some other time, I think," Michael said.

"Everything's some other time with her." Sonny made a face. "But you can't pay attention to anything she says. She's always dreaming up things that never happened."

Miss Fonda's arm was rigid against Michael. "It did happen." She turned to point at Sonny. "He killed her."

Sonny held his hands up in front of him. His face flushed red. "Whoa, Aunt Fonnie. Don't be telling people I killed somebody. The deputy here might take you serious."

"Enough." Michael stared back at Sonny again and put authority in his voice. "Be quiet and do what needs to be done for once in your life."

"That's all I am doing. What needs to be done when somebody lives too long." Sonny stared toward Miss Fonda.

Duct tape. That was what Michael needed. A strip of the stuff over Sonny's mouth, but unfortunately he didn't have any. Or any way to make the man quit talking short of shooting him, and that wasn't exactly in the deputy guide book. Ignoring him was his only choice, especially with Miss Fonda visibly wilting after her burst of anger.

Justin was waiting in the entrance hall. "Betty Jean said it was Geraldine Harper. Can that be right?"

Instead of answering the coroner, Michael gave his head a slight shake. "Miss Fonda's tired. She's ready to head back to Mrs. Gibson's. She doesn't want to miss dinner."

Justin's expression changed at once as he stepped over to take Miss Fonda's free hand. "How are you doing, Miss Fonda? Well, I hope."

Some people said Justin only took such interest in the older folks in Hidden Springs because he was the town's undertaker, but there was nothing fake about Justin. His business might be funerals, but he was never in a hurry to perform that service for anyone. He grieved right along with the families. Justin was also the town's coroner, a position he'd threatened to quit more than once in the last year. But the little man was civic-minded. Somebody had to do the job. The same as somebody had to enforce the laws in their county. But this was surely nothing more than a tragic accident.

After they exchanged a few words, Michael guided Miss Fonda past Justin out onto the wide veranda porch.

A phone rang in the house behind them. A sound like church bells. Geraldine's phone. A call she'd never answer.

Miss Fonda stopped at the edge of the porch steps. "My goodness, are we having a party?"

The driveway was full of cars. Geraldine's. Michael's cruiser. Sonny's BMW. It wasn't new, but even so, how did the man manage that with his spotty work record? Then Justin had eased his hearse around Sonny's car to get nearer the door. The bushes in front of the porch would take a while to recover. If that wasn't already enough, Hank Leland's beat-up old van pulled into the driveway. The newspaper editor had a nose for anything happening in Hidden Springs. And four vehicles in Miss Fonda's driveway were sure to set off his newshound instincts.

Hank clambered out of the van and jogged up the driveway, his camera bouncing against his chest.

Maybe Michael could get Hank to take Miss Fonda back to the home. That way she wouldn't be subjected to Sonny. Then again, if Hank heard Miss Fonda talk about a man making somebody fall down a flight of stairs, who knew what story might show up in the *Hidden Springs Gazette*. Hank liked headlines that grabbed attention on the paper stands.

Michael would just as soon Hank had no news to report other than the latest fender bender or the high school football score. He wasn't looking forward to seeing the headlines in next week's issue.

"Mike." Hank's shirttail was out and he was panting by the time he got to the steps. Those extra slices of pie at the Hidden Springs Grill didn't help his waistline. He took a breath and smiled at Miss Fonda as Michael guided her down the steps. "Miss Fonda, it's good to see you. Really good."

He must have thought Miss Fonda was the reason for Justin's hearse. Hank raised his eyebrows at Michael. "What's happening?"

Miss Fonda answered, "It must be a party, but I am entirely too exhausted to dance. Is there somewhere I can sit down, dear boy?" She peered up at Michael.

"Right here in this car." Michael tried the BMW's passenger side door. It was locked. He pulled in a slow breath to keep from yelling as he turned back to Sonny. "Miss Fonda is ready to go, Sonny."

"I'm not going anywhere until you tell me what's going on." Sonny stood at the top of the porch steps, his arms crossed over his chest again.

Hank raised his camera and took a picture. Then he pulled his infamous little notebook out of his shirt pocket and licked the end of the stubby pencil stuck inside it. "Nephew refuses to help aged aunt." Hank muttered loud enough for Sonny to hear.

"All right, already." Sonny jerked his keys out of his pocket and hit the unlock button. He pointed toward Hank and stomped down the steps. "I better not see that in the paper or you'll be sorry."

Hank shrugged. "I just print the news."

Michael settled Miss Fonda in the front seat as quickly as possible and turned, ready to step between the men if necessary. But Sonny and Hank were both more apt to fight with words than fists.

Felicia Peterson came around the house before either of the men could fire the next salvo. Sonny spotted her first. "Felicia, what are you doing here?"

Felicia blinked and looked around as though for an escape. She was slight in build, the kind of person who stayed on the outer fringes of any group, as though unsure of her welcome. Her straight brown hair was pulled back from her face and her red lipstick stood out extra bright on her pale face.

"I-I," she stuttered. She slid her gaze past Michael and caught sight of Miss Fonda in the car. "I was looking for Miss Fonda. I went to visit and one of the ladies said she was gone."

"Where's your car?" Sonny frowned. "You never walk anywhere."

"I was worried about your aunt." Felicia narrowed her eyes on Sonny. "Thought somebody should be. So I walked across the cemetery the way she usually goes."

If the two of them were keeping company the way Betty Jean claimed, they weren't showing much affection now. But couples didn't always "honey" and "dear" each other in public.

"Well, you're just in time." Sonny held out his keys. "You can drive her back to the home. And don't pay attention to anything she tells you. It's time you figured out you can't trust anything she says."

"You want me to take your BMW?" Felicia's hand trembled as she reached for the keys.

"Try not to drive like an idiot." Sonny didn't even pretend to be nice. "I told you I had to meet Geraldine this afternoon, but seems there's been some kind of accident."

"An-an accident?" Felicia's stutter came back. "Wha-what kind of accident?"

"You'll have to ask Michael that." Both of them turned toward Michael.

At the word "accident," Hank looked up from fiddling with his camera, news antennae raised. Justin settled down in a wicker chair on the veranda. He never got in a hurry. As he was wont to say, his clients weren't going anywhere.

Michael tried to take care of business in a professional manner in Hidden Springs, but somehow everything had a way of getting turned into a circus. Sometimes he thought ringmaster might better describe his job than deputy. But even as a ringmaster, he wasn't doing a very good job of keeping the show moving.

"Sonny can fill you in later. We don't want Miss Fonda to miss her dinner." He gave Miss Fonda one last smile, then shut the door, closing her in the car. He motioned Felicia toward the driver's side.

"Has something happened?" Her voice quavered as she looked toward Justin on the porch. "Something bad?"

Michael put his hand under her elbow and guided her around the car. He kept his voice low. "Geraldine fell down some stairs."

"Stairs," Felicia echoed Michael as she stared toward the house. "Is she, you know, okay?" She whispered the last word.

"I'm afraid not, but I'd rather you didn't talk about it to Miss Fonda. She was very upset when I got here." Michael opened the driver's side door for Felicia. "Something about it all brought up bad memories for her."

Felicia's eyes popped open even wider. That didn't make her prettier. Instead she looked the picture of an orphaned waif. "You mean she saw whatever happened?" Her voice sounded shaky again.

"Hard to know with Miss Fonda," Michael said.

"Yeah. Poor thing. She can't remember two minutes ago. She gets everything all mixed up." Felicia gave Michael a weak smile and slid into the car. "Don't worry. I'll take care of her."

She started the car and backed up with a jerk. Michael scrambled out of the way as she swerved off the driveway and around his and Geraldine's cars. When she scraped the side of the car against a forsythia bush, Sonny shouted.

Felicia gave no sign of hearing him. Instead, she gunned the car back up onto the driveway and out on the street without slowing down. A man in a pickup truck slammed on his brakes and blew his horn. Felicia waved and stepped on the gas. Sonny looked ready to faint.

"Remind me not to ask Felicia for a ride." Hank moved over next to Michael. "She seemed in an awful hurry to get away from here. You think it was us? Or him?" Hank nodded his head toward Sonny, who ran out on the driveway to watch Felicia's progress down the street.

"Who knows? At least I did fasten Miss Fonda's seatbelt."

"So what's this about Geraldine Harper? You say she fell? In there?" Hank pulled out his notebook again and nodded toward the Chandler house.

"She fell. In there." Michael headed toward the veranda steps.

Hank trailed along with him. "She hurt? Shouldn't you call an ambulance?"

"No ambulance needed. Justin will have to handle this one."

Hank stopped scribbling in his notebook. "She's dead?"

"She's sold her last house. You'll have to wait out here." Michael put his hand up to stop Hank from following him up the steps. He looked over at Sonny muttering under his breath as he headed toward the steps. "You too, Sonny."

"You can't keep me out of my own house," Sonny said.

"Your house?" Michael peered at him.

"Well, it will be when Aunt Fonnie passes."

"You'll stay right here until I say you can come in." Michael took his radio out and punched in the code for backup. Lester would be through at the school by now, and he could guard the door and give Michael the time he needed to check out the house. "Justin, stand here and don't let anybody in. Lester can take over for you when he gets here."

"If you say so, Michael." Justin took up a reluctant post by the door. "But it would be good to get on with it."

"I need a few minutes to check out the house."

"You're acting like this is a crime scene, Michael." Hank looked up from his notebook. "You suspect foul play?"

"I don't suspect anything. Just need to make a routine investigation."

Michael stepped into the house. The flash of emergency lights caught his eye out on the road. Lester took every opportunity to use his lights. At least his siren wasn't screaming too. Michael shut the door and resisted the urge to turn the lock.

5

The thick wooden door muted Sonny's protests. Inside the hall with Geraldine Harper's bags at the bottom of the stairs to indicate why he was there, the silence seemed to grow and surround him. It was too easy to imagine all the Chandlers from the past arrayed up and down the stairway. Watching him. Keeping their secrets.

Michael wasn't looking for secrets from the past, although Miss Fonda's words about her sister had tickled his curiosity. But she hadn't been talking about Geraldine Harper. Geraldine was who lay dead upstairs today. And it didn't matter that he had no idea what he was looking for or expected to find. He just wanted to make sure nothing was out of the ordinary.

Not that it wasn't already out of the ordinary. An untimely death like this was shocking. Tragic. Sorrowful. But never ordinary. And this one had some added oddities. Someone had seen Geraldine's body, had perhaps watched her fall, and then called to report it with the woman's own phone before propping that phone beside the dead woman's purse and disappearing. Had that person seen Miss Fonda come into the house? Had Miss Fonda seen whoever it was?

Questions without answers. His job was to find answers. So, whether those outside liked it or not, he had to check out the house. Without interference. Justin Thatcher might be a mild-mannered man, but given a task, he did it. Lester too. The blue lights of his patrol car bounced against the front windows. He started to radio Lester to kill the lights, but then again, maybe those flashing lights would keep Sonny in his place. Make him realize this was police business.

The back door was locked. He tested it. No windows were open or broken. The hardwood floors didn't show any dusty footprints. He swiped his finger on the table in the front room. Very little dust anywhere.

Upstairs, things were the same. Geraldine Harper at the bottom of the stairs. Her legs askew, with one stocking-covered foot stuck out toward him. Poor woman wouldn't like being so disheveled. Geraldine always looked ready to conquer the day. She wore her tailored suits like a uniform. The colors might vary, but the style rarely did. Her one feminine touch was a scarf precisely arranged around her neck. This day her suit was navy. A dark red scarf drifted across the floor beside her like a trail of blood.

Michael gingerly stepped over her body to the narrow stairs. He found Geraldine's missing shoe halfway up the steps.

The third-floor hallway was not large and airy like the halls on the bottom two floors. The ceilings here were only seven foot instead of twelve, and the narrow hallway was dim with no outside light. He flipped on the light switch and moved down the hall, checking each room. A floorboard creaked in front of the last room. Nothing unusual about creaking boards in a house this old. The unusual thing was how the rooms all seemed frozen in time. Waiting for something. Or someone.

The same way Aunt Lindy said the Keane house was waiting for him. Once he married. Somehow, thinking about that made the Chandler ghosts more real. He knew about the shadows of ancestors past.

When he stepped into this last room, a bit of glass crunched underfoot. A broken lamp. Broken today? Or weeks ago? Impossible to know, but no one had cleaned up the glass. It was simply pushed into a pile away from the door. Perhaps by Geraldine. She could have opened the door and knocked the lamp off the table that wobbled when he touched it. Then something, perhaps her phone ringing, could have sent her rushing down the stairs. A slip and a stumble on those steps and that was a call she never answered.

He could check her phone to test that theory, but Geraldine went full steam ahead all the time. She wouldn't have wanted to miss a potential sale if she forgot to carry her phone upstairs with her. That would be unusual for Geraldine. Her phone was generally plastered against her ear, but she could have forgotten to put the phone in her pocket while she looked over the house. Unless the other person took the phone downstairs to leave by Geraldine's purse.

That other person. What was sometimes called a person of interest in an investigation. A talk with whoever that was might clear up a lot of questions. But so far Michael had found no clues as to who that person of interest might be.

This room was small, like the others on this floor. Barely room for the rickety table, a four-drawer chest, a chair, and a black iron bed. The bed's plain blue spread was rumpled where one of the pillows was missing.

A shiver surprised him. The air in here was cooler than the rest of the house. A ghost, Betty Jean would say. She watched those ghost hunter shows on television where a burst of cooler air supposedly proved a ghost nearby. He wasn't concerned with ghosts, in spite of his earlier imaginings or the stories about the Chandler mansion being haunted.

People liked to imagine ghosts. Passersby sometimes claimed a woman stared out the upper windows or they saw smoke coming out of the old chimneys that hadn't been in use for decades. The storytellers would have new grist for their ghost story mills now.

Michael pulled the lace curtains back to check for an open or broken window. Everything intact. Nobody was likely to attempt to climb out these windows. It was a long way to the ground and the near-vertical tile roof would be almost impossible to navigate.

The cooler air must be coming from the tower room. Of course, that was where people claimed to spot the ghost too. A small octagonal room rose above the roofline like a turret on a castle.

He'd checked everywhere else. No need leaving this stone unturned. Slats nailed to the wall made a ladder up to a trap-door. Some of the steps gave a little under Michael's weight, but they didn't break away from the wall. He pushed open the trapdoor and stepped up higher to peer into the small room. No one there, but the missing pillow was next to a wooden box against the back wall.

Michael pulled himself up into the room and stepped with care on the old flooring. It took him a minute to realize what bothered him about the room. No cobwebs. No dust on the box. And there on one of the windowpanes was a spot someone had wiped clean to peer out. But who?

For a moment, he stood perfectly still in the middle of the room, as though expecting the walls to whisper an answer. But the walls kept their secrets.

Michael peered out the window. The clean spot was well below his eye level. So that ruled out Geraldine Harper. She didn't lack much being as tall as Michael. She wouldn't have climbed up into the tower room anyway and certainly wouldn't have carried a pillow up here to sit awhile. Geraldine rarely sat awhile anywhere.

A few new cars had joined the others in the driveway. Sonny's BMW wasn't one of them. Up here with little insulation, it was easier to hear the complaints rising from the men on the porch. Michael couldn't make out words, but the mood was easy to guess.

Time to quit hunting answers that might not even matter and take care of Geraldine's body. The person using the tower room surely had nothing to do with Geraldine's death. Unless. Whoever it was could have startled Geraldine. Made her fall.

He would have to ferret out the person who made the nest here to question them, but for now, it would stay routine. No need worrying what had to be an accident into something worse. Miss Fonda's words about somebody causing it were hardly reason to be suspicious. Not in her current state of health.

After climbing down the plank ladder, he settled the trapdoor back into place. Then he wasted no time heading back to the steps. The stairwell was dark. The bulb in the light above the stairs must need replacing. Geraldine might have missed a step and not been able to catch the railing nailed to the wall. She could have lost her footing. Perhaps her long scarf had come undone and tripped her up.

A few minutes later, that was what Justin decided when he examined the body. Steep stairs. Slick-soled shoes with two-inch heels. A trailing scarf. A woman perhaps going too fast. A woman who had hurried to her death. A regrettable accident. But an accident.

Why would it be anything else? Geraldine Harper might not have been the most popular person in Hidden Springs, but nobody had any reason to want her dead. Certainly not Sonny Elwood, the one person who knew for sure Geraldine would be at the Chandler house. He wanted her to sell the house.

Sonny had followed them upstairs after Michael let Justin in. Michael couldn't think of a reason to keep him out. It might not be Sonny's house, but he was the one handling Miss Fonda's business in the absence of his mother. Somebody died in that house. Insurance could be involved.

"I can't believe this," Sonny muttered when he saw Geraldine. His face went so white that Michael jerked a chair out of one of the rooms for Sonny to sit. The man sank down in it and held his head in his hands. "This can't be happening."

"But it did. Accidents happen all the time." Justin looked up from the clipboard he was writing on.

"She should have waited until I got here to come upstairs. It wasn't professional of her to be looking over the house without me with her, was it?"

"She must have had a key," Michael said.

"I did give her a key, but I didn't think she would fall down the steps and break her neck. Is that what happened?" Sonny raised his head to peek over at the body. "A broken neck?"

"Appears so," Justin said. "Or perhaps a blow to the head. Certain medications make falls extremely dangerous and more apt to be fatal."

"Was she taking that kind of medicine?" Sonny sounded hopeful. "That would keep her family from suing, wouldn't it?"

"I am not privy to Mrs. Harper's medications." Justin's voice was stiff. Sonny had obviously strained even Justin's vast supply of patience.

"But it's your job to find that out, isn't it?" Sonny insisted. "Things like that have to be determined. Cause of death and all. You can't overlook those possibilities."

"No, indeed. I will make a full report." Justin took a couple of photographs with his phone.

"Why are you taking pictures?" Sonny asked. "You aren't going to give them to Leland, are you? He'll have a field day with this."

"The photos are for my report." Justin didn't look around at Sonny. Instead he gave the stair railing a little shake. "This appears to be a bit loose. Perhaps a contributing factor."

"Loose? That could be a liability claim." With a groan, Sonny dropped his face down into his hands again.

"Anybody else have a key to the house?" Michael asked. "Felicia maybe?"

"Why would Felicia have a key to the house?" Sonny looked up with a frown.

"I don't know. You tell me."

"I haven't given her a key," Sonny said.

"So you and your mother are the only ones with keys."

Sonny licked his lips. "Aunt Fonnie still has a key. It's in her purse at the home. Mother said it wouldn't hurt anything to let her keep it. It's not like she can remember to bring it with her when she makes a run for it from Mrs. Gibson's."

"She was in the house when I got here. Had already found Geraldine's body."

"You wouldn't have thought she could have climbed all those stairs," Justin said. "Or would have wanted to. Doesn't she normally just sit down and wait for someone to take her back to the home?"

"When the door is locked. Sonny's right about her not remembering to bring her key. The door wasn't locked today." Michael shrugged a little. "Who knows why she came up the steps. But when she saw the body, she thought it was her sister, Audrey."

"I told you that you can't pay attention to anything Aunt Fonnie says, Deputy. The dementia makes her touched in the head." Sonny made a little circle with his finger next to his temple.

"Do you know anything about her sister?" Michael asked.

"I don't see what she has to do with anything. She died years ago," Sonny said.

"I remember her." Justin spoke up. "I wasn't coroner when she died, but I had started working with Mr. Fields, who had the funeral home before me. She died here in the house. An accidental fall."

"These stairs?" Michael asked.

"Not sure about that. It's been a long time ago. Let me see. That would have been around 1980. But I do remember Miss Fonda being beside herself with grief. The only person who could console her at all was Audrey's son, Brad. He was about nine at the time, as best I remember, but a brave little guy, considering everything."

"What happened to him?" Michael asked.

"What difference does any of this make?" Sonny stood up, his voice rising. "It isn't Audrey there now. It's Geraldine Harper." He pointed at the body.

Justin gave Sonny a cool look. "A little history of the house might be something you need to hear." Justin turned back to Michael. "Audrey's husband was Bradley Carlson. After Audrey died, he took little Brad and moved back to Indiana. He was from somewhere up there. He ended up serving as a representative in Congress. Not sure if he still is or not. Haven't heard anything about him for a while."

"Didn't he ever bring the boy back to visit or anything?"

"Not as far as I know. He might have thought the memories would be too distressing for the child. But Miss Fonda doted on little Brad. Broke her heart when his father took him away." Justin shook his head. "She never had much good to say about Bradley even before Audrey's accident."

"An unlucky house." Michael stared over at Geraldine's body, now draped with a black plastic cover Justin had in his bag.

"It's just a house," Sonny said. "So can we stick to the here and now? And not dwell on ancient history."

"Not exactly ancient history." Justin looked like he wouldn't mind having some of that duct tape Michael had wished for earlier as he peered over at Sonny. "But back to business. I'll get my gurney, but we'll have to carry her down the stairs on a stretcher. I'll need help."

Sonny held his hands up and backed against the wall. "Don't look at me. Not my job."

Michael let out a sigh. "Some of these days you're going to have to hire an assistant, Justin."

"You want the job?" The corners of Justin's lips turned up. "Pay's not too good, but your clients don't put up any fuss. There can be some bothersome background noise at times, though." He picked up his bag and headed for the stairs.

Sonny watched him disappear down the stairs. "A man has to have something wrong with him to be a funeral director."

"Justin's good at his job."

"Good at fixing up dead people." Sonny's turned his back to the body and shivered. "Creepy, is what I say."

Michael didn't bother responding.

"If we're through here, I need to find out if Felicia brought my car back in one piece. I can't believe she pulled out right in front of that truck. Last time she gets my keys."

Keys made Michael remember his question about the house keys. "Just one more thing, Sonny. You say you have a key. Your mother has a key and Miss Fonda has a key. So did you give Geraldine your key?"

"Mother left her key with me. That's the one I gave Geraldine, but I don't see what it matters how many keys I have. You can take a key to Jim's Hardware and get a dozen copies made if you want to."

"Have you done that? Had more keys made?"

"Not for the front door. I did for the back door after we took Aunt Fonnie to the home. We couldn't find any extra keys for it, and I had to give one to Mary Greene. She cleans the place once a month." Sonny stared at Michael. "Why do you keep asking about keys?"

"Somebody called to report the accident. They used

Geraldine's phone. Makes me think somebody was in the house when Geraldine got here."

"You think somebody broke in to steal something?" Sonny frowned.

"Hard to say. I didn't see any sign of forcible entry. You notice anything missing?"

"How would anybody know, with all the stuff in here?" Sonny looked around, but there was nothing in the hallway. "This place is the next thing to a museum. Or junk warehouse."

"Maybe your mother would know when she gets home."

"Who knows when that will be? She's out there enjoying the Arizona sun while I'm left here holding the bag with Aunt Fonnie." Sonny edged away from Michael toward the stairs.

Downstairs Justin's gurney banged against the door and then rolled to the bottom of the stairs. Sonny stepped a little closer to the stairs, obviously anxious to be gone before the body was loaded on the stretcher.

Michael gave up on getting any more answers from Sonny. "If you do notice anything gone, you can let me know."

"I'm still selling the place." Sonny looked back at Michael from the top of the stairs. "There are other real estate people. The ghosts can't kill them all off."

Michael didn't know if Sonny was being serious or not. But the man did turn and run down the steps as though some of those ghosts might be after him. A corpse could make a person jumpy. But it would be better if Michael didn't jump to conclusions. More than likely, Justin was right. Geraldine tripped on the stairs. Nothing more. Even if someone was in the house when she got here, that didn't mean the woman's fall wasn't still an accident. Or Audrey's death years ago either. The authorities would have investigated her death and must have declared it an accident too. Miss Fonda saying somebody caused it didn't change that. Sonny was right that nothing she said now could be considered fact without corroboration from other sources.

Whether Geraldine's death was something Michael could tie up in a neat package didn't really matter. Life was often messy. So was death.

6

The coffeepot was off and Betty Jean was on her feet, keys in hand, when Michael got back to the office. A look of relief flashed across her face as she dropped the keys down into her purple-and-pink purse. "Good. You can lock up."

Michael glanced at the big clock over the door. Seven minutes before five. "Out the door a little early, aren't you?"

"I'm not out the door. Just ready to be out the door, but now that you're here, the world won't come to an end if I leave a few minutes early. I put in plenty of extra time." She glared at him as though daring him to deny that. "Plenty of it."

Michael held up his hands in surrender. "Can't argue that."

Mollified, Betty Jean nodded toward his desk. "Your messages are under your stapler."

"Anything important?" Michael moved over to his desk but didn't pick up the notes.

"Miss Keane wants you to stop by her house before you go home." Betty Jean clicked off her computer monitor. "Why don't you tell your aunt to use your cell number?"

"I have told her that. Many times, but she has a thing against cell phones. Says we got by before everybody had a phone in their pocket, and barring an emergency, there's absolutely no reason for the things." Michael leaned against his desk. "Besides, she likes to talk to you. She says you are always in the know about what's going on around Hidden Springs."

"What is going on?" Betty Jean frowned and zipped up her purse. "I can't believe that Geraldine is really dead. I just saw her out in the hallway yesterday. Said she had the perfect house for me if I was thinking about getting married. I don't know where she got that idea." She fiddled with her purse strap and settled it over her shoulder.

"You're always thinking about getting married." And from the way she was acting like somebody had put itch powder down her collar, it appeared she had a groom candidate in her sights.

"Thinking about something is different than doing it. You don't see a diamond on my finger, do you?" Betty Jean held up her left hand to show no rings. "But what happened to Geraldine?"

"Looks like she fell down the stairs. Broke her neck or hit her head. Maybe both."

"Looks like. What do you mean, looks like?" Betty Jean's frown grew darker. "Did she fall down the steps or not?"

"I think we can safely assume she fell down the stairs. Not much doubt of that. The ones up to the top floor in the Chandler house."

"Those are steep. I've been in that house. We visited Miss Fonda some when I was a little girl. Beautiful old place. I used to dream about getting married there and gliding down that lovely stairway with the train of my wedding dress spilling out behind me. Not those top-floor stairs, but the broad curving ones down from the second floor to the entrance hall." Betty Jean sighed. "What fantasies!"

"You might still have a chance. Sonny claims he's selling the place, come what may. Maybe a handsome stranger will buy it. A handsome, single stranger."

"Yeah, and no doubt he'll be up in that tower room and just happen to see me walk by and fall madly in love with me." Betty Jean laughed.

"A fairy-tale romance." Michael went around his desk to sit down. "Did you ever go up into the tower room?"

"No. I wanted to like everything, but Mom would never let me ask Miss Fonda if I could." Betty Jean straightened her desk pad and picked up a stray paper clip to drop in her magnetic holder.

"I went up there today."

"Why?" Betty Jean looked over at him.

"To make sure nobody was there."

"You thought somebody was in the tower room?" Betty Jean raised her eyebrows with the question.

"I didn't know. Wanted to make sure." Michael's chair squeaked when he leaned back.

"Was there?"

"Not then, but somebody has been up there. Recently."

"You mean like today? When Geraldine fell?"

"Could be. Somebody called 911. Did you download the recording of the call?"

"It's on your computer." When Michael frowned at his monitor, Betty Jean shook her head at him. "It's not complicated. Just click on it." She took a quick look at the clock.

"I can't stay and pull it up for you. I need to get going." She grabbed her sweater off her desk chair and started for the door.

"Sure." Michael didn't argue, even though if he figured out how to pull up the call, it would be a minor miracle. "Did you recognize the voice?"

She stopped and shook her head. "The person only spoke four words when the dispatcher asked for a response. 'She can't. She's dead.' Sounded young and scared. Probably female, but the words were sort of whispered, so not positive about that. Could be a young boy." She pointed toward his computer. "Listen to it. You work with some of the kids at church. You might recognize the voice. Or play it for Miss Keane. She might know if it's one of the kids in her classes out at the high school." She shrugged her purse strap higher up on her shoulder. "Like I said, I'd stay and help you with it, but I'm meeting someone."

"Go." Michael waved her toward the door. "If I can't get it to work, it can wait until Monday. It's not like this is a murder investigation."

"Don't even say that word." Betty Jean shuddered. "Accident is bad enough."

"Accident? Somebody have an accident?" Vernon Trent poked his head in the door. "I hope not you, Betty Jean."

Betty Jean's face flashed pink. "Oh hello, Vernon."

"I know you said you'd meet me out front, but I thought I'd pop in to see if you were ready to go." He flashed a broad smile. "Hope that was all right."

"Of course." Betty Jean's answering smile was a little strained, and she looked like that itch powder was working on her again. A double portion this time.

Michael studied him as he stepped past Betty Jean into the office. A nice-enough-looking guy. Not a big man, only a little taller than Betty Jean, but one of those fellows who packed a lot of punch on his compact frame. He looked like a weightlifter, but it could be the antique furniture he moved around served as weights for the man. His dark hair, sprinkled with some gray around his temples, was cut short. Army-recruit style. He had the wide smile of a salesman or maybe a politician.

Michael stood up and leaned across the desk to shake Vernon's hand. "You two going out for dinner?"

Betty Jean gave Michael a look almost sharp enough to draw blood. It wasn't like Betty Jean to be so nervous about her romantic possibilities. But then, he wasn't sure she'd had any actual dates since he'd been back in Hidden Springs. Nothing but talk and no real guys coming through the door to take her somewhere. Michael narrowed his eyes a little on Trent and fought off the urge to third-degree him about his intentions.

Trent's smile didn't waver. "Yes sir. We're headed to the Country Diner for their Friday night catfish special. You want to come along? The more the merrier."

Betty Jean spoke up. "Michael has plans. Plans he can't change." Another pointed look.

"Sounds fun, but Betty Jean's right. Lots to do." He gestured toward his desk. He would have had to make plans for his own funeral if he said any different.

"Not surprising." Trent's smile faded away. "I just saw Hank Leland out on the street. He says Geraldine Harper is dead. An accident at the old Chandler mansion. Hard to believe."

60

"Yes," Michael said. News always traveled fast in Hidden Springs.

"I'm going to miss that Geraldine. She was a go-getter for sure." Vernon Trent shook his head.

"We'll all miss her, but we better hurry if we want to get a table at the Country Diner." Betty Jean looked ready to grab the man's arm and tug him out the door. "It's best to get there before the tourists start showing up from the lake."

"The girl knows." Trent's smile came back. He winked at Michael. "She's volunteered to help me get some of my antiques online. Teach me some computer skills."

"She's a computer whiz." Michael kept a smile on his face, even though it wanted to slide off. Something about the man bothered Michael. So much that he almost decided a fish supper was what he needed, but Betty Jean would never forgive him.

Their footsteps rang in the hall as they headed outside. Betty Jean's chatter drifted back to Michael as he went to the door to watch them leave. He didn't need to act like an overprotective brother. Betty Jean could take care of herself.

Michael locked the office door and went back to his desk. No sense inviting anybody else in. Without interruptions, he might still get home before dark. He flipped through the stack of pink notes. Nothing that couldn't be put off until Monday except Aunt Lindy. He'd go by there on his way home.

He pushed the messages aside and jotted down a few quick notes about Geraldine. The full report could wait. No reason to think her death was anything but an accident. Except for the missing caller. Young and scared could explain why they didn't hang around until somebody came.

He turned on his computer and stared at the icons popping up. He wished he'd made it back to the office five minutes earlier so Betty Jean wouldn't have been in such a rush to get out the door. She was definitely not excited about Michael knowing she was meeting Vernon Trent. He had to wonder about that.

He clicked several things until the computer made that irritating sound signaling he'd hit something he shouldn't. He shut the thing off and called Sally Jo who covered the dispatch desk after office hours.

She played the recording over the phone.

"She can't. She's dead."

Whispered. Scared sounding. Understandable, since the caller did sound like a kid, the way Betty Jean said, and that kid had just seen a dead body.

Michael shut his eyes and listened while Sally Jo played the words over again, but no face came to mind. After he gave up on recognizing the voice, he called Geraldine's son and got his voice mail. Michael left his cell number.

Outside, the sun was still a ways from sinking below the horizon. After he checked on Aunt Lindy, he might yet have daylight enough to drop a line in the water off his dock. Sally Jo could reach him on his radio if she needed him.

He touched the phone in his pocket. He didn't always have a signal inside his house, but out on the dock on a clear night, calls generally came through. He could call Alex. They hadn't talked for almost a week.

A couple of months ago, they pledged to do better, to talk every day, to find a way to make loving each other work. He'd loved Alex forever. She claimed to love him too, but once she was back in Washington, DC, on the attorney fast track, things slipped back to not enough time and too many miles apart. She was busy. Too busy for him, he was beginning to think.

Alex said it wasn't all her. And maybe it wasn't. He was tied to his hometown. Roots down into the bedrock. Could he pull up those roots for the woman he loved? He'd worked in a big city once. Hated it. Came home. But it could be time to try again to live among the skyscrapers with nearly every inch of ground paved over and too many lights to see stars at night.

Thinking about that gave his heart an uneasy jolt. But the thought of giving up any chance to be with Alex split his heart in two. Sometimes there were no easy answers.

Or maybe he didn't want to accept the easy answers. Just like with Geraldine Harper. Why not simply accept she slipped and fell? Justin thought it happened that way. But here he was doing his best to worry it into something more than just a tragic accident.

He needed to squelch his uneasy suspicions about Geraldine's death before he got to Aunt Lindy's. No need having her worry about another murder in Hidden Springs.

To even think the word "murder" about Geraldine was taking things to the extreme. It had to be Miss Fonda looking up from the woman's body and saying she was dead because of this Bradley that had awakened his suspicions. But the old lady hadn't even been talking about Geraldine.

Aunt Lindy might know about Miss Fonda's sister. Whether she was pushed or not. Then again, the reason for her death would have been determined long ago. Miss Fonda coming to a different conclusion than the authorities didn't change facts. People had a way of ignoring the evidence if it contradicted their ideas of what happened. He couldn't afford to be one of those people.

He was ready to block it all out of his mind and let the sparkling lake water bring peace back to his soul. The night promised to be clear. Looking up at the moon and stars in a night sky had a way of making a man remember life was a gift and not a guarantee. A gift this man wanted to treasure.

When his phone jangled awake in his pocket, he looked for a place to pull over. He didn't want to be driving while he broke the news to a man that his mother was dead. But it wasn't Geraldine's son. Instead Aunt Lindy's name flashed on the screen. Not good. Not if she was actually calling his cell. The turn for her street was in sight, but he punched the on button anyway.

He didn't bother with hello. "What's wrong?"

She didn't waste words either. "It's Reece. That's why I wanted you to come by. When I came in from school, he was out sweeping leaves off his walkway. Didn't look good. Face too red."

"That was a couple of hours ago." Michael's hand tightened on the phone.

"Yes, but I just came back over here to check on him. He's not making sense and his mouth is drooping on one side. I fear he's having a stroke."

"Call the ambulance."

"It's on the way. But somebody needs to go with him. That somebody will have to be us with Alexandria hours away. We'll have to fill in as family until she can get here."

"Right. I'm almost there." Michael disconnected the call.

Sirens screamed the ambulance's progress through town,

and the lights were in sight by the time Michael braked in front of Reece Sheridan's house. Reece and Aunt Lindy had been neighbors since before Michael was born. When she was a kid, Alex visited her aunt and uncle every summer. That was when Michael had fallen in love with the girl next door, even if she was next door only a few weeks out of the year.

7

Malinda Keane let out a relieved breath at the sight of Michael's patrol car. He'd know what to do. Well, she had known what to do. She'd done that at once when Reece opened the door and said, "Hello morning." Morning was long past.

Way past the morning time of their lives too. Reece was seventy-one if she was doing the math right, and she always did the math right. She knew numbers, but sometimes those age numbers surprised her. Not because she couldn't do the math but because of how swiftly the years had flipped by. A couple of years ago, she'd stared sixty square in the face. People told her she should retire. Live the good life. Travel to Europe. Tend her roses. Read till her eyes crossed.

Be nothing but an old lady with a cat. She had the cat, but she didn't have to be the old lady. She would retire from teaching when they made her or when she could no longer do the math. Not one minute before. A person needed a purpose in life, and the Bible gave honor to teachers. That might be teachers of Scripture and not math, but a person needed to know numbers too. Plenty of numbers in the Bible.

Reece hadn't retired either. At least not completely. He went to his office almost every weekday. Picked and chose his clients, but he was still practicing law. When he wasn't fishing.

She looked at him in his recliner. At least she'd convinced him to sit down. The man had aged in the last year. She supposed she had too. A person couldn't deny forever how the years added up. And then with all that had happened here in Hidden Springs the last couple of years, it was no wonder she often felt her age.

Reece hadn't wanted her to call the ambulance. Said he was fine. A little tired but fine. That was what he intended to say anyway. If his words hadn't gotten jumbled up. Obviously they didn't sound jumbled up in his ears.

She told him straight out he must be having a stroke. That got his attention. Nobody wanted to have a stroke. When a body reached a certain age, the threat of infirmity or dementia had a way of lying in wait to make a person question every wobbly step or forgetful moment. Malinda prayed each day the Lord would take her home before she lost her ability to reason. She had no doubt Reece felt the same. The concerned look on his face now told the story.

After Adele died ten years ago, some of Malinda's lady friends thought she and Reece should start keeping company. But it wasn't an idea either she or Reece favored. That would have done nothing but spoil a lifelong friendship. The ones they wanted to get together were Michael and Alexandria. Those two were meant for each other. They were simply too stubborn to make room for love in their lives. Surely a sorrowful thing.

Much worse than how she'd loved and lost when she was young. Hanley had gone to the service with every intention of coming back to Hidden Springs to settle down with her, but he'd always been something of a risk taker. After all, he had risked loving her. His helicopter went down in Vietnam. So many brave boys died in those jungles. Reece had come out better. He and dear Adele had many good years together before cancer stole her away.

"Michael's here, and I hear the ambulance." Malinda put her hand on Reece's shoulder.

"You and everybody and his brother," Reece grumbled. "Entirely unsavory. Every bucket of it."

His words were a little slurred and a dribble of saliva rolled down his chin. Malinda considered dabbing it off and thought better of it. He was unhappy enough with her already. She'd let Michael handle it.

Dear Michael. It was so good to have him right here in Hidden Springs. They had been through so much together. His weeks in a coma when he was a teen after the auto accident that killed both of his parents. His slow recovery. The tragedy of all that story. But now he was strong and healthy.

She thanked the Lord for Michael's life every day. Michael thought she was the one who brought him back from near death, but his waking from the coma was the Lord's doing. Not hers. The Lord had work for Michael to do. What that was, Malinda didn't know. She wasn't concerned about it. She'd lived enough years and struggled through enough challenges to know the Lord often had a different timetable for things than she did.

Sometimes that was the hardest thing to accept. The Lord's timing. *Dear Lord, please don't let it be Reece's time.*

Glen Andrews and Gina Peak followed Michael in, carrying their bags. They overfilled the room, sucking the ordinary right out of the day. One look was all they needed to send Glen rushing back out for the stretcher. Time mattered with strokes and they were a good half hour from the Eagleton Hospital, even with the sirens screaming.

"Don't call Axel," Reece told Michael after they finally convinced him to get on the stretcher. "I'll be normal. I will."

They followed the ambulance in Michael's patrol car. Not Malinda's favorite ride. She'd never been that pleased about Michael being a policeman. She was almost positive that wasn't the Lord's plan for him. Oh, it was good to protect the public, keep the peace. Somebody needed to enforce the law or things would go haywire. But that didn't mean Michael had to be out there risking his life.

Selfish thinking on her part, but it did little good to pretend something that wasn't true. Especially in front of the Lord. Better to simply admit it and ask forgiveness. The problem was that while she might ask forgiveness for selfishness, she couldn't repent of the desire to see Michael in a job that didn't require carrying a gun.

One wouldn't think there'd be much danger to a deputy sheriff in a little town like Hidden Springs. That was what she'd thought when Michael came home from Columbus to work here, but bad things happened everywhere. When those kinds of things happened, an officer of the law couldn't step back out of danger. He, or she in these liberated days, had to be on the front line.

They didn't talk much on their way to Eagleton. It didn't seem right to chat about this or that while speeding along behind an ambulance with lights and sirens going full blast. Michael didn't use his siren, but he kept his lights flashing and stayed right with the ambulance. Malinda grabbed the armrest and hung on. She was thankful most of the way was on the interstate, with no intersections to fly through until they got off at the Eagleton exit.

There were all kinds of ways of dying. Stroke. Heart attack. Getting shot. But being T-boned while in a police car was a way too. She jerked her seatbelt tighter and tried to remember to breathe.

Michael didn't appear bothered at all. Routine for him, she supposed. She definitely needed to increase her prayers for him.

At the emergency room, Reece looked the worse for the ambulance ride, but he seemed resigned to his fate. Not dying, but enduring whatever the doctors said must be done. He tried again to get Michael to promise not to call Alexandria, but that wasn't a promise he could make. Michael did agree to wait to see what the doctors said. They wheeled Reece away to do some sort of test on his head. The whole thing made Malinda tremble. Not just for Reece, but for what might lie ahead in her future.

Maybe Geraldine Harper falling down the steps and meeting a quick end wasn't all bad for her. That wasn't so. Geraldine, poor woman, would no doubt have wished for that ambulance ride and a chance to keep breathing.

She didn't know about Geraldine until Michael gave her the news while they waited in the ER room for Reece to come back from getting his head scanned or whatever.

"Such a shame," Malinda said. "Hard to take in. You don't think about people falling down steps and dying."

"Statistics show falls as a leading cause of accidental deaths."

Michael looked tired. A stressful day and ending up here

in the ER made everything worse. She thought about getting up to go kiss the top of his head the way she used to when he was a boy and things were hard for him. But he wasn't a boy anymore.

"Maybe so, but it's still not something you think about happening," she said. "Unless the person is old and infirm. Certainly not the way you expect a robust person like Geraldine to meet her end. What do you think happened?"

"Hard to say without an eyewitness." Michael shifted in the plastic chair and made it pop. He ran his hands up and down his thighs and kept his eyes focused on the far wall. A clear sign something was making him uneasy.

"And you don't have one of those?" Malinda studied his face. "Or do you?"

"None that I know of."

"Wouldn't you know?"

"Maybe. Miss Fonda was there at the house." He sighed and quit avoiding her eyes. "She made another escape from Mrs. Gibson's."

"Oh dear. Poor old thing." Malinda shook her head. "The last time I stopped in to see her, she didn't know who I was. A terrible thing to lose your memory."

Malinda felt the sadness of it all through her. Seemed to be even worse than usual in this sterile room. Her darkest fears were being shoved right in her face. First, Reece rushed to the hospital with a stroke and then the worry of someday being like Fonda Elwood.

The thought of getting old had been stalking her recently. She kept pushing it away. She wasn't that old. She was hale and hearty. She didn't even take a blood pressure pill, and that could be considered amazing since she spent a good portion of her days cracking open teenagers' reluctant minds to pour in some algebra. But then Geraldine Harper had been hale and hearty yesterday too.

"Yes. Miss Fonda seems to forget everything but the way back to her house," Michael said.

"Do you think she saw Geraldine fall?"

"Hard to say. When I got there, Geraldine was dead and Miss Fonda was crouched over her. Very distraught."

"I suppose finding someone dead in your house would be distressing whether you knew the person or not, but I'm surprised Fonda would remember Geraldine."

"She didn't. She thought Geraldine was her sister, Audrey."

"Ah yes. Audrey." Malinda rubbed her hand across her forehead. Her head was beginning to ache. That happened when she forgot to drink enough water. "Then no wonder Fonda was so upset."

"Justin said Audrey died from a fall too. Maybe down those same stairs. Do you remember when it happened?"

"Of course. It was a long time ago, but those kinds of tragedies have a way of knitting themselves into the fabric of your memories." While that was true, Malinda didn't particularly want to unravel those threads to recall something that happened so long ago. Besides, she wasn't sure anybody knew the whole story.

"Tragedy?" Michael looked puzzled. "It was an accident, wasn't it?"

"That didn't keep it from being a tragedy. It certainly seemed so to me at the time. Audrey was so young. Older than me, but still only in her thirties. And there was little Brad to consider. Perhaps my heart went out to him because I knew how it was to lose a mother at such a young age."

She looked over at Michael and felt a tug at her heart. "As do you."

"But this happened a long time before the wreck, didn't it?"

"Oh yes. And little Brad was even younger than you when you lost your parents. Only nine, I think. Losing his mother at such a young age had to be difficult no matter what sort of mother she was."

"What do you mean? Wasn't she a good mother?" Michael looked surprised by her words, as though he thought all mothers were good.

If only that were true, many of her students would be better for it. Malinda pulled in a breath and tried not to think about her headache. "Perhaps I shouldn't have said that. I'm sure she did her best, although Fonda never thought Audrey paid proper attention to the boy. Audrey was something of a socialite. Always off to this or that event in Eagleton. She and her husband wanted to be jet-setters. Not enough action in Hidden Springs to suit them."

"Then why did they live here?" Michael asked.

"A good question. Could be Audrey felt duty bound. Her parents moved to Florida after signing the Chandler house over to her when little Brad was born, with the condition that she couldn't sell it. If she moved, she had to give it to Fonda. There were only the two girls. And them ten years apart. Fonda was oldest, but she didn't marry until after little Brad was born. That's why Audrey got the house. Some said Audrey stayed just to spite Fonda. There was always friction between those two. But Fonda did love that place."

"Still does."

"Indeed. And she loved little Brad even more. You'd have thought she was the child's grandmother the way she spoiled him." Malinda's head began to thump. She certainly hoped strokes weren't catching. Of course, they weren't. She was being silly. All she needed was something to drink. With the worry about Reece, she had foregone her cup of tea after school.

"Are you all right, Aunt Lindy?"

Michael was watching her, ready to leap to her aid.

"I'm fine." Now she was sounding like Reece, saying she was fine when she wasn't. "I just need a drink."

A stainless steel sink was in the corner behind her. Stainless steel. The whole room was white and steel except for the black television screen suspended on an arm from high on the wall. Thank goodness, it wasn't turned on. She got up and went to the sink. She could sip water from her hand if necessary, but she opened the cabinet over the sink. If they didn't want the cabinets opened, they should lock them. A stack of Styrofoam cups was a welcome sight. She ran the water a minute before she filled the cup and drank every drop. Next thing she'd have to find a restroom, but she'd worry about that later. She filled the cup again and sat back down.

"Are you sure you're okay? I can get a nurse."

"No need in that. I'm fine," she repeated. She sipped more of the water and did feel better. "Shouldn't they be back with Reece by now?"

Michael glanced at the clock on the wall. "It's not been that long."

She looked at the clock too, with no idea of how long they'd been there. She generally had an internal clock that ticked off the minutes from long practice of knowing how much time was left in her classes at school. But this with

Reece and then talking about Audrey and thinking about Geraldine had thrown her off-kilter.

"Why do you want to know about Audrey?" she asked.

"When Miss Fonda thought Geraldine was Audrey and then Justin said Audrey died in a fall too, it made me curious."

"I don't see how the two deaths could be connected."

"Only by place."

"Yes, well." Malinda took another drink. "It's just so odd."

"What is?"

"I hadn't thought about any of this for so long. And now you're the second person to ask me about Audrey in the last week."

8

Michael looked at Aunt Lindy. "Why would anybody be asking you about Audrey?"

"Why indeed?" Aunt Lindy massaged her forehead with the tips of her fingers, as though trying to erase a headache. Or maybe her memories of whatever had happened to Audrey.

He wasn't surprised by her reluctance to talk about Audrey. Aunt Lindy was a one-woman booster club for Hidden Springs. Bad things that happened in the town weren't exactly forgotten, just swept back out of sight. A lesson to learn from but nothing to dwell upon. He tried an easier question. "Then who?"

"Lana Waverly." She pulled in a deep breath and let it out. "Have you met her yet? She opened that tearoom venture on Main. An attractive woman. Ambitious. Obviously capable."

"I've met her." Could the day get any weirder? "How would she even know about Audrey? Isn't she from New York?"

"She grew up in Indiana. South Bend, she said. Moved to New York and got a job with a publishing company. Worked her way up to content editor at one of the big-name companies. She resigned to have time to write. She wants to write mysteries and she thinks living in a quaint little town like Hidden Springs will be good for her muse. At least that's what she claims." Aunt Lindy looked as if she wasn't sure she believed the woman.

"That doesn't explain her asking about Audrey. Or even knowing about Audrey. I didn't know anything about her until today."

"That might be because you didn't pay attention. I'm sure I have mentioned in the past that Fonda had a sister who died young." Aunt Lindy took another sip of water. "As for the Waverly woman, she didn't mention Audrey or the Chandler house when she called. Not that newcomers aren't often curious about that old house. It is quite grand. But no, she claimed to want to see our collection of antique books."

"Those dusty old books on the shelves in the front room?"

"I'm sure some of them are rare books of historical value." Aunt Lindy gave Michael a look. "Anyway, since I'd heard she has plans for a bookstore along with her tea shop, I thought perhaps she had an actual interest in literature."

"She doesn't?"

Aunt Lindy shrugged a little. "I can't say for certain, but she barely glanced at any of the books except the history of Keane County that Willard Jefferson wrote back in the fifties. Someone told her I had a copy. Probably that Vernon Trent." Aunt Lindy's eyes narrowed. "I'm not one to discourage new businesses on Main, but that man needs to learn boundaries. I've told him I'm not selling anything to him. I don't care what he says Grandmother's china cabinet is worth."

"You don't have to sell him anything."

"I certainly do not. The man's a leech. Stealing the heritage of people here in town."

"Stealing?" Michael raised his eyebrows at her.

"Same as. Most people have no idea what their antiques are worth." Aunt Lindy sounded disgusted. "But I don't suppose you can arrest a man for taking advantage of people. Anyway, back to Lana Waverly. She latched onto Willard's book. Pretended she wanted to read it to find out more about her new hometown."

"Pretended?"

"It's dull as dishwater. I doubt if any but the most diehard Hidden Springs citizens read past page ten. Besides, if she wanted to read it, she could get a copy at the library. No need acting like my copy is a town treasure." Aunt Lindy made a face. "A person should simply be straightforward about what she wants."

"I'm surprised you didn't kick her out." Michael twisted his mouth to hide his smile.

"Her apparent deviousness would have been no excuse for rudeness on my part. Besides, when she didn't give any of the old books much notice, I did begin to wonder why she had come. She beat around the bush awhile. Asking about things in town. Clubs and such and whether there were any writers in Keane County. But eventually she got around to the real reason she was there."

"Which was?" Michael prodded when Aunt Lindy fell silent.

"Bradley Carlson. Audrey's husband. You may have heard of him. He moved from here to Indiana and was eventually elected to the House of Representatives. Lana Waverly says he's still serving in spite of being well into his seventies now.

Lana claims to have known him when she lived in Indiana. Not sure that explains why she showed up on my doorstep asking about him." Aunt Lindy rubbed her fingers and thumb together, something she did when she was working out a difficult problem.

"Could be somebody told her you were the town historian. The one person in Hidden Springs who knows everything."

Aunt Lindy waved away his words. "I hardly know everything, and even if I did, that doesn't mean I'd tell it. But as for Lana Waverly, it may have been nothing more than idle curiosity. Somebody told her Bradley Carlson once lived here. Add onto that the story about his wife dying in a tragic accident. A potential mystery writer might be looking for plot ideas."

"Was Audrey's death a mystery?" Michael remembered Miss Fonda's accusing words. *She's dead because of him.*

Aunt Lindy fiddled with the crease in her slacks. "No."

"You don't sound totally sure."

She sighed and looked up at him. "There was talk, but there is always talk in Hidden Springs. You know that. And Fonda was so distraught about it all. While she and Audrey had their issues, they were family. But Fonda never considered Bradley family. He was the outsider who appeared to want to entice Audrey away from Hidden Springs. Then that didn't happen, but he took her nephew away instead. Fonda was heartbroken over both the loss of her sister and young Brad. In her mind, Bradley Carlson became the villain of the piece." She started to say something else, but then pressed her lips together and kept quiet.

"Justin said they never came back for a visit. That seems sort of harsh."

"Yes, perhaps Bradley thought a clean break from such tragic memories was best for the boy. A new life for both of them. He didn't really have any reason to come back, since the house went to Fonda per her parents' will. Not sure if the will continues through the next generation, but if it does, once Fonda passes, the house would be little Brad's. I suppose he's not so little now. He'd be in his forties."

"If that's true, Sonny Elwood must not know it. He plans to sell the house."

"I'd be surprised if he can legally do that. Even if his mother is Fonda's power of attorney. I doubt Fonda can sell it. The Chandlers didn't intend the property to be owned by anybody out of the family. Of course, they thought Audrey and Fonda would have more children. If not Chandlers in surname, a branch of the Chandler family."

"Can wills be drawn up like that? That prohibit the sale of property?"

"I'm not sure. That would be a question for Reece." Aunt Lindy looked at the door out into the hallway. "What in the world are they doing to the poor man?"

Michael stood up. He put his hand on Aunt Lindy's shoulder as he passed by her. "Thanks for telling me about Audrey."

"You know I'm ready to answer whatever questions you have about the past here in Hidden Springs. But some memories are more distressing than others." She pressed her cheek against his hand. A rare affectionate gesture from her. She was not one for hugs.

"Do you think there was anything to what Miss Fonda said? That he caused her to fall."

"I've been up and down those stairs a time or two. Easy to imagine someone falling, but you would hope it wouldn't be fatal. Entirely possible however. I guess that was proven today with Geraldine." Aunt Lindy sat up straight and shook her head. "So hard to believe. That's how it felt with Audrey too. Hard to believe. But Bradley gave every appearance of a man deeply mourning his wife. Didn't take him long to remarry however. Barely six months after Audrey died."

"People grieve in different ways." He didn't know why he was taking up for a man he didn't even know.

"True," Aunt Lindy said. "And some seem to have more than their share of trouble. Lana Waverly said Bradley's second wife also came to a tragic end some years ago. An overdose of pills. Lana said she knew the second wife well. That she could never agree with the coroner's finding of suicide." Aunt Lindy looked up at Michael. "I doubt Bradley Carlson ever got her vote."

"Do you think she came to Hidden Springs to find out more about him? To try to connect the deaths of Audrey and the other wife?"

"Why would she wait so long if that was her intent?" Aunt Lindy frowned. "That would seem very strange, don't you think?"

"Very." Michael agreed with her, but the fact was, people did strange things all the time.

A nurse pushed open the door and rolled Reece's bed back into the room. Reece looked ready to be swallowed up by the sheets and blankets draped around him. When had he gotten so frail? But perhaps it was only the hospital that was siphoning away his strength. He needed his fishing pole and lucky hat. Then he'd look right. But his mouth still drooped. As much as Michael hated it, as much as Reece hated it, the man was right where he needed to be.

While the ER doctor thought Reece would recover from

the initial stroke little worse for the wear, they couldn't be sure another stroke might not follow on the heels of the first. Prevention was the best treatment, and that called for more tests and observation.

"They just need to let me go fishing." At least Reece did seem to have his words back. "But appears like I'll have to let them poke and prod some more. Time they get through, I'll feel like a poor fish reeled in and flopping around in the bottom of the boat."

"Maybe it won't be that bad." Michael patted his arm.

"Probably worse." Reece looked miserable. "Guess you will have to call Alex after all. She'd give me heck if nobody told her."

"I'd be the one in trouble. Not you."

"True enough." Reece almost smiled. "So call her, but tell her not to come. Once they add a few pills to the handful I already take, all will be well."

"Nonsense." Aunt Lindy joined Michael by the bed. "She needs to be here."

"Now, Malinda. Alexandria is busy."

"If she's too busy to come see about you when you're in the hospital, she's way too busy." Aunt Lindy didn't give an inch. "Besides, she hasn't been home for weeks."

"This isn't her home," Reece said. "Washington is."

"That's something that needs to change." Aunt Lindy glared at Michael.

"Don't look at me like that." Michael held up his hands in defense. "I'd drive the old truck up there and help her move anytime, but you know Alex. She does what she wants." And he was pretty sure moving to Hidden Springs wasn't on her to-do list anytime soon.

Reece did manage a smile this time, but only one corner of his mouth turned up. "That's our Alexandria."

Aunt Lindy didn't smile or let her glare waver. "Have you ever asked her?"

Michael was relieved when a nurse bustled in to take Aunt Lindy's attention away from him so he didn't have to answer her. He hadn't asked Alex. At least not straight out. He was too afraid of hearing that final no.

After Reece was settled in a room, Aunt Lindy reluctantly agreed to leave. On the elevator down to the exit, she said, "It's sad. People like Reece and me. With so little family."

"You have family. Me. Right here if you need anything."

"I know." She reached over and touched his arm. "I don't know what I'd do without you, but at the same time, I don't want to be a burden on you."

Michael scowled at her. "Where's all this coming from?"

"I don't know. Seeing Reece looking so alone in that bed when we left." She stared at the elevator doors as they descended to the first floor. "Thinking about Geraldine with nobody to see to her arrangements."

"I talked to her son." Michael had finally reached him on the phone and broken the sad news. "He's flying up here tomorrow."

"But he's not married. No children. Geraldine didn't get to enjoy any grandchildren." Aunt Lindy sounded sad.

They bounced to a stop on the bottom floor and the elevator doors slid open. "She never seemed like the grandmotherly type anyway."

"People might say that about me too, and while I can't be a grandmother, I would dearly love to be a great-aunt." Aunt Lindy didn't look up at him as she stepped out of the elevator.

Her words found an answering yearning inside him. "I guess I haven't held up my end of the bargain on that."

"Oh, don't pay attention to me. I'm simply feeling maudlin for some reason. You'll have those children someday when you and Alexandria come to your senses."

Michael didn't say anything as he tried to imagine Alex a mother and couldn't. He had a hard enough time picturing her in a wedding dress. Perhaps it was time they both stared reality in the face and admitted it would never work. Agree to move on. Both of them find people better suited to the life they wanted to live. Her in the high-powered political world and him here in the small-town world of Hidden Springs. No sooner did that thought surface in his mind than he pushed it away. Not yet. Maybe someday, but not yet.

He'd called her while the nurses settled Reece in his room. Got her voice mail, as usual. Left a short, to-the-point message, while he wondered if she was having dinner with that better someone.

Aunt Lindy walked ahead of him out the front entrance. "But her biological clock is ticking. She's almost thirty."

Michael laughed. "Good thing she's not here to hear you say that."

"I assume she knows how old she is." Aunt Lindy used her no-nonsense tone. "But as far as that goes, I suppose all our clocks are ticking. None of us knows how much more time we have on this good earth. Just like poor Geraldine today and Audrey years ago."

"Come on, Aunt Lindy. You're going to live to be a hundred and five." He leaned down to get a better look at her face in the glow of the parking lot lights. "Hank Leland will be coming to take your picture to put in the paper if he's still around."

"Hmph. The way that man eats, he'll never make it another forty-three years." Hank wasn't Aunt Lindy's favorite person. He was too ready to publish less-than-favorable stories about Hidden Springs in his newspaper.

"Maybe he'll change his ways."

"When pigs fly."

Michael laughed again as he opened the patrol car door for Aunt Lindy. But that's how he sometimes felt about his and Alex's chances. When pigs fly. But tonight he'd talk to her. Hear her voice, and if she came home to see about Reece, he'd see her. He couldn't give up on those flying pigs yet.

9

Have you asked? Aunt Lindy's question stayed with Michael. Alex knew he loved her. She had to know. But he wasn't sure he'd ever told her straight out in so many words. Three words, to be exact. *I love you.*

Michael stared down at the container of mealy worms as if he'd never seen fish bait. The morning sun was warm on his shoulders. The lake water shimmered with promise. Fish lurked below the surface, but his mind was up in the air. With Alex. Who was flying to Eagleton. Now. Right now.

He had talked to her last night, but only long enough to share the necessary information. What happened. Which hospital. What the doctors said. No "I love you" from either of them. No "will you marry me" from him. No time for that. Alex was anxious to get off the phone to call the hospital and then schedule her flight. She had things to arrange. None of the arrangements included Michael.

"Do you need me to pick you up at the airport?" Michael had asked.

"No, I'll get a rental car."

That was the trouble. She didn't need help. She didn't need him.

"Michael, did you find the bait?" Karen Allison walked up from the dock. Her dark blonde hair was yanked back in a ponytail and she had on blue jeans with a hole in one of the knees. She never worried much about how she looked. "The kids are ready to start drowning some worms."

She was smiling. Karen was always smiling. She said everybody who knew Jesus should be smiling. Karen was the pastor of the local Presbyterian church. For a while, the two of them had played at dating. Long enough that some of the local people thought they might be headed for the altar. But they had always been more friends than a romantic couple. Then after he and Alex danced closer to not just admitting their feelings for one another but doing something about it, he and Karen decided to forget dating and stick to being friends. Karen was all wrapped up in her church and he was all wrapped up in Alex.

Karen just wanted him to keep helping with her youth group. Something he was glad to do. Most days. But this day he wanted to be at the airport waiting for Alex's plane to touch down.

He'd talked to Reece that morning. Early. He sounded good. Resigned to more doctor prodding. Aunt Lindy had brought him the newspaper. She was sitting by his bed grading papers. Michael had no reason to cancel on this fishing outing Karen had arranged weeks ago. Not with Reece well cared for at the hospital and no emergencies at the sheriff's office.

While he still had questions about Geraldine Harper's death, the search for answers could wait until after the kids went fishing. So could talking to Lana Waverly to find out why she was curious about Audrey Carlson's death. No emergency there either. Not for something that happened so long ago.

Actually, his questions would have to wait even longer, because he planned to head to the Eagleton Hospital as soon as the kids caught a few fish. Chief Sibley, the town's police chief, and Buck Garrett, the state policeman for the Keane County area, could handle things.

It wasn't like he couldn't be found. His radio, clipped to his belt, chattered now and again to let him know he was in range. Sometimes he thought it might be good to be out of range. Out of reach. He fingered the power button on his radio, but he didn't push it. It was his job to be there. To be found.

Karen took the container of bait from him. "I hope you bought plenty. These guys are planning on catching every fish in the lake." She headed back toward his dock where some of the kids were checking the hooks and sinkers on their lines while others looked as if they'd never seen a fishing pole.

One of the boys grabbed a mealy worm and dangled it in front of a girl, who shrieked on cue. Karen's laugh carried up from the dock. She didn't put up with any foolishness, but she let the kids be kids.

Ten kids had come in the big van Karen talked the church elders into buying. Aunt Lindy claimed that was practically a miracle, but Karen had a way about her. Everything she did was wrapped in such caring and love that people wanted to help her.

Michael liked working with the kids. Sometimes he thought that might be his purpose in life Aunt Lindy kept saying he needed to find. She didn't think that purpose was keeping the peace in Hidden Springs. She didn't think being a youth leader was it either, but the kids were enough for Michael.

He might not be able to keep every kid off the road to trouble, but he wanted to. His gaze went to Anthony Blake down on the dock with one of the girls.

The two of them had gone some rounds together, but now Anthony was like a little brother. Showed up to bed down on his couch at least once a week. Sometimes to go fishing with Michael. Sometimes just to take a hike with Jasper. The dog had taken to the kid from the first, when Anthony was a very troubled teen. Now if Anthony was around, Jasper was generally not far away. Just like now. Jasper sat right behind Anthony, his tail sweeping across the grass.

The girl with Anthony was new to the group. Maggie Greene. She was a couple of years younger than Anthony, but the boy looked more than a little besotted. She was a pretty girl. Straight brown hair in a long ponytail. Hazel eyes with dark lashes. She didn't wear the latest trendy fashions or have a cell phone in her hand all the time like some of the other girls. Maggie appeared to be more comfortable hanging on the fringes of a group.

Michael knew about that. He'd felt that way often enough in high school while he was recovering after the wreck that almost crippled him. It had been a long time before he was able to walk without a limp. Anthony knew about staying apart from the crowd too. He'd had more than his share of struggles. Probably would have plenty more. But for now he was off Trouble Road and checking out scholarships, since he would graduate in the spring.

Anthony saw Michael looking at him and waved him down to the dock. A smile lit up his face.

"This girl has never been fishing. Can you believe that?" Anthony pointed at Maggie. His smile got even brighter.

"Don't let him poke you about that, Maggie. He didn't know how to bait a hook a couple of years ago." Michael grinned at Maggie, but she flashed her eyes away from him.

She had been laughing and talking to Anthony, but she seemed almost afraid to look at Michael. Maybe she was simply feeling shy, but she hadn't acted shy with Michael at their Sunday meeting last week. He'd sat down beside her and she told him about her classes at school. She had actually seemed more comfortable talking to him than to the other kids that night. But today things were different.

"Don't listen to him," Anthony said. "I'm an expert with worms. Catching them. Squishing them on hooks."

Maggie kept her eyes down.

"I get the feeling the girl don't like worms." Anthony spoke in a stage whisper.

She giggled and looked up at Anthony. "I'll have you know I used to make pets of worms. It's just the squishing them on hooks that doesn't sound so good."

"Anthony," Karen yelled over at them. "Help! Billy's got his line all tangled up and I'm hopeless with it."

"Pastor Karen calls." Anthony let out an exaggerated sigh. "My expertise is needed everywhere. But I'll be back to help you bait that hook so you can catch the biggest fish of all."

After Anthony ran off to help Karen, Maggie peeked up at Michael and then back at the ground.

"Glad you were able to come today, Maggie."

"Yeah, well, Pastor Karen said we'd be back early enough if my mother needed me to help her clean." She ran her hand up and down the fishing pole, avoiding the hook. Her gaze went everywhere but toward Michael.

When the girl said "clean," Michael made the connection. Sonny said Mary Greene had a key to clean Miss Fonda's house. That was Maggie's mother.

"That's right. Your mother cleans for people, doesn't she?"

"She has a few places, but she works out at the Fast Serve too. She says I'm too young to get a job there, but I've been helping her dust and stuff forever." She pushed out the words all in a bunch, as though she thought she had to explain everything.

People had a way of doing that when they were nervous. Something was obviously bothering the girl. Sunday she had been easy with him. Today she wished he would disappear.

"Your mother's right. Better to concentrate on school if you can."

"I'll probably get a job next summer. We can use the money. My father got laid off."

"It's tough right now with the economy." Empty words.

"Yeah." Maggie looked out at the lake.

The girl probably didn't care that much about the state of the nation's economy. The economy in her family was what mattered to her. Last he'd heard, Curt Greene was drinking too much. Some men didn't deal well with unemployment.

"Your mother cleans the Chandler house, doesn't she?"

Her gaze shot back to him and then slashed away as if he'd said something startling. After a second or two, she nodded.

"Then that must be where you learned to dust." Michael tried to keep his voice light. "Miss Fonda has a lot of keepsakes. Must take a while to clean that house."

"Yes." Again her answer was short. She stared toward where Anthony was working to free Billy's line from a bush.

"Do you know when your mother cleaned there last?"

Maggie shook her head. "I'm not sure. It's been a few weeks." She looked back toward Michael but kept her eyes on his shirt buttons.

Michael was searching for a way to put her at ease, but she spoke first in a voice so low he could barely hear what she said. "It's bad what happened to Mrs. Harper, isn't it? You don't think about anybody dying from falling down steps. Even steps like those."

"Accidents happen."

"Yeah." She ran her hand up and down the fishing pole again. This time she forgot to watch for the hook and jabbed her finger. "Ouch." She dropped the pole and stared at the drop of blood on her finger. "Guess I'd better go see if Pastor Karen has something I can put on this." She put her finger in her mouth and moved past Michael.

From the look of relief on her face as she took off toward Karen, Michael suspected she'd jabbed her finger on purpose.

Could be he'd found the person who had been using the tower room. And the one who had called 911. Young. Scared. Both of them fit Maggie Greene. More telling, he didn't think Karen had mentioned that Geraldine had fallen down stairs that morning when she asked the kids to remember to pray for Geraldine's family.

10

Maggie's heart pounded as she walked away from Michael. She shouldn't have come. She knew Michael would be here. She knew he was a policeman. But she didn't think about him being the one to get the 911 call. If he did, he might recognize her voice. He might know she was there.

She was in so much trouble. Breaking into somebody's house was against the law. She hadn't actually broken in, but she had gone into the house with nobody there to say it was okay. Trespassing was a crime too. She'd seen "Trespassers will be prosecuted" signs. None at Miss Fonda's house, but that didn't matter. She had still been a trespasser.

They might send her to juvenile detention or something. Some girl at the high school had gone to a place like that last year. Nobody had seen her since.

When she swallowed, her throat felt tight. She looked out at the road. They were miles from anywhere here at the lake. She couldn't take off and walk home. Pastor Karen would never allow that. She would insist on knowing why Maggie had to leave. She'd see right through Maggie claiming she was sick, even if she felt like she was about to throw up.

Maybe she should throw up. As embarrassing as that would be in front of her friends. In front of Anthony. People believed you were sick if you threw up. No questions asked. She could call her mother to come get her. Except her mother was working at the Fast Serve today. It would have to be her father. She'd better be bleeding if she called him to come get her. A lot. Not only that, but by now he'd probably downed a couple of beers. The last thing they needed was her father getting a DUI. The very last thing.

Even if he wasn't drinking, he'd be mad if she begged a ride home. He hadn't wanted her to sign up for the fishing trip in the first place. He said she should stay home and watch her little brother. Her mother and father had a big argument about it that ended with her father slamming out of the house and her mother banging pans in the kitchen. Maggie told her mother she didn't have to go. She could stay home. Her mother had glared at Maggie and said indeed she would go. She didn't want to hear another word about it.

That was last Sunday night. Before Friday afternoon. Before Mrs. Harper fell down the steps and Maggie called 911. Before whoever else was there had left without calling anybody. Why couldn't she have been like that? Or maybe she should have sent a text message. Nobody would recognize what finger typed in a text. *She's dead.*

A shiver walked up Maggie's back. She couldn't get the sight of Mrs. Harper at the bottom of the stairs out of her head. If she could talk about it, that might help. But she couldn't tell her mother or anybody else.

She thought about telling Miss Fonda. She wouldn't remember after ten minutes, but she might pat Maggie's hand and tell her it was all right. That might make Maggie feel better. Except somebody else was always around when she went to see Miss Fonda. And it might upset Miss Fonda, talking about Mrs. Harper dying in her house, even if she couldn't remember who Mrs. Harper was.

So she couldn't tell anybody. Not without getting in trouble.

Michael was watching her. She knew he was, even without glancing back at him. It was funny how you could feel somebody watching you. Actually feel it. Not that the feeling was always right. Sometimes you just imagined it. Like that morning.

She'd felt sure somebody was watching her when she took the shortcut across the graveyard to the church. She always went that way. It had never bothered her. But that was before she saw a dead person with eyes open and everything. When her grandmother died, she looked like she was lying there in the casket sleeping. Peaceful. Ready for heaven.

Mrs. Harper hadn't looked a thing like that. Not a thing. She looked like she might stand up and chase Maggie. Maybe that was what spooked Maggie that morning on the way to the church. Not only the feeling that somebody was watching her, but that it might be Mrs. Harper mad about being dead and ready to take it out on Maggie.

She shook her head. That was dumb. She didn't believe in ghosts. She didn't care if people did say they saw ghosts at Miss Fonda's house. She never had. Never. And she'd been there a lot. In the very room people claimed they saw a woman peering out the window. Sometimes Maggie wondered if it was her shadow they saw in the window. But then, the ghost stories about the Chandler mansion had been around way before she started sneaking into the house. Trespassing.

More likely a guilty conscience was what had been stalk-ing her that morning. Pastor Karen said that could happen. She claimed something you did that wasn't right could weigh down on you. Or something you didn't do when you knew you should. Either one could cause somebody to think all kinds of wrong things. Like a ghost haunting them.

"Hey, Maggie, where's your pole?" Anthony was running toward her, a big smile on his face.

Anthony was the reason she asked to go on the fishing outing. He was why she started going to Pastor Karen's youth group. Anthony had asked her to.

He was so cute. It seemed impossible he could be interested in her. She was just a sophomore. He was a senior. Maybe he was simply recruiting kids for the youth group for Pastor Karen. But he did have a way of looking at her with those deep blue eyes that made Maggie have trouble breathing. He was the best-looking boy at high school. The very best.

"I left it back there." She remembered her finger that she jabbed on the fishhook to have a reason to stop talking to Michael. "I stuck my finger. I thought maybe Pastor Karen would have a bandage or something." She held out her hand. Her finger had stopped bleeding.

When Anthony took her hand in his, her heart began pounding even harder. "You have to be careful with hooks."

"Yeah, but it's okay now." Maggie pulled her hand away from his and then wished she hadn't. She liked him holding her hand.

"I could kiss it and make it well." He stared straight into her eyes with a tease of a smile.

Her cheeks flashed hot and her tongue felt too big for her mouth. She had no idea what to say. She'd never flirted with a boy. At least not since she was in third grade and chased a boy named Lonny around the playground. She hadn't caught him. He could run fast, but that was okay. She hadn't really wanted to catch him anyway. The chase was the fun part then. But staring up at Anthony, she sort of wanted to be caught. She was already caught. Caught by his eyes.

Michael came up behind Maggie, carrying the fishing pole she'd dropped on the dock, and broke the spell between them. "Is your finger okay, Maggie?"

"Yeah." Maggie managed to push the word out as she held up her finger.

"Well, then here's your pole. It's best not to leave it where somebody might step on it."

"Sorry. I guess I don't know much about fishing." Maggie took the pole. She didn't know much about anything, but she did wish her heart would stop galloping in her chest. She felt like she'd just run a mile.

"No problem." Michael grinned at Anthony and punched his shoulder. "And you best keep your mind on the fish in the lake, kid."

"I'm here to catch fish." Anthony laughed, obviously a little embarrassed.

Michael looked straight at Maggie. "Could be we should talk before you leave today, Maggie."

He wasn't smiling. Not a bit. Maybe she would throw up. "Am I in trouble?"

She shouldn't have said that. It was like an admission she had done something wrong. She should have just thrown up on her shoes. But Anthony might never want to be within ten feet of her again if she did that.

"What's going on, Michael?" Anthony stepped a little

closer to peer at Michael's face. "You don't have to warn her off from me. I know how to act."

Michael surprised Maggie by laughing. "This is between Maggie and me. Nothing to do with you. If she wants to let you teach her how to catch a fish or two, then she'll just have to take her chances." Michael winked at Maggie. "Play your cards right, Maggie, and he'll do the worm squishing on the hooks for you. And no, you're not in trouble. Not with me. I just thought you looked a little worried about something. Something we might need to talk about."

Maggie moistened her lips. "Okay."

She was relieved when Pastor Karen yelled at Michael to see if he had more bait. She let out a shaky breath when he walked away.

Anthony touched her arm lightly. "Don't let him scare you. He's a good guy."

"He's a policeman."

"As long as you haven't broken the law, that won't matter."

Anthony was joking. She knew he was, but it was all she could do to push a smile out on her lips to answer his. "Yeah. I don't know what he could want." That wasn't exactly true, but she wanted it to be.

"Don't worry about it. He used to be on my case. We went some rounds, let me tell you, but he's all right. And he's got a great place to fish here." Anthony put his arm around her shoulders and turned her toward the lake. "So let's get at it. Time for you to learn all about worms and catch your first fish."

She could smell the clean scent of his shirt mixed with a little sweat. His arm, light on her shoulders, felt just right. They moved together without bumping into one another.

Walking smoothly side by side, their steps matched. He was a head taller than her, but that seemed the perfect height too.

It was almost enough to make her forget about Michael wanting to talk to her. Almost, but not quite. But she was still glad she hadn't thrown up on her shoes. She was very glad Anthony was going to show her how to catch a fish. She would find a way to avoid Michael for the rest of the day. Maybe he'd forget about wanting to talk to her.

11

It was late afternoon by the time Michael headed to Eagleton. The kids had fished and taken turns out on the lake in his rowboat. Michael was surprised a few hadn't "accidentally" fallen in the lake. But Karen told them no swimming and none of them wanted to get on her bad side. They seemed less worried about Michael's bad side. He was the errand boy today, fetching more worms, untangling lines, making sure all the boys and girls stayed in sight.

Maggie Greene stayed in sight, but she made sure to stay well away from Michael. It was plain she didn't want to talk to him about cleaning Miss Fonda's house or anything else. Once or twice he considered cornering her, but Karen would read him the riot act if he did anything to chase Maggie away from the youth group. Anthony wouldn't be happy about that either. He was obviously smitten by Maggie.

So those questions had to wait. He'd ask them. Just not today. Seems that was what he was doing with everything. Shoving it off until Monday. There was really no reason to spend the weekend making an accident into more than it was just because of one nervous kid. Along with the uneasy feeling that kept nudging him and bringing to mind even more questions.

Answers. That was what he needed. Not questions. But then Aunt Lindy's question kept circling in his head. *Have you asked?*

He couldn't just blurt it out. *Will you marry me?* These days women wanted elaborate proposals. Alexandria Sheridan deserved the most elaborate proposal any man could dream up. Maybe he should rent a sign in Washington, DC. Put his love for her in lights. Or buy two plane tickets and take her to dinner at some famous Parisian restaurant. Or carve a heart in the tree in front of Reece's house and put their initials in it.

He might have done that years ago when he got his first pocketknife, but if so, the memory was lost to him now, the way so many others were after his head injury when he was a teen. If he had carved that heart, Alex had never helped him recall that forgotten memory the way she had others. Things like how, when she was seven, she named her pet cat Dog, because she wanted a dog, not a cat. That was Alex changing life to meet her expectations. Reece had taken in the cat when Alex's father got a new coaching job and the cat named Dog had to go.

Michael didn't remember the cat at all. Even though it had lived at Reece's right next door. He'd been in a coma for weeks after the wreck. That blackness had soaked into his brain and made some memories too hard to dig out.

Not that a heart carved on a tree trunk when they were kids or now when they weren't would ensure her saying yes. Or even dinner in France or on the moon. But he hadn't tried any of them. If he never actually asked in so many words, then she could never say no in one word. But she couldn't say yes either.

The very idea of her yes made his knees go weak. *Will you be my lawfully wedded wife?*

He hoped Alex was still at the hospital. He had tried her cell number with no answer. His heart began beating a little faster when he stepped into the elevator to go up to Reece's room. Where Alex might be. His pulse rose along with the floor numbers.

As soon as he exited the elevator, he spotted her at the nurses' station, her back to him. Her dark hair was loose around her shoulders, the way he liked it best. She had on an oversize sweater with black tights that somehow made her legs look even longer. She was up on her toes talking to the nurse at the desk, like an exotic cat ready to pounce or perhaps run. He couldn't hear what they were saying, but it was plain Alex was not happy, nor was the nurse, if the stony look on her face was any indication.

"Alex." Michael wanted to rush down the hall and take her in his arms.

She was turning toward him even before he spoke as though she sensed him there. Instead of him running to her, she covered the space between them in a few strides and practically fell into his arms.

"Oh, Michael. I'm so glad you're here. I wanted to call you, but Malinda said you were doing something with the church kids." She hesitated a bare second or two. "And Karen." Her face was burrowed into his shoulder.

"A big fishing outing. Planned forever." He heard the hint of a question behind Karen's name, but he simply tightened his arms around her to answer that. "I talked to Reece this morning and he seemed okay. Has something happened? Not another stroke?" He looked down the hall toward Reece's room. He should have called again.

She leaned back from him and shook her head. "No, no. Nothing like that. It's just Uncle Reece. He's throwing a fit to get out of here and go home."

"Reece throwing a fit? That I would have to see." Reece was about the most laid-back person he knew.

"He's not happy. And that makes me unhappy."

She looked tired. Shadows under her gorgeous blue eyes. Makeup gone but never necessary to Michael's eyes. She must not have slept any last night and then spent the day here with nobody doing what she said. Not Reece. Not the nurses. Not something she was used to happening in her world.

"And that makes me unhappy." He tightened his arms around her again and she leaned against him. Needed him. A good feeling. "So we're all unhappy. What do we do about it?"

"I don't know. They won't listen." She didn't lift her head. Instead her lips moved against his shirt, her breath warming him.

"You want me to arrest somebody?"

That was supposed to make her laugh and it did. She pulled away from him. "I think you left your deputy badge at home. You look like a regular Joe off the street in your jeans. No gun. No handcuffs. No power against these by-the-rules nurses."

"I've got my radio."

"On duty, huh?"

"Always. Got to keep the peace in Hidden Springs."

"Not been all that easy lately, has it? Malinda said something else has happened. The real estate lady met an untimely end. Accidentally?"

"So it appears."

"Uh-oh. That sounds like more investigation is in order." The corners of her lips curved enticingly up, and then as quickly her smile was gone. "But can it wait until you help me convince Uncle Reece another ten hours in the hospital won't be the death of him? I've never known him to be so contrary."

"You've never been around him away from Hidden Springs."

"That's it. He's threatening to move to a cabin by the lake where he can lie down and die without interference." She tried another smile, but her lips were trembling. As close to tears as he'd seen her in years. She looked down the hall toward Reece's room. "Do you think he's going to die? I mean actually die?"

"It happens to all of us sooner or later, but I'm guessing later for Reece." He put his arm around her. "He's got more fish to catch."

"Do you really think so?" She stepped away from him to move down the hall.

He matched his steps to hers. "I do. More important, that's what the doctors say too, isn't it?"

"Yes, as long as he takes care of himself and does what they say."

"So see? This is just a little rough water for him. He'll get better." He peered over at her. "But how about you? Are you going to be okay?"

She managed a little laugh. "Maybe. Now that you're here. It's just that I really do not like hospitals." She shuddered. "Goes back to visiting some kid I thought I was in love with way back when. All those wires sticking out of you."

"Not good." Especially the part about *thought* she was in love. He wanted her to *know* she was in love with him.

She was still back in time, remembering. "I begged you to squeeze my hand, but your hand was so limp. No response at all."

"I'm sure I was trying to hold your hand." Michael reached over and captured her hand. He wanted to ask her if she was in love right now, but the words stuck in his throat.

"That's what Malinda told me, but it scared me to death. I've never gotten over it." She tightened her fingers on his hand. "I don't think I ever will."

"Is that why you keep running away from me?"

"Me?" Her eyes flashed up to his face. "I thought it was you doing the running."

"I'm right in Hidden Springs. Where I've always been."

"Where you'll always be?" She raised her eyebrows at him.

He was saved from having to answer by the nurse stepping out from behind the desk in front of them.

"I'm very sorry you are upset, Miss Sheridan. We certainly understand your uncle's frustration. And yours. Few people want to spend time in a hospital." The nurse was several inches shorter than Alex. A little dumpy in her loose-fitting scrubs decorated with balloons. She looked concerned as she slid her gaze from Alex to Michael.

Perhaps she thought Alex had called in reinforcements. He smiled a little to put the nurse at ease but didn't say anything.

All traces of a smile fled Alex's face as she squared her shoulders and fixed cold eyes on the woman. "Hospitals are not jails. If a person wants to go home, there should be no locked doors."

The nurse met her look without flinching. "We don't have locked doors, but we do have rules. A doctor releases a patient when it is determined the patient no longer needs hospital care. As I told you, your uncle's doctor has not yet done that. Of course, your uncle can sign himself out, but that is not something we advise." Her words said one thing, but she looked as if she knew exactly where those papers were and wouldn't mind handing them to Alex.

"We'll keep that in mind, Nurse. Thank you." Michael ended the standoff between the women before it escalated. He put his arm around Alex's waist and turned her away from the nurse. "Come on, Alex. Let's go see how Reece is doing. Then you can decide what to do."

Alex looked up at him. "I just want him to be okay. To be sitting in his easy chair wearing his fishing hat. He and Aunt Adele were always home to me. You know how my parents stayed on the move. Dad was forever chasing after a better team where he could win all the championships."

"How are your folks?"

"Fine. Did I tell you Dad signed on as a coaching assistant with a pro basketball team in Italy? They left a couple of months ago. The best team Dad's ever coached." Alex made a face. "He said that every time we moved when I was a kid. The best team ever."

"You did move a lot."

"That's why I loved coming to Hidden Springs. A place that didn't change. When I got to come stay with Uncle Reece and Aunt Adele, that was home. I can't imagine losing that if something happens to Uncle Reece." The waver was in her voice again.

They stopped in front of Reece's room. The door was

closed, but instead of pushing it open, Michael put his hand on Alex's arm. "You can always come home to me."

"Can I?" She stared up at him.

He could drown in those eyes. "Yes."

She smiled and slid her fingers across his cheek. Her touch lit a fire inside him. "Thank you."

He thought about going down on one knee right there in the hospital corridor, but she turned away from him and went through the door. The moment was lost. Or perhaps only delayed. He would ask. Before she flew away again.

12

Maggie was practically floating on air by the time they got back to the church from the lake. She didn't know when she'd had so much fun. Even squishing worms on hooks was next to dreamy with Anthony helping her. And when he put his arm around her and his hand over hers to teach her how to cast her line, she thought she might faint. But she didn't. She didn't want to miss a second of being that close to him. Anthony beside her had even been enough to make her almost forget about Michael wanting to talk to her. Almost.

Anthony liked Michael. She liked Michael too. Last Sunday at the youth meeting, she talked to him a lot. She didn't think about him being a policeman then. Just somebody easy to talk to, even if he was way older than her.

But today she wanted to hide behind something whenever he looked her way. She kept imagining him saying she was under arrest. For trespassing in Miss Fonda's house.

It wasn't really trespassing. Maggie practiced the words in her head about how Miss Fonda told her it was okay. That she could use the tower room whenever she wanted. But she wasn't sure he'd believe her.

At church, Anthony offered to give her a lift home, but Maggie knew better than to show up in a guy's car without her parents' okay. They thought she wasn't old enough to date. Even if she was fifteen. That had never mattered to Maggie until now. She hadn't met a boy she wanted to go anywhere with. But that had changed.

A little sigh wanted to escape her lips, but she didn't let it. She glanced over at Pastor Karen, who was taking her home instead of Anthony. Maggie told her she could walk, but Pastor Karen said it was no trouble to give her a ride.

Maggie sincerely hoped Pastor Karen wouldn't want to go in and talk to her dad or something. No telling what he might say. Worse, he might decide Maggie couldn't go back to youth group. She had to go to youth group. To see Anthony.

She should have insisted on walking home. But even with her worry about upsetting her father, she was still relieved she didn't have to walk through the graveyard again today. Not after the spooky feeling that morning.

"Looks like you got a little sun at the lake." Pastor Karen smiled over at Maggie.

"Oh." Maggie touched her cheeks. They did feel warm, but she wasn't sure if it was from the sun or thinking about Anthony.

"Not enough to hurt. It just gives you a pretty blush."

"Um, thanks." For some reason, Maggie felt tongue-tied around Pastor Karen. Like she might look at Maggie and see all the things she wasn't doing right.

"I'm glad you went with us today. Anthony told me you'd never been fishing."

Maggie's cheeks got warmer at the mention of Anthony. "No, I hadn't."

"Did you like it? Fishing?"

"It was okay." Maggie cringed. That didn't sound very polite. Like she hadn't had a good time.

"Fishing's not for everybody. I'm not that big a fan myself." Pastor Karen laughed and gave Maggie a quick glance.

"I didn't mean to sound like I didn't like it. It was great. Thank you for letting me come." Maybe that would show she did have a few manners.

"Anytime." Another smile over at Maggie. Pastor Karen smiled more than anybody Maggie knew. "So what do you like to do? For fun."

"Read." That should be a safe answer.

"That's right." This time Pastor Karen kept her eyes on the road. "Michael said you told him Language Arts was your favorite class. Especially the creative writing section."

"Yeah, I guess."

Why had she ever told him that? She never talked about her writing.

As luck would have it, they were passing right in front of Miss Fonda's house. Maggie's heart started beating faster. Not the pleasant heart-pounding feeling when Anthony was teaching her to cast her line, but the worried, in-trouble pounding. She couldn't keep from staring out the window at the house.

Pastor Karen slowed down and looked over at the house too. "It is a beautiful old house. Have you ever been inside?"

Only all the time. The last time on Friday when Mrs. Harper fell down the stairs. Maggie flashed her eyes back toward the road and licked her suddenly too-dry lips. Or maybe they were sunburned.

She had to say something. Pastor Karen was waiting for

an answer. "My mother cleans the house for Miss Fonda. I usually help her." All true. Every word.

"Miss Fonda is a dear, isn't she?"

"Yes." Maggie didn't look back at the house.

"It's too bad about Mrs. Harper, though. Such a tragedy."

Maggie nodded without saying anything. She barely kept from shuddering as she thought about the dead woman's eyes.

Pastor Karen practically stopped the car as she peered up toward the roof. "I love that turret room. Every house should have one of those."

"It would look pretty funny on top of our trailer," Maggie said.

"Or my little house." Pastor Karen laughed and stepped on the gas.

Maggie wanted to look back at the tower room. Her room. But she kept her eyes on the road in front of them.

Pastor Karen turned down the street to the trailer park. Park. It must mean like parking a car. Here and there a tree shaded a trailer and bright-colored mums bloomed on some of the stoops. But it wasn't a park. Just a place to live when you didn't have money enough to live somewhere better.

For about the tenth time, Maggie wished she'd walked home. It wasn't raining and she didn't have any reason to hurry. She'd just have to clean up the kitchen when she got there, with no time to read or sneak away to Miss Fonda's house. Not that she would dare do that. Not yet.

She might never get to do that again. Maybe never climb back up into her little hideaway room. She thought about her notebook of stories hidden in the wall, and a funny, lost feeling opened up inside her. She ignored it as she pointed out her driveway to Pastor Karen. She clicked her seatbelt loose and grabbed the door handle before the car came to a complete stop.

"Thanks for the ride." She rushed out the words as she climbed out of the car.

"Sure thing, Maggie." Pastor Karen leaned across the seat to peer out at her. "See you tomorrow? At church?"

"Yeah. Okay. Bye." Maggie shut the car door and ran for the house. At least her father wasn't watching from the door or, even worse, sitting on the stoop with a beer. At the door, Maggie turned and waved. Pastor Karen was already backing out of the driveway. Thank goodness.

Maggie wasn't exactly ashamed of her father or where they lived. She loved her parents and her little brother, even if he was a pest at times. They were a family. Things were rough right now, but her father hadn't wanted to get laid off. It wasn't his fault the factory closed down. Her mother said everything would be better when he got another job. They just had to hold on and try not to get on his nerves right now. Her getting caught trespassing in Miss Fonda's house would definitely upset him. Michael showing up to talk to her wouldn't be good either.

"Hi. I'm home," she called as she went inside. Their little dog came bounding to greet her, his front feet popping up and down, his tail almost spinning. When she knelt down to pet him, he licked her chin. Then Bertie got serious about sniffing her, probably smelling Michael's dog. Jasper had followed Anthony around all day. And Anthony had followed her around all day. A smile slid out on her face in spite of her worries.

Jesse looked around from his spot on the floor in front of the television. "Hi."

She hoped he hadn't been watching television all day. At seven, he was into cartoons. "Did you have lunch?" she asked.

"Popcorn."

Maggie sniffed the air. "Smells like you might have burned it."

"Yeah, but we ate it anyway. Except the black ones. Bertie wouldn't even eat those." He got up to show her the clump of blackened popcorn in the scorched microwave bag.

"You have to watch that when it's popping, Jesse." Maggie frowned at him. "That stuff can catch on fire, you know."

"Dad said it was okay. We didn't burn down the house."

Maggie took the bag and wadded it closed. "Where is Dad?"

"I don't know." Jesse shrugged. "Changing clothes maybe. He said he had somewhere to go when you got home. If you ever got home. I told him I was big enough to stay here by myself."

"No, you're not," Maggie said flatly. "And I couldn't come home until Pastor Karen was ready."

She glanced at the clock. It was after four. Her mother would be there soon. But the place didn't look too bad. A newspaper folded open to the want ads. That was a good sign. No beer cans. That was a better sign. She peered toward the kitchen. A few dishes in the sink, but not too messy. She could have it all straightened up fast as anything, throw some clothes in the washer, and have time to jump in the shower.

Jesse wrinkled his nose. "You smell sort of yucky."

"Fish smell like fish. Burnt popcorn smells like burnt popcorn." She hoped Anthony didn't think she smelled yucky. But then he probably smelled like worms and fish too. That was okay in the wide-open air at the lake.

"Did you catch any fish?"

"A few."

Jesse peeked around behind her. "Then where are they?"

"We threw them back in the lake. The ones I caught were too little to keep anyway."

"I wish I could go fishing." Jesse's mouth drooped.

"Maybe you can go with me if I go again." Maggie tousled his hair. Her parents might let her go fishing with Anthony if they took Jesse along. She could make sandwiches. Have a picnic. How dreamy would that be?

"So no fish for supper." Her dad came up the hallway.

"Sorry I'm later than I said." She watched his face, expecting a blowup, but he didn't look mad. He'd shaved, slicked back his hair, and even had on a clean shirt. She didn't smell any alcohol on him, but maybe her fish smell was stronger.

"Can't be helped." He nearly smiled. "Look, I've got to go see a guy about a job. Tell your mother I don't know for sure when I'll be back. Might be late. That Sonny Elwood called and wants her to clean the Chandler house. Things probably got messed up when that woman died over there."

Maggie nodded. She couldn't say anything. The thought of going back in the house made chills run up her back, but then she did want to get her notebook. If only she didn't have to climb up those stairs to get to the tower room. But she would have to help her mother and act like nothing was wrong. She had to stop imagining Mrs. Harper's ghost peering over her shoulder.

"Can we go fishing sometime?" Jesse asked their dad.

"Sure, kid. Sounds like fun. But we'll bring home what we catch. Have fish for supper." He picked up the newspaper and was out the door.

"You think he meant it?" Jesse looked hopeful. "That he'll take me fishing."

"I don't know. Maybe. We better worry more about him getting that job." She didn't know where he could be applying for a job on Saturday afternoon, but wherever it was, she hoped he got it. She picked up a couple of dirty glasses and an apple core and headed for the kitchen.

The phone jangled on the kitchen wall, but her hands were full. "Get that, will you, Jesse?"

Jesse answered the phone, then held out the receiver toward Maggie. "It's for you. Some guy."

Maggie put the glasses in the sink and wiped her hands on her pants. A guy. Had to be Anthony. A smile turned up her lips as she took the phone. "Hello."

"Maggie?"

"Yes." It wasn't Anthony. She didn't know who it was. "Who is this?"

"That doesn't matter. You listen and you listen good. If you know what's good for you, you will forget whatever you saw at the Chandler house yesterday."

Maggie's heart started racing. "I didn't see anything."

"That's smart, Maggie. You stay smart like that and nobody will get hurt. Not you. Not your little brother. You understand?"

"Yes." She could barely push the word out loud enough to be heard.

"Remember, Maggie. I'll be watching."

Her hand shook so much she had to try twice to hang up the phone. Jesse had gone back to his cartoons. She was alone in the kitchen. She put her hands flat against the cabinet top to try to stop them from trembling, but the trembles were all through her.

What was she going to do? She hadn't seen anything. She'd

115

only heard a voice. She shut her eyes and tried to remember how the voice sounded. Nothing like the man on the phone. It could have been a woman at the house. She wasn't sure. But she was sure whoever was on the phone was a man, even if he did sound funny. Like how she sounded when she read storybooks to Jesse and made the voices fit the story.

Only this wasn't a storybook. This was real. She was in trouble. And she couldn't tell anyone.

13

With Reece being uncharacteristically cantankerous and Alex obviously exhausted but refusing to leave, Michael stayed at the hospital with her. At least that was the reason he said out loud.

After they got Reece's solemn promise to stay in bed, they went to the hospital cafeteria. Not exactly a date-night location. Certainly no place to ask someone to share the rest of your life. But at least he could feast his eyes on her.

"You should have gotten the fish special." Alex picked at her salad and looked across at the chili and sandwich in front of him.

"You obviously have no idea how many hooks I worked out of fish mouths today." Michael smiled. "I've seen enough fish for one day."

That made her smile. "So the fishing was good?"

"Reece wouldn't think so. Mostly little fish, but the kids had fun."

"Did you? Have fun?" Alex took a bite and studied him while she chewed.

"I like being with the kids, but today I was sort of distracted."

"By the realtor lady's demise?" She picked up her coffee cup.

"Some. But mostly because you were here and I was there." He bit into his sandwich.

She sipped her coffee. "I wish I had been there instead of here."

"So do I. You could have helped with the fishhooks and the worms."

That made her laugh the way he intended. "Don't act like you don't think I could. When we were kids, I could impale a worm on a hook faster than you."

"But you didn't like taking the hooks out of the fish." He didn't really remember that, but made a lucky guess.

"Well, no. The slippery things kept wriggling out of my hands. Besides, it made you feel manly to do it for me." Her smile settled in her eyes.

"Michael to the rescue." He pushed his sandwich aside and reached across the table to capture her hand.

"Indeed. And here you are, still rescuing people." Her smile slipped away as she pulled her hand back to take another bite of her salad.

If she needed rescuing now, would she call him? So many things Michael wanted to ask her. But instead he dipped his spoon into his chili and ate in silence.

After a couple of minutes, she pushed her half-eaten salad away. "Speaking of your rescues, how's Anthony?"

"Doing great. I think he's in love with a girl named Maggie."

She pretended a wounded look. "And I thought he had a crush on me."

"That he did, but I guess he's growing up. Decided to chase a girl he might catch."

"And has he caught this girl's affections?"

"They appeared to have plenty of fun today with Anthony showing her how to cast her line. She's a cute girl." Michael's smile faded a little.

"Uh-oh." Alex raised her eyebrows. "From the look on your face, I'm thinking you've found a new rescue project."

"Maybe. Somebody was in the house when Geraldine Harper fell yesterday. I think it might have been Maggie."

Alex frowned. "Why wouldn't she tell you if she was there?"

"I don't know, but today when I tried to talk to her about it, she stuck her finger on a fishhook to get away from me."

Alex laughed. "You always were a charmer."

"True enough." Michael managed a sideways smile. "And it could be she's just worried because her family is having some problems right now. Her father lost his job. That sort of thing."

"You'll figure it out. You always do." This time Alex reached over to take his hand.

For just a moment, with her looking straight into his eyes, he thought he could figure it out. Not just what had happened at the Chandler house, but also how to keep Alex in his life. But then she looked at the clock on the wall and pulled her hand away to stand up. The moment slipped away.

Later in the hospital room whenever Reece drifted into a restless sleep and the nurses stayed out of the room, they talked in muted tones about everything but what he most wanted to talk about. Their future. Instead, they shared memories of crazy things they did when they were kids. When being in love was easy.

In the middle of the night, she dozed off, and he watched her with a deep yearning to see her sleeping beside him every night. Belonging with him.

His feelings must have shown on his face because Reece spoke up. Michael had thought he was asleep too.

"She is beautiful." Reece's voice was weak but clear.

Michael flicked his gaze over to Reece and then back to Alex. "The most beautiful woman I've ever seen." Her long lashes lay softly on her cheeks and her lips looked way too inviting. His fingers twitched to reach over and brush a stray lock of hair off her face.

"You know, Michael, she might never choose love over her career."

"Does it have to be a choice?" Michael kept his eyes on Alex. She showed no sign of hearing them.

"Sometimes. I think maybe this time."

Michael let Reece's words settle in the air between them for a long moment. "Do you think I should turn her loose so she can find somebody to love in the city?"

Then it was Reece's turn to be silent as he considered his answer. "I think Alex would do what she wanted to no matter what you did. The question is, should she quit letting you think it possible?"

"It has to be possible." The words seemed to be jerked from somewhere deep inside him.

Reece let out a slow breath. "Adele and I had such hopes for the two of you. And you know Malinda felt the same."

The resignation in Reece's voice stabbed Michael. He sounded like it had been already decided, when Michael hadn't even found a way to ask Alex.

Reece went on, almost as though talking to himself. "It

would have been good to have seen Alexandria settled before I passed on."

"This is just a little bump in the road for you, Reece." Michael was relieved to shift the focus from him and Alex to Reece's recovery. "You'll be back fishing in no time."

"That could be, but death is something we all face. Just like Geraldine Harper. Malinda told me about her accident at the Chandler House." Reece moved his head back and forth on his pillow. "None of us would have expected that. And think about how close both you and Malinda came to death last summer. Alex too, for that matter. Thank God that turned out all right. What happened to that man?" Reece peered over at Michael.

"Still awaiting trial. Behind bars. The judge didn't set bail."

"No judge in his right mind would set bail for that man."

Reece shut his eyes and Michael thought he had drifted off to sleep again. But then he said, "I suppose the Hidden Springs gossips will say Audrey's ghost pushed her. Geraldine, I mean."

"Then who pushed Audrey? Aunt Lindy says she died from a fall down those same stairs years ago."

"That would be according to whether you asked Fonda or the coroner."

"Who was right?"

Reece didn't give Michael a direct answer. "Best to go with the coroner report. Seems little need in opening up that can of worms after all these years."

"The statute of limitations doesn't run out on murder."

"True enough. But it was all investigated then. Truett Johnson was sheriff when it happened. Do you remember Truett?"

"Can't say that I do."

"Well, he's been gone a long time. Had a heart attack. Anyway, Truett liked his investigations wrapped up fast and with a neat bow. Kept life simpler."

"Are you saying he was wrong? That somebody did push Audrey the way Miss Fonda thinks?"

"She didn't just say somebody pushed Audrey. She said Audrey's husband, Bradley Carlson, pushed her. On second thought, I'm not sure she ever actually said he pushed Audrey, but she had no doubt he was to blame."

"She didn't say pushed when I found her beside Geraldine either." Michael replayed Miss Fonda's words in his head. "She said Audrey was dead because of him. She didn't say who he was."

Reece frowned. "You think she saw somebody there?"

"I don't know. Poor woman was barely coherent when I found her by the body. She'd gone back in time. She thought Geraldine was Audrey."

"Odd how dementia works." Reece shook his head a little. "A sorrowful disease. But that would explain why she was so upset. She was distraught when Audrey died. When Truett wouldn't listen to her, Fonda came to me. She wanted me to press charges against Bradley, but there wasn't anything I could do. I wasn't part of the prosecutor's office then, and even if I had been, I couldn't have done anything. There was absolutely nothing to indicate Audrey's fall was anything but an accident."

"Why was Miss Fonda so sure it wasn't?"

Reece breathed in and out slowly, as though gathering his thoughts. "She didn't like Bradley. Claimed he wasn't good for Audrey, but he gave every appearance of being a loving husband. He did make no secret of his disdain for small-town life. A man with his aspirations wanted to be where the action was. The house was all that kept them in Hidden Springs."

"Aunt Lindy said the sisters, Fonda and Audrey, didn't always see eye to eye."

"Very different personalities. That made things even more complicated. Audrey felt having the house proved she was the favored daughter. She couldn't quite give that up even though Bradley hated living there. He said you didn't have to believe in ghosts to know the place was haunted. By memories. By family expectations."

"I can understand that." Michael knew about the weight of family expectations. He and Aunt Lindy were the last Keanes in Keane County. If he didn't have children, the family line would end. Something Aunt Lindy would consider a tragedy, but Hidden Springs would continue on whether a Keane was in residence or not.

"I suppose you can." Reece hit the button to raise the head of his bed and reached for the glass of water on the table by his bed. "All this talking has dried out my mouth."

"I'm sorry. I should be letting you rest."

Reece waved away Michael's words. "No, no. I have a hard time sleeping at home in my own bed. No way can I sleep here." He looked over at Alex. "Looks like Alex is managing fine."

"I doubt she slept much last night. Worried about you."

"She's a sweet girl."

Sweet wasn't a word Michael had ever thought to use to describe Alex. Striking. Electrifying. Determined. Maddening. Adored. But when he thought about it, she was very sweet to Reece.

Reece went on in a musing tone. "But I suppose it's natural

that Geraldine's death would make Audrey's death come to mind for those of us who remember her. Both falling to their deaths down those stairs, but accidents do happen."

"All the time."

"Nothing about Audrey's accident aroused suspicions except Fonda's accusations that somehow Bradley was at fault." Reece sat his plastic water glass down and twirled it around. "The only red flag at all was the large life insurance policy Bradley took out on Audrey the previous year. That did supply some grist for the gossip mill. But it's not unusual to buy insurance for one's spouse." He was silent for a moment. "I had a policy on Adele. Nothing like what Bradley had on Audrey, but a fair amount. That didn't mean I ever wanted to cash it in. I do miss that woman."

"Do you think Bradley missed Audrey?"

"Hard to answer for someone else. He did give every appearance of being grief stricken at the funeral. Shocked by her death as everyone was. But then he went home and packed his and little Brad's things and left the next day. It wasn't long before we heard he had remarried. Never came back to Hidden Springs. Left it up to Fonda to do whatever she wanted with Audrey's things. Fonda wasn't in any shape for it either. She wandered around in a daze for weeks. Much the way she is now. Not sure about anything except how much she disliked Bradley."

"But she was married then, wasn't she?"

"True. Gilbert was one of those men ready to go along with whatever his wife wants. Like me, I suppose." Reece laughed a little. "While Adele was alive, people often accused me of being henpecked, but that wasn't it. Not at all. I was just relaxed. Not sure that was the case with Gilbert."

"Why's that?"

Reece's smile was gone. "I don't know that I could ever put my finger on it. The two of them, Fonda and Gilbert, didn't exactly fuss and fight. Gilbert didn't seem to care enough to fight, if you know what I mean. There were times I wondered if he only married Fonda to find the treasure he was so sure was hidden in the walls of the Chandler mansion. As a way of coming into money."

"Do you think there's treasure to find?" Michael had heard all the rumors about hidden treasures in the old house.

"Who knows? The house goes back a ways. Might be a secret cubbyhole somewhere. Fonda used to laugh about Gilbert tapping on the walls trying to find something like that. She put up with it, but she refused to let him tear into any of the walls to search. She took preserving the house exactly as it was while her parents were alive very seriously."

"It definitely has an antique feel."

"With good reason. Her parents and grandparents before them were collectors and acquired some fine things. That's probably where the treasure is. In the paintings and antiques. I'm surprised Vernon Trent hasn't been trying to mine that treasure. But then with Fonda not exactly in her right mind, I suppose he can't."

"It wouldn't matter. Miss Fonda wouldn't sell anything to him any sooner than Aunt Lindy would."

"Or me." Reece took another drink and wiped his mouth on an edge of the sheet. "But you're right. Fonda clung to her memories. She got the house solely in her name after Audrey's death. Bradley and little Brad didn't get any part of it then. That was the way the Chandlers had their will drawn up. A rather odd document, but legal enough. Hardly seemed completely fair, but I suppose if Bradley or the boy had inherited the house, it would have been sold. Fonda and Audrey's parents were determined that not happen. So they wrote all sorts of conditions into their will."

"Guess it was good Bradley had the big insurance policy then." Michael shifted a little in his chair and made the plastic covering squeak. He glanced at Alex to see if the different noise woke her. Her eyes were still closed but he had the feeling she was no longer asleep.

"I'm sure it helped him get established in Indiana. You knew he was a representative in Congress for his district up there, didn't you?"

"Aunt Lindy told me that."

"Was still serving last I heard. Wonder if Alex knows him up there in DC?"

"Ask her." Michael leaned over and touched her knee. "I think she's playing possum."

She flicked her eyes open with a slightly abashed smile. "Maybe. I didn't want to interrupt your conversation."

"And just how long have you been eavesdropping?" Michael hoped she hadn't heard Reece talking about their chances to make love work between them. Or lack of chances.

She sat up and stretched. Even with her hair mussed and her clothes rumpled, she still looked like a sleek cat. "Not long."

But she avoided looking at Michael as she quickly stood up to fluff Reece's pillow and straighten his covers. She must have heard Reece. How come everybody was losing hope even before he found a way to ask? He wanted to take her hands. Make her look at him. Really look at him. Make her believe they could love one another. But first, he might have to make himself believe.

14

Sunday morning, Reece was dressed and ready to leave the hospital fifteen minutes after the doctor gave the go-ahead. Then he fidgeted while a nurse mostly ignored him and went over home care instructions with Alex. Michael stood to the side, almost glad to hear the nurse go on and on about this or that reason Reece would need assistance. Reasons for Alex to stay in Hidden Springs for at least a few days.

On the way to Reece's house, he drove through the Fast Serve for coffee and sausage biscuits. Mary Greene was working the drive-thru window.

"Good morning, Mrs. Greene. Thanks for letting Maggie go fishing with us yesterday." He handed her the money for his order.

Mary Greene was an attractive woman even with the silly Fast Serve hat perched on her short brown hair and the weary lines on her face. Probably pulling extra hours with her husband out of work. She smiled and that erased a few years from her face and made Maggie's resemblance to her more evident.

"She had fun." The woman handed change out to Michael.

"Good to hear. But I got the feeling she was worried about something. Did she mention anything to you?"

"You know teenagers." The woman avoided his eyes. "Always something going on with them."

With mothers of teens too, it seemed. "You've got that right, but if there's any way I can help, let me know."

"Thank you." She handed out the coffee in a cardboard tray.

His rearview mirror didn't show anybody behind him to hurry him on his way. A good time to find out some things. "She said you cleaned the Chandler place."

"Right. I've been cleaning for Miss Fonda for years. I miss her being there now. The house feels so empty when we go over there." She handed out the sack of food.

"When was the last time you were there?"

She paused, thinking about her answer. "About three weeks ago. I only clean once a month now, but Sonny Elwood did ask that I clean again as soon as I have time. No reason I shouldn't, is there? After Mrs. Harper's accident, I mean." She sounded a little worried.

Behind Michael, a car pulled up to the speaker to order. "No. Clean whenever you want." Michael put the cruiser in gear. "Tell Maggie hello for me."

She smiled and waved before she turned to speak into the microphone hooked to a headpiece. Her voice squawked out of the box behind him, almost unrecognizable.

Reece was inside settled in his recliner when Michael got there. Alex raised her eyebrows at the fast-food sacks.

"We need coffee," Michael said. "And there's yogurt and fruit cups if you aren't a sausage biscuit fan, but Fast Serve makes good ones."

"They do indeed." Reece held out his hand. "I'll take one and that coffee."

"Uncle Reece, do you think you should? They said to watch your diet."

Reece leveled his eyes on Alex. "You can fix chicken soup later. Right now coffee and sausage biscuit is on my list. So hand them over, Michael."

Michael did his best to ignore Alex's disapproving look as he handed Reece one of the biscuits.

"They said you might have trouble swallowing for a while." Alex looked so worried Michael began to regret stopping at the Fast Serve. "You don't want to choke."

"I heard them, Alexandria. I was there even if that starched hankie nurse acted like I was deaf and blind. But a man has to eat. I'll take teeny bites and chew ten times before I swallow." He took a bite to demonstrate and then sipped his coffee. "Ahh, so good to be home. A man should have the right to pick his place to die."

"Nobody has said a thing about you dying." Alex narrowed her eyes on Reece. "You're too ornery to die. Unless you commit suicide by way of fast food with the help of those who should know better." She turned her scowl on Michael.

"Sorry." Michael backed up a step. "I guess I missed the doctor's diet directives."

"I guess you did." Alex's glare didn't get any softer.

"Don't worry about it, Michael." Reece gave a little shrug. "She's a lawyer. She's rewriting the facts to suit her case. That doctor never said one thing about sausage biscuits. He said I needed protein and fruit. Sausage equals protein." He held up his coffee. "This came off some kind of bush, didn't it? So fruit."

She made a face at Reece. "I do not rewrite the facts. I search out the right facts!" Her smile was back for Reece as she gave up the fight over the food, but when she turned back to Michael, the smile didn't seem as easy. "Don't you have to go home and feed that dog of yours?"

Michael took a sip of coffee. "Are you trying to get rid of me?"

Reece quit chewing to watch them.

"No, not at all. Well, maybe a little. Uncle Reece needs to rest. He can't say the doctor didn't tell him that." She shot a look over at Reece, then packed the remaining sausage biscuits back in the paper sack and shoved it at Michael.

Things were not going exactly as he hoped. "Okay." He fastened the top down on his coffee. "I'll go peacefully if you walk me to the door."

He sat the coffee and food sack down on the table by the door and took Alex's hands. She didn't pull away from him, but she wasn't exactly relaxed either. "We need to talk, Alex."

"We always talk, Michael."

"But do we ever say anything?"

"Sometimes and we will again, but not today. I'm tired. You're tired." She slipped her hands away from his and lifted up on her toes to brush her lips across his.

It was all he could do not to grab her and pull her close. "You're not going to disappear back to Washington on me, are you?"

"How can I? Not until I find a nurse or housekeeper, somebody to help Uncle Reece." She kept her voice low as she looked back toward Reece.

Two Bits, his cat, came out of hiding to climb into Reece's

130

lap. Reece stroked the cat and fed him a crumb from the sausage biscuit.

"What am I going to do?" Alex looked back at Michael, a hint of desperation in her voice. "There's no way I can make chicken soup." A tear slid out of her left eye.

Michael reached to brush it away. "Call Aunt Lindy. She's not the greatest cook, but she knows how to make soup." He knew she was talking about more than chicken soup, but he didn't have answers for her other worries.

"Dear Malinda. She did say she'd help however she could." She surprised him by capturing his hand and kissing his fingers. "Thank you, Michael. I don't know what I'd do without you here. You and Malinda."

He didn't like the way she paired him with Aunt Lindy. But then, there were a lot of things he didn't like. A lot of things they needed to make clear. He'd been afraid to ask too long. Still, she was right. They were tired.

He brushed her hair back from her face and kissed her forehead. "Get some rest. I'll come by after church tonight."

"If it's not too late," she said.

If it's not too late. The words trailed after him to his cruiser. Was it too late?

———— ◆◆◆ ————

Malinda came around her house carrying a pot of vegetable soup to Reece's just as Michael came out of the house. She called his name, but he didn't hear her. His head was down, staring at the ground. No energy to his steps. Her heart gave a little lurch. Alexandria must have sent him away.

Those two infuriated Malinda. She had thought for sure after the trouble last summer they would finally admit they were meant to be together. For a few weeks, her prayers for them seemed to be seeing fruition. But the long arms of Alexandria's attorney firm had reached out and pulled her back to Washington, DC. Michael hadn't gone after her.

Now Michael wheeled his car around to go the other direction, still without giving any sign of noticing her there. His powers of observation were lacking.

She wanted to set the soup pot down in the grass and run after him. Make him talk to her the way he used to when he was a boy. But boys grow up. Shoulder their problems on their own. As they should. Even so, when he hurt, she hurt. No way could she change that. That was how mothers were. No matter that she hadn't actually given birth to him, he was her son. That might have been different if his parents hadn't been killed when he was a teen. Might have been.

No need to think about might-have-beens. Things happened and life went on. Sometimes you could make things better and sometimes you couldn't, no matter how much you wanted to. Just like now. Reece had had a stroke. He couldn't go back a few days and avoid that somehow. And whatever Alexandria had said to Michael to make his shoulders slump like that had been said. The words couldn't be taken back.

Standing there in the yard like a clothesline post, wishing things different while the soup got cold, wasn't helping a thing. She could at least send up a prayer for the silly children. That's what they were acting like. Children. Fighting and making up and fighting again. You'd think they would have grown out of that long ago.

As she headed on toward Reece's house, she looked up and whispered her plea. "Lord, you know best. I know you do. But can't you give those two a little shove or something? Please."

15

Michael checked in with Sally Jo before he headed home. Nothing going on, she reported. No wrecks. No crimes. No fights. Although she was sure speeders were burning up the road out around the interstate.

"Somebody else will have to catch them today. I just hope they don't run into one another."

"If things go haywire, you'll be the first to know." Sally Jo laughed. "So don't get too comfortable down there fishing off your dock."

"Yeah, thanks." Michael signed off.

Things had already gone haywire. Geraldine Harper dead. Reece having a stroke. Alex in Hidden Springs. That had changed his plans. Fishing wasn't on the top of his list anymore. Alex was.

But she had practically pushed him out the door. She was tired. He was tired. She was glad he was there. She wanted him to leave. She loved him. She didn't love him enough. He felt like he was plucking the petals off a daisy. She loves me. She loves me not.

At his house, Jasper bounded off the porch to greet him. At

least somebody was glad to see him. He looked past the dog toward the log house and imagined Alex in the door waiting for him. Maybe a little girl on a swing hanging from a maple branch. A little boy pushing a truck in the dirt by the porch.

He must be asleep. That was a dream, for certain. The chances of Alex living here on the lake were nil to none.

Jasper made short work of his food while Michael downed a couple of the cold sausage biscuits. He was kicking off his shoes to grab a nap when the radio crackled awake. Sally Jo was sorry but T.R. Boggess said somebody filled up at his station out by the interstate and took off without paying.

Michael looked at his bed with longing, but even though the guy would be in the next state by the time Michael got there, he pulled his shoes back on. T.R. should stop trusting people and make them pay before they pumped, like the new Stop and Go with its bright lights and self-serve drinks.

T.R.'s drink machine was so ancient it only took quarters. When he started losing money on the sodas, he unplugged the machine and loaded a shelf inside his station with canned drinks. They weren't cold, but they were wet. T.R. didn't do convenience. He had his wrecker and a few customers at his gas pumps to keep him going. But he couldn't stay in business if people didn't pay.

T.R. told him as much when Michael got to his place a half hour later. Loudly and more than once. Right after he told him a business owner shouldn't have to wait an hour for the police to show up when he'd been robbed.

Michael nodded now and then and let T.R. get it all out. When the man finally calmed down enough that Michael could write up a report, he didn't have much to report. His surveillance camera had gone on the blink a month ago, and he hadn't gotten around to fixing it. He was busy changing the oil in Mrs. Paxton's Ford and had barely looked at the man at the pumps. He did know it was a blue Plymouth. Or maybe a Dodge. 2002 model. Or 2003. He hadn't paid much attention until he heard the guy slam his door and start the motor up. Then he'd run to the door to get the license plate. Except he hadn't been wearing his glasses. Didn't need them for changing oil but he did for reading license plates. He thought it might have been a Tennessee tag.

Michael took it all down but both of them knew the only way T.R. would get paid for that tank of gas was if the guilty party had an attack of conscience and came back. That wasn't likely to happen. Attacks of conscience seemed to be out of style.

The day went downhill from there. A fender bender in the First Baptist Church lot after a deacons' meeting. Both Stanley Campbell and Bill Ridner claimed the other man should have been paying more attention. But that was the way of parking lot accidents. Nobody was ever at fault if you listened to the drivers. Then he drove downtown and saw Betty Jean's car parked behind Bygone Treasures. He resisted the urge to stop and do a security check on the store.

He didn't know what bothered him about Betty Jean and Vernon Trent, but something did. He shook off the feeling. If Betty Jean had found love or at least was tiptoeing toward it, that was good. Better than good. The girl had been hunting love a long time. His foul mood had more to do with the feeling that love was tiptoeing away from him. No, not tiptoeing. Walking away. Maybe running.

He considered turning toward Keane Street, but he had

called when he left T.R.'s. No answer. He left a message to call him back. Alex hadn't.

That didn't mean he couldn't go to Aunt Lindy's and catch a nap before church. No time to drive to his house. But Aunt Lindy would ask about Alex. She'd think it was simply a matter of adding one plus one to equal two. Alex plus him. The formula worked for Michael. But he was pretty sure Alex was adding a few unknown x's and y's to the equation.

The same as he seemed to keep adding a few unknowns to Geraldine Harper's death. He was passing the Chandler house and on impulse turned into the driveway. He should make a drive-by now and again since the place was empty. Could be he might catch whoever had been in there on Friday.

After the fishing outing yesterday, he was pretty sure who that was. Could Geraldine have caught Maggie Greene in the house and that was why she was rushing down the steps? To throw Maggie out. Maybe threatening to call Maggie's parents.

The girl might have been scared silly even before Geraldine fell, but he couldn't believe Maggie had done anything to make the woman fall. Even so, she needed to admit being there if she was in the house.

Michael climbed out of his cruiser, relieved to see the front veranda empty. Miss Fonda must be safely ensconced at the Gentle Care Home. When a blue jay squawked a warning overhead, Michael looked up. No way to spot anybody in the tower room from here. If Maggie was the intruder the way he suspected, she probably wouldn't be brave enough to come back for a while. At least, not alone.

The house wasn't all that far from the street, but the old trees in the yard gave it a secluded feel. The cemetery that bordered the side yard increased that feeling. Quiet neighbors for sure. An archway in the wrought-iron fence had a gate that opened into the graveyard.

When Miss Fonda's calico cat darted out from under a forsythia bush to race past him, Michael followed it around the house. There, on the back porch, a woman leaned close to a window with her hands cupped around her face to peer inside. Perhaps he was wrong about Maggie being the intruder after all.

The cat that paid no attention to Michael ran straight for the woman to rub against her legs. The woman jerked back from the window to look around. Lana Waverly, tea shop owner and aspiring mystery writer, gasped and slapped her hand against her chest when she saw Michael. As she stepped back, she tripped over the cat and grabbed at an old lawn chair to keep her balance. But it folded and fell with her. The cat scooted out of the way.

Michael ran up the porch steps to lean over the woman. "Are you all right?"

"Oh my! How embarrassing." She laughed slightly as she pushed up to sitting position. "I'm not usually so klutzy." She reached up toward Michael. "If you could give me a hand."

"If you're sure you're not hurt." Michael took her hand.

"No damage to anything other than my dignity." With his help, she got nimbly to her feet and looked around. "Wherever did that cat come from? And where did it go?"

If any dignity had been lost, Lana Waverly had recovered it. She didn't seem a bit concerned to be caught trespassing on someone else's property. She lightly smoothed down her shoulder-length blonde hair before she brushed off her crisply pressed pants. She was an attractive woman at that age where it was difficult to guess exactly how old she was. Forties, maybe. Everything about her was polished to its highest gloss.

"Miss Marble has a way of appearing and disappearing at will."

"Miss Marble. What a delightful name for a calico cat!" She flashed him a smile. "Does she live here even though the place is deserted?"

"The cat's usually around somewhere." He kept his eyes on Lana. The cat belonged here. Lana Waverly did not. "But why are you here?"

Her smile didn't waver. "I suppose I am trespassing. But when I saw the gateway out of the cemetery, I couldn't resist the urge to take a peek at the house." She held up her hand to stop him from speaking. "Wait. I know your next question. Why was I in the cemetery?" Her smile got a bit wider. "I thought it would be a good way to get a feel for the history of the town."

"Oh?"

"Come now. That's not so strange." Her smile dimmed as she looked toward the graveyard. "What better place to get to know about the people here? Their names. Their heritage." Her eyes turned back to Michael. "Since I plan to use your town for the setting of a whole series of mystery novels, the more I know about this place, the better. Don't you think the town's name practically shouts mystery? Hidden Springs." She drew out the name in the air with her graceful hands. "I can hardly believe some of the things I've been told happened here in the last couple of years. Definite inspiration for a mystery writer."

"Bad things happen everywhere." That didn't mean Michael

wanted to talk about them. Could be he was getting more and more like Aunt Lindy. Wanting to bury everything except the good about Hidden Springs.

"Sadly, that's true, as Mrs. Harper's tragic fall proves." She looked toward the house again. "They say it was an accident." Her words carried an unspoken question.

"Yes." Michael spoke the word flatly.

"So sorrowful for her family." She kept her eyes on the house as she spoke. "Do you think history repeats itself, Deputy?"

"What do you mean?"

She pulled her gaze from the house to look at him. "You do know that another woman died in a fall in this house, don't you? Down a flight of stairs too."

"So I've been told, but that happened a long time ago."

"Yes." The lines of her face tightened as her hazel eyes grew more intense. "But I'm sure you are aware there is no statute of limitations for murder."

16

"Murder?" Michael didn't like hearing that word. Never mind the uneasy feelings that had been poking him ever since Friday. "Whose murder?"

"Audrey Carlson's."

He shouldn't have been surprised by her answer. Aunt Lindy had already told him the woman had asked her about Audrey. But it seemed so strange. As if Geraldine's death had shaken awake long-forgotten ghosts in the Chandler house.

"The coroner determined her death was accidental." Michael stressed the word "accidental."

"Coroners make all sorts of convenient findings." Lana lifted one perfectly shaped eyebrow. "Especially if the death investigation involves a person of importance."

"Decisions are based on the facts available." He didn't like what the woman was implying.

"Please, don't misunderstand. I don't mean to disparage your current coroner, who no doubt performs his duties to the best of his ability. Did he rule Mrs. Harper's death an accident?" This time both of her eyebrows shot up.

"Yes." While Michael didn't care for her condescending tone, he had no reason not to answer her.

"Perhaps it was. People do fall down steps, I'm told. Accidentally at times, even in mystery stories." Her smile returned. "Or not. A murder mystery must have some sort of wrongful death, now doesn't it?"

"If you say so. I don't read mystery novels."

"You don't like mysteries?" Again the lifted eyebrows. This time with an amused look.

"I see enough of that on the job. I prefer history."

"Truth rather than fiction." She pulled a little face. "How disappointing. I was thinking you'd make the perfect first reader for my books. To check the accuracies of police procedure."

"Not qualified for that."

"How better qualified could one be? A bona fide police officer." Her smile changed as she stepped closer to him. "I could make it worth your time. A dinner out perhaps? Your aunt says you aren't married."

He didn't back away from her, even though she was near enough for him to catch a whiff of her perfume. "I doubt my aunt told you that."

She laughed. "Come to think of it, I don't think it was Miss Keane who gave me that information. But plenty of the ladies in my shop discuss their handsome deputy sheriff and his bachelor ways."

He did step back then. Time to get this encounter on firmer footing. "You spoke about Audrey Carlson. What makes you think her death was anything other than an accident?"

"I'm acquainted with Bradley Carlson." The woman's flirtatious smile was gone in an instant. Now her face looked hard enough to crack. "Too acquainted."

"Do you want to explain?"

"He killed my mother too."

"Your mother?" Michael frowned. "Are we talking about the same Bradley Carlson?"

"The one and only. Longtime member of Congress. A man of importance. Good at getting rid of wives."

"What happened to your mother?"

"Which do you want? The coroner's version after his long talk with my stepfather or the true version?"

"Which do you want to give me?"

"It hardly matters." She stared off toward the cemetery. "No one wants to listen. They never have."

Michael didn't say anything, simply waited her out. She wanted to tell him.

The silence that wrapped around them must have encouraged Miss Marble to come out of hiding. The cat sauntered back up on the porch but kept her distance. The woman didn't notice her. She was peering into the past.

Finally she spoke. "The coroner said my mother committed suicide. An intentional overdose. That could have never happened. Not my mother. She loved me. She wouldn't have hurt me that way. Bradley Carlson did it. Ready to move on to another woman. Another step up. That's all his wives were for him. A step up. First, Audrey here with her family fortune." The woman waved her hand toward the house. "Then my mother with her inheritance and property from my father. My father's death in a private plane crash devastated Mother. She had married young and didn't know how to live alone. That made her easy pickings for a man like Carlson." Her words crackled with bitterness, but she didn't allow any expression to show on her face when she turned back to Michael. "It takes money to get elected these days."

"What makes you think Audrey's death wasn't an accident?" He moved the conversation away from her mother.

"A man kills once, he will do it again." She seemed to dare Michael to deny that. "Especially when he not only gets away with it but wins the sympathy vote. Believe me. Bradley Carlson knows how to play the part of a grieving widower. Voters love that."

"How long ago did your mother die?"

"You mean was murdered?" The harsh lines of anger aged the woman. As if she realized that, she smoothed her hand across her face and regained her earlier composure. "I am sorry, Michael. It is all right if I call you Michael, isn't it? Everybody here in Hidden Springs seems to be on a first-name basis. Makes for a chummy place, don't you think?"

"Part of the charm of a small town, Miss Waverly."

"Oh please. If I call you Michael, you must call me Lana." She laid her hand lightly on Michael's arm. "Chummy can't be one-sided, can it?"

"I guess not." Michael shifted just enough to move away from her touch. "But you didn't answer my question about your mother."

"It's been over ten years ago." Again her gaze drifted to the cemetery. "In ways it seems much longer and in other ways, as though it happened yesterday. She was a lovely woman and Bradley Carlson killed her."

"Do you have any proof of that?" Michael had no reason to involve himself in something that happened in a different state. He should have tamped down his curiosity, but the question came out.

A. H. GABHART

"Some things are difficult to prove, but that doesn't mean they didn't happen." She looked back at Michael. "But no, I have no proof that could be set down in front of a jury. But I have no doubt my mother is dead because of Bradley Carlson."

Her words echoed Miss Fonda. *She's dead because of him.*

"Is he remarried now?" Another question he had no reason to ask.

"No. He did have another woman in his sights after Mother, but the woman broke it off. Perhaps she didn't like the political life or who knows?" She raised her hand to stare at her red fingernails, as though looking for a chip in the polish. "It could have been the letter I felt compelled to send her advising her to be careful. Very careful."

"Did you know his son, Bradley Jr.?" Again, Michael tried to shift the conversation.

"Of course. Little Brad was quite a handful when my mother married his father. Kept the household in an uproar with one crisis after another. I made a mad dash for New York the minute I was out of school. Young Brad eventually grew up and took off for California. Wanted to be in the movie business."

"Do you keep in touch?" When she gave him an odd look, he added, "With Bradley Jr."

"Why do you care?" A frown etched lines between her eyes.

"No reason. Just curious."

"Curiosity killed the cat, you know." She frowned at him, then shrugged slightly. "But I don't mind telling you. He used to hit me up for money now and again when his father pulled back his wallet. I did send him some a few times. For my mother's sake. I didn't want Brad Jr. showing up on her doorstep again. But once Mother was gone, I stopped. I doubt he could track me down now."

"He probably wouldn't expect to find you here in Hidden Springs. His hometown."

"He might think it a delightful surprise. He had good memories of Hidden Springs. Of his aunt Fonda and the house." She turned back to the house. "It is a beautiful place, but it surely has its dark memories. And now it has more."

"How so?"

She looked surprised by his question. "Geraldine Harper, of course. Such a tragic end for her." She bent down to stroke the cat that was rubbing against her legs again. "I talked to Geraldine last week about possibly buying the house when it went on the market, and she warned me a cat was in residence. I'm not sure why she thought that necessary, but I suppose the cat has proven to be a tripping hazard. What happened today perhaps happened Friday. Do you think Geraldine was tripped up by a cat?"

"The cat wasn't in the house."

"Someone could have let her out." She kept her eyes on the cat. "But then again, Geraldine may have simply been warning me in case I had allergies."

"Do you?"

"Not to cats." She smiled up at Michael and stroked Miss Marble head to tail one more time before she stood up. "Perhaps Geraldine did. She didn't sound as if she cared much for cats. Or dogs either. Claimed they were nothing but a bother when she was trying to sell a house."

"She did enjoy her business," Michael said.

"Selling houses was her life, or so she told me. You can't imagine how excited she was about Sonny Elwood contracting with her to sell this one. He's a strange little man, isn't he?"

"All of us have our moments."

"Michael, I do think you're jabbing me with that." She laughed then, a practiced tinkling sound, as fake as her tears earlier.

When he didn't say anything, she went on. "I don't suppose you know where a key is hidden around here? I would dearly love to take a look inside."

"You haven't been inside?"

"Why would I be acting like a peeping Thelma if I had already been inside?"

"I don't know. You tell me."

"I did tell you. All the stories I've heard about the house since I got to Hidden Springs have piqued my interest. The lovely antique furnishings. Not to mention the treasure rumored to be hidden in the walls."

"You can't believe everything you hear."

"True enough." Her voice changed. "That's the reason I need to see for myself."

"You'll have to talk to Sonny Elwood about a key."

"Or sweet Fonda. She does like to talk about how things used to be in the house. When she was young. Too bad she has difficulty separating now from then. Mrs. Gibson was quite clear in telling me not to put too much stock in anything Fonda said."

"Guess that won't matter if you're looking for grist for your fiction mill."

"Come, come, Michael. You make it sound so commercial. Writing murder mysteries takes skill, the same as catching murderers. I hear you're good at that. Catching the bad guys."

"Sometimes I manage to catch a trespasser."

"So you do." She held out her wrists with a sly smile. "Are you going to handcuff me and take me in?"

"I think a warning will do." Michael kept his smile in neutral. No need giving her any encouragement. "But if you want to see the house, I'm sure Sonny would be glad to give you a tour."

She dropped her hands back to her side. "I'll have to check with him." She laughed again as she moved past Michael to the porch steps. "Come by the shop sometime and have a cuppa. On the house. And the apple walnut muffins are to die for." She glanced back over her shoulder. "Not to worry, Deputy. A mere figure of speech."

He watched her pass through the cemetery gate and move out of sight among the headstones. Miss Marble, now that the woman was gone, wrapped around his legs. When he leaned over to pet the cat, she pushed her mottled black and orange head up to meet his hand. A purr rumbled through her.

"If only you could talk, you could tell me what you saw on Friday."

Nothing. The cat saw nothing because there was nothing to see. He straightened up and shook his head. The lack of sleep was getting to him. He could lean against one of the porch posts and doze off in a minute. Maybe sooner. But no time for that.

He pulled his phone out of his pocket. Almost church time. No calls. Not from Sally Jo. Not from Alex. She was probably sleeping. Or making chicken soup. What she wasn't doing was calling him.

He took another look around. Tried the doors to be sure

they were locked. Considered peeking in the window like Lana Waverly, but the house was empty. Nothing to see but ghosts. And he didn't believe in ghosts.

On the way to the church, he passed Mrs. Gibson's Gentle Care Home. Mrs. Gibson was usually good for a cup of coffee and he had just enough time before church for a quick visit to Miss Fonda. He pulled in the driveway just as Felicia Peterson was backing out of a parking spot in her old Chevy. It was doubtful she'd ever get to drive Sonny's BMW again after her wild trip away from the Chandler house on Friday.

Michael moved to the side to give her plenty of room. She gave him a jerky wave and then stared straight ahead as she slowly drove past him. He checked in his rearview mirror to see if she stopped before turning out on the highway. The brake lights came on and her turn signal flashed. She appeared to be taking no chances that Michael would have reason to stop her.

When he rang the bell, Mrs. Gibson came to the door with a dishtowel in her hand. "Sorry about the locked door, Michael, but I guess I'll have to keep it locked all the time now. Either that or lose my license if the inspectors hear about you-know-who getting away on me." She lowered her voice and glanced toward the women clustered around the television set in the spacious front room. Three of the four had nodded off. Miss Fonda wasn't among them. "So many rules and regulations sent down by the government these days. Makes a body's head swim. I'd give it up and start a cake baking business if it weren't for the ladies. I can't imagine what might happen to them."

"It's not that much trouble to lock your doors."

"I suppose not." She fanned herself with the towel. She was a generous woman in spirit and size. "Did you come by to see Miss Fonda?"

"And to get a cup of coffee if you have any made."

"For you, I'd make a fresh pot. But as it turns out, I haven't poured out the pot I fixed for Florence Stamper's son who ate dinner with us a while ago. He's such a nice boy."

Michael managed not to smile. Gary Stamper had to be in his late fifties, but Mrs. Gibson who was pushing seventy had probably known him when he was a boy. "Where is Miss Fonda? She not in the mood for television tonight?"

"Oh no. The dear thing hasn't been the same since Friday when, well, you know." She glanced over at the ladies again. "Has quite taken to her bed. I've half a mind to call Ellen tomorrow about having the doctor take a look at her. I know Ellen's in Arizona, but it does absolutely no good at all to talk to Sonny. That boy." She clamped her lips together. "Never mind. I shouldn't be talking about him. And he does send Felicia over to check on his aunt most every day. Felicia's a bit flighty but she's company for Fonda."

"I saw her leaving just now." Michael nodded toward the parking area.

"Right. She didn't stay long. She said Fonda kept dozing off on her, so she thought it best to let her sleep."

"Was she here Friday when Miss Fonda made her escape?"

"Well, no, dear. She's very good with Fonda. She wouldn't have let her get out the door. If only. Poor dear. It had to be quite a shock for her to find Geraldine like that. So like her sister." Mrs. Gibson dabbed her forehead with the dishtowel. "I made a pot roast tonight and the kitchen is steaming. But come on and I'll get your coffee."

He started to say something, but she waved away his words. "No trouble. No trouble at all."

He trailed her to the kitchen. "I can't stay long, so if you could put it in a Styrofoam cup, that would be great."

"Sure thing." She rummaged in the cabinet and came up with a cup. "You take it black, don't you?"

When she handed him the cup, he took a sip. "Just what I need. You're a lifesaver. I might make it to church now."

"So nice of you to help Pastor Karen with those kids. That age can be a challenge. Except that sweet Maggie Greene. She comes by and reads to Fonda now and again. Fonda thinks she's her daughter sometimes."

"Miss Fonda didn't have a daughter." Michael peered at Mrs. Gibson over his cup.

"That doesn't mean she can't think she does now. Everything is all a jumble for her. Real and imagined mixing together." Mrs. Gibson frowned. "It doesn't help when that woman comes by and tries to make her remember what the poor thing can't remember."

"Felicia?"

"No, that new woman. What is her name?" Mrs. Gibson shut her eyes as though that would help her think. "Waverly. Lana Waverly. Fonda was in a state after she visited yesterday. Worse even than when Felicia brought her back Friday. I can't imagine how awful that would be. To find somebody dead. Well, somebody you weren't expecting to die. I have seen a few of my ladies pass over, but that's just an easy letting go. Geraldine dying is different. She wasn't even sixty yet."

"What does Lana Waverly want with Miss Fonda?"

"She claims to be interested in the history of the Chandler

place. But I can't be letting her make my clients sick. If Fonda wants to talk, that's one thing. But that woman was peppering her with questions. Had Fonda in a state."

"What sort of questions?"

"I'm sure I don't know. I don't eavesdrop on my clients and their guests." Mrs. Gibson pushed her hair back from her forehead and flapped a little air toward her face with the dishtowel.

"Maybe you should tell her Miss Fonda isn't up to visits right now."

"Oh, I couldn't do that." The woman shook her head a little. "I don't run a prison. In spite of the locked door. My ladies like visitors. And Fonda likes talking about the past. You should hear her when that child, Maggie, comes by. You can almost see her dancing with her fellows back in the day. And climbing up to that tower room. To hear Fonda tell it, she spent half her time up there when she was Maggie's age. It was her getaway place."

"What about Felicia? Does she like talking to her about the past?"

"Felicia is more into the here and now. Hasn't much patience for the back-when stories. Not that she's not nice enough to Fonda. She is, but you can tell it's a job. No more." Mrs. Gibson sighed. "I just don't understand this young generation. It's like they can't give one iota more than what they think they're being paid to do." A timer went off in the kitchen. "Oh dear, I need to give Etta her evening meds. You go on back and see if Fonda's awake. Maybe it'll cheer her up to see you."

Miss Fonda opened her eyes when Michael stepped up beside her bed. She looked tired. No, more than tired. She looked weary of breathing. When she lifted her hand off the covers toward Michael, he set his coffee down and took it. "Hello, Miss Fonda. I dropped by to see how you're doing."

"Not good." She gripped his hand with more strength than Michael would have thought she had. "And don't say that they are, Gilbert. You're always trying to make things better than they are."

Michael knew who Gilbert was. Miss Fonda's long-dead husband. He mumbled some kind of answer. It seemed cruel to tell her Gilbert had been gone these many years.

"But I know what happened and whose fault it was." She dropped her hand back down on the covers and turned her face toward the wall. "I know. And sometimes I don't think I can stand it."

Michael patted her shoulder. "There, there, Miss Fonda. It will be all right after you rest awhile."

"How can you say that? It will never be all right again." She didn't turn her head to look back at Michael. "It was his fault. All of it. His fault." A tear made its way through her wrinkles down her cheek. "And don't say it wasn't, because it was. No matter how it happened."

"Shh." Michael stroked her arm this time. "Maybe things will look better in the morning."

"Morning only brings more trouble. Nothing but trouble since she married. Nothing but trouble." The last words were a whispered mumble as her eyes closed. But she was still breathing. She hadn't given up on that completely quite yet.

He picked up his coffee and made his way out. Mrs. Gibson waved at him from the television room. By the time he got to church, he was running on coffee and fumes. He searched through the kids gathered in their meeting room. Anthony was there, but no Maggie.

For some reason, that worried Michael. Worries piled on top of worries. But right in the middle of them, poking him the hardest, was his silent phone.

17

"Aren't you going to youth group tonight?" Maggie's mother asked her when she came home from work Sunday afternoon. She sank down on the couch and kicked off her shoes. "I'm beat."

Maggie looked up from the algebra book in her lap. Jesse was watching yet another of those dumb cartoons, but that was her fault. She wouldn't let him go outside. Not after their father ate the fish sticks she fixed for lunch and took off. She'd wanted to ask him not to leave, but what was she going to say? That some man might be watching them because she was somewhere she wasn't supposed to be on Friday. That some man threatened her. Threatened Jesse.

I'll be watching. The man's creepy voice echoed in her head. She was almost afraid to let the dog outside and now was relieved Bertie lay at her feet.

He'd bark if anybody strange came to the door. But what if he did bark? What if someone was outside? Watching her. She didn't know what to do.

"I had homework." Maggie held up her book. Didn't matter that she'd been staring at it an hour without figuring out the answer to the first problem. If Miss Keane had a pop quiz on Monday, she'd flunk for sure. Nothing was adding up in her brain today.

"You had all day. You should have done it earlier." Her mother rolled her head around to stretch out the kinks she got from wearing that Fast Serve microphone all day. "You can't skip the church meetings if you want to go on their outings."

"That's not it, Mama. I wanted to go." She really, really did. Anthony would be there. He might have sat by her while they did their Bible study. He might have reached over and touched her hand. Little shivers tickled through her at the thought. "But I have to keep up my grades if I want to get a scholarship." And stay out of trouble.

"What's wrong, Maggie?" Her mother raised her head up off the couch and fastened her eyes on Maggie. "Did something happen yesterday to upset you?"

"Nothing's wrong." The words almost choked her. She didn't like fibbing to her mother, but what else could she do? Her mother might call the police. Maggie couldn't take that chance. If she just stayed quiet, the man would leave her alone. Leave Jesse alone too.

Jesse deserted his television show and came over to lean against his mother. He was still a baby in so many ways. The youngest could be that way. The oldest had to grow up and do what had to be done. Maggie bit the inside of her lip. Keeping her mouth shut was what had to be done, even if she did want to confess the whole mess to her mother. Or to somebody. Anybody.

Anthony came to mind. Maybe she could tell him. But no, he'd want her to talk to Michael.

Her mother pulled Jesse up on the couch beside her. "You

haven't been watching television all day, have you? It's a pretty day. You should be outside riding your bike."

Maggie's blood froze. Around the block on his bike where she couldn't see him? She couldn't let that happen. She was trying to come up with something, any excuse for passing up the nice day outside. Jesse beat her to it.

"Maggie wouldn't let me go outside. She's been acting weird all day. Daddy said she was as jumpy as a frog in a hot skillet when the phone rang." Jesse grinned over at Maggie. "Said she must have caught more than fish yesterday, but a boyfriend too."

Relief swept through Maggie even as her cheeks got hot. Her father had said that. She hadn't paid much attention at the time. She was too focused on who might be on the phone. But her father said it was just one of those pesky sales calls. And Maggie could breathe again. She hadn't thought about it being Anthony. She had been hearing that man's voice in her head.

"Don't tease your sister. Nothing wrong with having a boyfriend. As long as she doesn't get too serious too soon." Her mother shut her eyes and leaned back against the couch. "Where's your father?"

"I don't know," Maggie said. "Said he had some things to do."

"Did he say when he'd be back?" Her mother opened her eyes to look over at Maggie.

"No. He just put on a clean shirt and went out." Maggie kept her eyes on her book. The numbers danced in front of her eyes. She tried to change the subject. "I can't get these formulas in my head." It didn't work.

"A clean shirt, huh?" her mother said. "Surprised he could find one unless you threw some clothes in the washer."

"I was going to, but Dad beat me to it. He loaded the washer right after breakfast."

"You don't say. That's a first." A hint of bitterness sounded in her mother's voice. "I didn't think he knew where it was."

"Can I go dig for worms?" Jesse asked. "Daddy said he would take me fishing."

"Did he now?" Maggie's mother made a sound that could have been a laugh if she hadn't sounded so tired. "That daddy of yours is full of surprises today. So go hunt your worms. Maggie can help you. Your mama needs to rest a few minutes before supper."

"I don't want to dig worms." Maggie scrunched down lower in her chair. "Daddy can buy bait if he takes you fishing."

"Then take a walk or go study out on the stoop while Jesse looks for worms." Her mother punched the couch pillow and swung her feet up to lie down. "And turn that TV off."

Maggie picked up her book and clicked off the television. She couldn't let Jesse go out by himself anyway. She had to keep her eyes on him. Make sure he was all right.

She was almost to the door when her mother said, "Oh, and before I forget, you need to head over to Miss Fonda's house after school tomorrow. You can get started on the dusting before I get off work. Else we'll be there all night."

Maggie had to force her legs to move on toward the door. She couldn't go to Miss Fonda's house by herself. She couldn't.

"You know where the key is." Her mother sounded half asleep.

Maggie went outside and sat down in the late afternoon sunlight. She wouldn't think about it. She'd think about algebra instead, x's and y's. Maybe she could make them add up. Nothing else was adding up. She wished she was at church. And not just because Anthony would be there. But it might be easier to pray about what to do if she was at church. She knew a person could pray anywhere, but right now she just felt sick. And scared.

———◆◆◆———

The next morning, when Maggie got to school, Anthony was leaning against her locker. Her heart skipped a beat and then took off like it was in some kind of race. He was so handsome. Especially when he was smiling like that. At her.

"Hey, Maggie. Missed you at church last night. I was worried all that funky fish smell maybe made you sick." Anthony pushed away from the locker.

"I'm fine. I just had homework. Algebra." She hugged her book bag to her chest and made a face. "If Miss Keane gives us a pop quiz today, I'm in trouble."

"I used to think algebra was tough, but Miss Keane tutored me to keep me from flunking when I was a sophomore. Then one day, the light came on and it all made sense. So maybe I could come over sometime and help you study." He hesitated. "Or maybe we could go to the movies or something."

"Oh, wow, that would be great." Maggie grabbed the handle of the locker, glad for the cold feel of the metal. That might keep her from fainting. He'd just asked her for a date. A date. Not that she could go. She felt about five years old, but there was nothing for it but to tell him. "I'd love to go to a movie with you, but my parents say I can't date until I'm sixteen."

"Oh." He looked disappointed. "Well, okay, I understand.

But I could still maybe come over and help you with that algebra."

"Maybe. Probably."

"Great." He reached over and put his hand over hers. "And we can see each other at youth group. I'll save you a seat."

She looked up into his wonderful blue eyes. "I'd like that." It was good the first bell rang to bring her feet back down to the ground. She grabbed a couple of books and shoved them into her book bag. "I got to run or I'll be late to class." She started down the hall.

"Sure thing. Why don't I come by your house after school? We can work on that algebra." He called after her, sounding like algebra was the last thing on his mind.

Her heart skipped another beat or two. She wasn't thinking about algebra either, but she had to turn him down again. She looked over her shoulder. "I can't today. I have to help my mother clean the Chandler house."

She waved and took off in a near run. She didn't want to get a tardy. Another peek back showed Anthony watching her and in no hurry at all. That's how it was with seniors. They never looked rushed. But this one did look gorgeous.

How did she get so lucky that a great-looking senior guy actually wanted to come see her? She wouldn't think about why he couldn't. She wouldn't think about going to Miss Fonda's house after school. She'd just think about Anthony's smile and how he wanted to help her with algebra.

But she couldn't completely block out the memory of that phone call. If Mrs. Harper's fall was an accident, why was that man worried about what she might have seen? Things weren't adding up. Or maybe they were. Maybe they were adding up to something she didn't want to think about.

Whoever was in the house might have pushed Mrs. Harper. Made her fall. Made her die. Somebody who did that might do more. Might carry through the threats he made over the phone. No, not might. Would.

She shook the thought away and tried to focus on the teacher. She was safe at school. Jesse was safe at school. It was when school let out that she would need to worry. That's when she had to go to Miss Fonda's house. If only she could forget seeing Mrs. Harper at the bottom of those steps with her eyes wide open and not seeing anything.

Mrs. Harper would want somebody to pay for killing her. People weren't supposed to get away with murder.

18

Monday morning when Michael got up, he was way too aware of his silent phone. It was good Sally Jo hadn't needed to call him out during the night. Not good at all that Alex hadn't returned his call. He could bear her silence when she was in Washington, DC, but not when she was in Hidden Springs. Just moments away.

He went in early, without breakfast, to drive by Reece's house. No lights on. All quiet in the neighborhood. Aunt Lindy was already off to school. She was an early riser and liked to get to school long before the first bell rang. Reece was generally an early riser too. That almost made Michael put on the brakes and go knock on the door. Maybe something had happened and Alex had taken Reece back to the hospital without telling Michael.

But no, the rental car was in the driveway. He hadn't heard an ambulance called out on the scanner. All was well. All except his silent phone.

He considered banging on the door. He could bundle Reece up and take him fishing. Let Alex decide if she wanted to come or not. But he couldn't do that today. Duty called. Sheriff Potter was on vacation. Michael had to show up for work.

Betty Jean's car was in her usual spot behind the courthouse when he parked his cruiser in the sheriff's reserved spot. He checked the time and then called Betty Jean as he headed up the street to the Grill. "I'm grabbing some breakfast at the Grill. You want me to bring you something? A chocolate doughnut?"

"No, I'm fine. I've got some yogurt."

Yogurt. He knew what that meant. Betty Jean was dieting again. All to impress a certain antique dealer. Michael glanced over at Vernon Trent's store. Shuttered. The closed sign on the door.

"I won't be long," Michael promised.

"Take your time. Everything's fine here."

That didn't sound like Betty Jean. Not on a Monday. Not with her starting a new diet. "Are you all right?"

"I'm wonderful."

He didn't detect even a hint of sarcasm as she disconnected. Obviously her weekend had gone better than Michael's. He stared at his phone a minute, then shoved it in his pocket.

After he scooted into one of the booths, Hank Leland slid off his stool at the counter, picked up his coffee, and came over to squeeze in the other side. "They need to make these booths bigger," he complained.

Cindy poured Michael a cup of coffee and gave Hank a look. "Maybe you need to be smaller, Hank."

"I might be if you didn't make such good pies." Hank held up his cup for a refill.

Cindy laughed and poured his coffee. "You want the usual, Michael? Omelet loaded down?"

"Sounds good. I need something to get me going this morning."

"So toast and blackberry jam too. Coming right up." Cindy headed toward the kitchen.

Hank tore open three sugar packets and stirred them into his coffee. "Rough weekend?"

"Could have been better. How about you?" Michael picked up his cup.

"I would say same old, same old, but Geraldine coming to such an end wasn't the same. I hear her son is supposed to be here today. Looked him up on the internet. If I found the right Grant Harper, the guy's super rich. Wouldn't have guessed that, the way his mother was always scrambling to earn an extra buck. Do you know him? He was gone from Hidden Springs before I moved here."

"I don't remember him. Betty Jean says Grant was a couple of years ahead of her in school, so he would have graduated before I started high school. How did he get so rich?"

"Came up with a better mousetrap." Hank slurped his coffee. "Not actually a mousetrap, but some kind of electronic gizmo. Don't ask me what. Not an engineer. Anyway, bingo. Money rolling in. Took some of that money and started an online flower shop. Figured out how to get flowers there fast to save a guy's bacon. Not that those flowers are helping me much."

"Barbara still not ready to come home?" Hank's wife had gone to her folks' in Georgia last summer.

"She's not coming back." Hank stared at his coffee as he ran his finger around the cup's rim.

"Has she told you that?"

Hank let out a long breath. "Not in so many words, but

some things don't have to be out in the air between a couple. You just know. Things had been sort of iffy with us for a while anyway. You know, before all that other stuff last summer gave her an excuse to leave. Barbara likes it in Georgia. She enrolled Rebecca Ann in school down there. She wouldn't have done that if she planned to come back here."

"I'm sorry, Hank."

"Yeah, well, it's not your fault." Hank stared at the cowboy picture over the table. "Nobody's fault. Isn't that how divorces are these days? No fault. The thing is, I don't believe in divorce. People get married and have a kid, they're supposed to stay married."

"Maybe you should go to Georgia. Find a paper down there."

Cindy came over and slipped the omelet and toast in front of Michael. She must have heard Hank too, because she put her hand on his shoulder. "You want a doughnut, Hank? On the house?"

"I'll take a rain check and just stick with the coffee, Cindy. But thanks." He waited until she headed back to the counter before he waved at Michael's food. "Don't let me crying in my coffee keep you from chowing down. I don't want people feeling sorry for me. I'm fine. Not as fine as I could be. But fine enough."

"That's good to know." Michael attacked his omelet. "Rebecca Ann doing all right?"

"She sounds okay when I talk to her on the phone. No tears or anything. Not from her anyway." Hank took another long sip of coffee. "I might think about heading down to Georgia if I thought that would do the trick. Place doesn't matter all that much if you've got love."

"No, I guess not." Hank's words hit Michael hard. Place seemed to be all that was keeping Alex and Michael apart.

As if Hank read Michael's mind, he said, "How's things going with you and that gorgeous lawyer friend of yours? I hear she's in Hidden Springs. Too bad about Reece's stroke."

The news line was obviously working in Hidden Springs. "The doctors think he'll be back fishing in no time."

"So Alex won't be hanging around that long?" Hank gave him a long look. "Maybe you should have taken some doughnuts over to eat breakfast with her."

"Not likely she'd want any doughnuts." Or him at her breakfast table, if his silent phone was any indication.

"Guess neither of us is scoring high on the happy meter today. At least Betty Jean is finding romance."

"So it seems." Michael smeared some jam on his toast and took a bite, but some of the sweetness seemed lacking.

Hank frowned a little. "Can't fault Vernon's ambition. He says a man tries, a man can make a lot of money selling old stuff. That there are treasures in these old houses. He wants me to do another article about some of his finds. Free advertisement, I guess." Hank shrugged. "But I have to fill the pages with something. Even if the *Gazette* does only come out once a week."

"Coming up with news hasn't been a problem lately."

"Ain't that the truth? Some of those hopping news weeks were enough to make me ready to go back to scraping up stories like Farmer Brown's cow having twins. Some news isn't so good. Sells papers though." Hank put another packet of sugar in his coffee and shook his cup a little to mix it in. "Guess I'll have plenty to fill the front page this week too with Geraldine's untimely end. What do you think happened there, Michael?" He fingered the little notebook in his pocket but didn't pull it out.

"She fell. Broke her neck. Died." Michael finished off his omelet. "Not much story there."

Hank did take out the notebook then to jot something down. Michael had peeked into the notebook a time or two and couldn't make heads or tails of Hank's scribbling. But Hank knew what was there. He got his facts straight and his quotes accurate.

"Maybe not, but everybody knew Geraldine. They'll want to read what happened." He looked up from whatever he was writing down and fixed his newsman stare on Michael. "So a few details would be helpful."

"You can get Justin's report." Michael pushed his plate away from him.

"He'll probably sit on it until after I have to print."

"It takes a while to gather all the information, but I gave you what it will say. Accidental death due to a fall."

"Are you sure that's all? You spent a long time in there looking around before you let Justin in." Hank narrowed his eyes on Michael.

"Making sure no surprises were going to jump out at us."

"And did something jump out at you?" Hank leaned toward Michael. "Ghosts? Boogeymen? Skeletons in the closets? That old house looks to be full of surprises. I've been hearing rumors about it ever since I came to Hidden Springs."

"Rumors are just that. Rumors." Michael wadded up his napkin and tossed it on his plate.

"But sometimes rumors start from a grain of truth. Do you think some long-ago Chandler did hide treasure in those walls somewhere?"

"I guess it might have happened." Michael finished off his coffee. "But you have to remember that Miss Fonda has always laughed at the idea, and she should know."

"But it could be a treasure she doesn't recognize. Like those stories you hear about people buying a priceless work of art at somebody's garage sale. Something that was stuck up in their attic. I figure there's plenty of ancient stuff in the attic of the Chandler house."

"Could be. I haven't been up in the attic. If there is one."

"There's always an attic in an old house. Always. And secrets hidden there for the finding." Hank smiled as he tapped his pencil on the table.

"Probably nothing but cobwebs and dust." Michael threw down a tip and stood up to pay at the register.

Hank stuck his notebook in his pocket and scooted out of the booth to follow him. "You might be right, but I bet Vernon Trent would like to do some dusting and take a look. He's been buddying up to Sonny Elwood. He must think he can get first chance at anything valuable that way. On the other hand, he may be selling Sonny short. Sonny's got dollar signs in his eyes when he thinks about that house. They tell me he still aims to list the house for sale. Geraldine's ghost and all, notwithstanding."

"It's not ghosts he has to worry about. It's Miss Fonda. The house is still hers."

"True." Hank leaned against the counter as they waited for Cindy to come take their money. "And scuttlebutt about town says Sonny can't sell it anyway. That Miss Fonda couldn't either. That when she dies, it goes to her sister's kid. The sister who died after falling down those same stairs as Geraldine. Sounds like a legal nightmare to me."

"Some kind of nightmare anyway. Who's been telling you all this?" He handed his money to Cindy, who punched the buttons on the ancient register.

"You know a good newspaperman never reveals his sources."

Cindy spoke up as she gave Michael his change. "If he won't tell you, I will. It's that Lana Waverly. That's all she wants to talk about. The Chandler house and what happened there."

"She's just looking for a background for the mysteries she wants to write." Hank handed her his ticket and money.

"Hmph. She's making trouble, if you ask me. Her and her tea and muffins. Thinks she can waltz in here and make over Main Street." Cindy slapped Hank's change down on the counter. "Well, I'll tell you what. Some of us think Main Street is fine the way it is. And pie and coffee beats a dry old muffin and a snooty cup of flavored tea any day of the week. Don't have to hold your pinkie right or anything." Cindy held up her hand with her pinkie crooked.

"Whoa, Cindy." Hank gingerly picked up his change and backed away from the counter. "You know I'm in the pie corner."

Michael laughed. "Come on, you two. There's room on Main Street for tea and coffee."

Cindy turned her glare on Michael. "And murder mysteries too, I guess."

"As long as they're just stories. We've had more than our share of the real-life kind lately. Don't need any more. Ever." Michael put his wallet in his pocket and checked his phone again. Still no calls. He barely resisted the impulse to punch a few buttons to see if the thing was working.

"You can say that again," Hank said. "Even if those

headlines were selling papers. But a mystery writer is a different thing. Lana gets a book published with a Hidden Springs setting, that would make a great headline, don't you think?"

"Each to their own, I suppose." Cindy shoved her red hair back from her face. "But I can't see why anybody would want to make up stories about people getting killed. Plenty of better things to write about in Hidden Springs. Plenty of them."

Cindy grabbed her towel and went back to clean off their table. Hank watched her. "You think she's still sore over me not making headline news of her nephew winning that ribbon for showing his Holstein at the fair?"

"You missed your chance for big slices of pie with that one. You always said cow pictures sold papers."

"Yeah. That and murder."

"I'll take the cow pictures." Michael kept the smile on his face, but something still bothered him about Geraldine. He was getting paranoid about everything. Geraldine's fall. Maggie or maybe Lana sneaking into the Chandler house. Vernon Trent's interest in Betty Jean. Alex's silence. Could be she was simply tired, like she said. He'd come back and get a few plates of Cindy's finest this afternoon and take them to Reece's.

First he had to head to the office and hear what Betty Jean had to say about her weekend. Hank took off toward the post office and Michael headed to the courthouse. Bygone Treasures still had the closed sign turned out on the door.

19

"Michael." Lana Waverly stepped out her shop door in front of Michael.

Michael held in a sigh. He wasn't in the mood for another round of her flirting. Even so, he couldn't ignore her. "Good morning, Miss Waverly."

"Come, come, Michael. We got past all that formality yesterday. Why don't you come in and sample my Irish breakfast tea?" She held her hand out toward her door that sported a new sign. Steam rising from a cup formed a *y* in Waverly Tea Room. The same design was appliquéd in blue on Lana's crisply starched apron. "On the house."

"Thanks, but I better get to the office before Betty Jean sends Lester after me."

Lana laughed. "Lester is a gem. He will find his way into my books for sure. A bit of small-town color."

Maybe that was what bothered Michael. The feeling that they were all just small-town color to her. "That might make him happy."

"You sound a bit dubious." Her smile lingered. "Don't

worry. If I put you in my story, you'll be one of the good guys."

"That's reassuring. When are we going to see this book?"

"Not for a while. I'm still working on the storyline and the killer's motive. Motive is very important, but I'm sure you know that from investigating real-life crimes. And accidents." Her eyes sharpened on him as her smile vanished. "I hope you do a better job investigating Mrs. Harper's death than the former sheriff did when Audrey Carlson died."

"I try to be thorough." The woman wasn't going to give up her suspicions.

"But isn't it true that even the most thorough investigations can miss important, even vital, evidence?" She didn't give him a chance to answer as she went on in a friendlier tone. "Oh, never mind. I shouldn't be trying to make a mystery of everything. But I did contact Sonny Elwood, as you suggested, and he's going to meet me at the house later today. If I uncover any clues, I'll let you know."

"Clues to what?"

"The truth. What else?"

"As long as you don't try to turn fiction into truth." Michael didn't smile as he said it.

"But truth is so very elusive at times." She met his look straight on. "And sometimes it's swept into a rat hole and never allowed to come to light."

"Look, Miss Waverly." He intentionally didn't use her first name. "Audrey Carlson died years ago. The investigation is closed, the investigators no longer alive."

"Two who know what happened are." She paused. "Those two are the only ones who probably ever knew what really happened. Bradley Carlson and Fonda Elwood."

"Miss Fonda is past telling. Illness has wiped away her credibility. And Carlson supported the verdict of accidental death."

"I'm sure he did." Lana didn't hide her sarcasm. "But there could be something in the house that might shed light on what really happened." She looked away from Michael as if she could see all the way to the end of town where the Chandler house stood.

"What happened is that the stairs are steep. Audrey must have tripped and fallen the same as Geraldine did." Michael was ready to brush away any suspicions of anything else. Even, maybe especially, his own.

"Those deadly stairs." Her smile came back as she laid her hand on his arm. "I'll watch my step."

"That would be wise." Michael casually shifted away from her and then smiled as he said, "I'll take you up on that cup of tea another day." He turned to go down the street.

"Anytime," she called after him. "If Audrey's ghost points out anything to me, I'll be sure to let you know."

He looked back over his shoulder. Her smile showed she was all too aware she made him uneasy. "You do that. Just remember to be careful. We don't need any more accidents." He stressed the word "accidents."

At the courthouse, Betty Jean's laugh drifted out to meet Michael when he went in the back entrance. Vernon Trent must be searching out antiques in the courthouse. Searching out something anyway. He needed to corner the man and ask his intentions. Michael might not actually be Betty Jean's brother, but he was close enough.

A little squeal of a laugh topped Betty Jean's. Stella Pinkston. She must have come down from the county clerk's office to join in the fun. Maybe she had eyes for Vernon too. That suited Michael. Stella claimed being married didn't mean a girl had to quit looking. So if she was ready to shift her eyes from Michael to Vernon Trent, that would be good.

A man's low voice rumbled and the laughter stopped. Didn't sound like Trent. Certainly wasn't Lester, although it was almost time for him to be back from his school crossing job.

No need standing in the hall doing a guessing game. Better to find out.

The man looked around at Michael when he stepped into the office. Nothing like Vernon Trent. This man was a couple inches taller than Michael. His dark hair didn't show any gray, but his hairline was receding a bit. His nose was a little big, but it didn't detract from his looks. Maybe because his hazel eyes were so full of life and almost commanded attention. No wonder Stella barely glanced Michael's way. Betty Jean's cheeks showed a flattering touch of pink too.

The man's clothes were a little rumpled, as if he'd been wearing them for a while.

"You must be Grant Harper." Michael held his hand out toward the man, who took it in a firm grasp.

"I wasn't sure you'd remember me, Michael." The man's smile was that of a successful, confident man.

"Can't say that I do. Lucky guess."

Harper's smile didn't waver. "To be honest, I don't remember you from our school days either, but your uniform gave you away. But I do remember Betty Jean and Stella from those days." He glanced back over at the women. "We were just rehashing old times."

"Come on, Grant," Stella spoke up. "You make us sound ancient."

"Oh, sorry about that, Stella. But I guess I'm feeling sort of ancient today. Losing my mother like this. I thought she'd live to be a hundred." The lines of his face deepened as his smile disappeared and his eyes looked moist with unshed tears.

Michael liked the man more at once. "Her death had to be a shock to you."

Betty Jean came around her desk to put her hand on Grant's shoulder. "It was a shock to us all. Your mother was such a strong person."

Stella looked uncomfortable in the face of Grant's grief. She wobbled a bit on her too-high heels as she backed away from him. "Gee, I'm sorry too, Grant. But I better get back to work before I get in trouble with the boss." She headed for the door without a backward glance. Her heels clicked on the tiled hallway up to the county clerk's office.

Grant didn't look around at her. His eyes were on Betty Jean. He rubbed the corners of his eyes with his fingertips and managed a shaky smile. "Now don't start saying what a wonderful woman she was. I know how my mother was. Demanding. Obnoxious at times. Pushy all the time."

"But she was your mother and she was so proud of you. You should have heard her when you got in at MIT. That's all we heard about for weeks. Her brilliant son." Betty Jean had a tender smile.

Michael knew Betty Jean had a soft heart, but she rarely allowed anybody a glimpse of it. Now this guy had been back in Hidden Springs ten minutes and she was touching his shoulder. Maybe Michael's uneasy feelings about Vernon Trent weren't as big a problem as he thought.

She was still talking, peering up at Grant Harper. "I think she sold ten houses that month. Had everybody ready to move just to help with your tuition." Betty Jean shot a look over at Michael. "You remember that, don't you, Michael?"

"Can't say that I do. But if anybody could sell ten houses in a month, it would have been Geraldine." Michael put his hands in his pockets and leaned back against his desk.

Grant sighed. The tears gone. "I should have come back to see her more. But I was always so busy and she said she liked coming down to Florida." He looked over at Michael. "Do you think I could see where she died?"

When Michael didn't answer right away, he rushed on. "I guess that sounds sort of morbid, but it just seems like I should know."

"Of course you should." Betty Jean tightened her hand on his arm. "Michael will be glad to arrange it." She shot a glance over at Michael.

"Sure thing. If you think that will help you."

"You said it was the Chandler house, didn't you?" Again Grant didn't wait for an answer. "I remember that place. A beautiful old Queen Anne–style house."

"Yes. She fell down the upper stairs," Michael said.

"Rushing too much probably." Resignation was in Grant's voice. "She was always in a hurry. I'm sometimes the same way. Always more to do. Never enough time, but maybe I'll learn something from this. To take time. To smell the roses." His eyes went to Betty Jean again.

Her cheeks got pinker. "We should all do that."

The phone rang and jerked Betty Jean off that cloud she looked ready to float away on.

"Want me to get it, Betty Jean?" Michael asked.

"You don't have to ask my permission to answer the phone." She gave Michael a look. "But no, I'll answer it." She turned back to her desk, punched a button, and picked up the receiver.

As she went through her sheriff's office spiel, Michael asked when Grant wanted to go to the Chandler house. "I'll have to talk to the owner's nephew to get a key."

"Not today. I just got to town and need to make Mother's arrangements at the funeral parlor. I came here because I thought maybe you might have Mother's handbag with her house keys."

"Justin Thatcher took your mother's things with her body to the funeral home. Do you need directions?"

"No." The man pressed his lips together for a moment. "Simply courage. I'm having a hard time wrapping my mind around Mother being gone. It just doesn't seem right. But it has to be faced."

He waved to Betty Jean, who punched the call on hold to tell him goodbye.

Michael waited until his footsteps went up the hallway before he said, "Nice guy."

"Yes." Betty Jean stared toward the door without picking up the call again. "He's changed a lot since school. Wore glasses back then. Always studying."

"Guess that turned out well for him." Michael sat down behind his desk. "Must not be Vernon on the phone."

"Who?" She looked at the phone in her hand.

"Vernon Trent. You know. The antique dealer. The one you spent the weekend with."

"I didn't spend the weekend with Vernon. I simply helped him list some of his items online to sell." She glared over at Michael. "If it's any of your business. Which it isn't."

She punched the button and began talking into the phone again as she jotted something down on a notepad. "Yes, ma'am. Cows in the road can be very dangerous. I'll send somebody right out."

Betty Jean put down the phone and handed Michael the note. "You get to be cowboy this morning."

Michael looked at the address. Miles out in the county. By the time he got there, the farmer would probably have the cows back in the pasture and the fence fixed. "Why don't you call Lester? He could use his lights."

"Lester is taking his mother to the doctor this morning. We're getting low on deputies around here, so looks like you're it." Betty Jean grinned.

"You think you can hold down the office all by yourself with all these guys courting your favor?"

"I'll manage." She pointed toward him and then the door. "Go chase some cows. Oh, and be careful not to step in anything."

20

Maggie tried to pay attention in class and not think about going to Miss Fonda's house after school. But no matter how hard she tried to block it away, the sight of Mrs. Harper's body at the bottom of those steps had a way of popping into her mind like a jack-in-the-box somebody kept winding up to scare her.

It did scare her. A lot. What scared her even more was that phone call and how it was making her wonder if Mrs. Harper hadn't simply tripped and fallen. Maggie couldn't bear to think what that might mean. Except she did know she was in trouble. If she talked, she was in trouble. If she didn't talk, she was in trouble.

A different kind of trouble but trouble nevertheless. Trouble with her conscience. A person was supposed to do what was right. If whoever had been in Miss Fonda's house pushed Mrs. Harper, then Maggie could be aiding and abetting a murderer. That was what police called it when somebody helped out a criminal. She wasn't exactly helping anybody out. Except by being quiet and not telling what she knew.

She hadn't seen anything. She had heard somebody. A

voice that sounded nothing like the man on the phone. But she hadn't seen anything.

The person obviously saw her. The person must have still been in the house when she went out the back door. She'd been so sure she heard a door open and close before she climbed down from the tower room. Maybe her ears had tricked her. That didn't matter now. What mattered was that he must have been hiding somewhere. Watching her.

A creepy chill swept through her. She stared at her algebra book and tried to concentrate on the problems, but the numbers on the page blurred. She hoped Miss Keane wouldn't call on her. She'd never come up with the right answer. Not the way her head was spinning.

She had to tell somebody. Trouble for her or not. But then, if the man had killed once to make sure Mrs. Harper didn't call the sheriff, he might carry through his threats if Maggie went to the police.

It wasn't just her she had to worry about. She had to think about Jesse. The man had sounded dead serious. Dead. She tried to push that word out of her head, but it sank claws down and wouldn't let go. Dead. Mrs. Harper was dead. Eyes-open-staring-at-nothing dead. Another shiver ran through Maggie.

If something happened to Jesse because of some dumb thing she did . . . She couldn't stand to even think about that. That would be worse, much worse, than getting in trouble for being in Miss Fonda's house. She could weather that.

Maggie jumped when the final bell rang. She hadn't heard what Miss Keane had assigned. She'd have to call somebody to find out. When she shut her book and stood up, Miss Keane stepped in front of her.

"Is something wrong, Maggie?" Miss Keane's intense look froze Maggie in her tracks. "I don't think you heard a word I said today."

"I'm sorry, Miss Keane." Maggie stared down at her shoes. "I'll do better tomorrow."

"If you're concerned about not understanding the lesson, you can stay after school and I'll help you. You don't want to get behind."

Miss Keane sounded almost friendly. Miss Keane never sounded friendly. Everybody in school was afraid of her. Everybody but Anthony. Maggie peeked up at Miss Keane. Anthony must have said something to her about Maggie having problems with algebra, but Maggie didn't dare ask if that was true. Never in a million years. She shifted back and forth on her feet and clutched her algebra book close to her chest. "I can't today. I have to help my mother this afternoon."

"I see. But remember, if you need help, just ask." Miss Keane smiled. "You have a good mind, and if you trust your ability a bit more, I believe you can be very good at math. You might even find it fun. Mrs. Frost says you excel in your Language Arts class. So if you pull up math to comparable levels, you'll do very well on the ACT test and be a prime candidate for some excellent scholarships."

"I hope so. I'm going to need a scholarship." Maggie kept her eyes on her algebra book as she stuffed it into her book bag. She hefted the bag up to her shoulder. "I got to run or I'll miss my bus."

"Of course." Miss Keane touched Maggie's arm. "But if something is bothering you, please discuss it with someone here. Sometimes when things are happening at home, it makes it hard for students to concentrate on their work."

"We're okay." That hadn't come from Anthony. Michael must have talked to Miss Keane about her too. He was her nephew. That might make Miss Keane know about police things. Maybe Maggie should forget about missing the bus and talk to her. Tell her about the phone call.

The words were right there on her tongue, but she swallowed them down. Miss Keane would tell Michael and then the man might find out. She couldn't take that chance.

"That's good." The teacher tightened her fingers on Maggie's arm for a few seconds. Her smile disappeared. "The assignment is page forty-seven. Your father was very good at math when he was in school. He can help you."

"Dad?" Maggie was surprised. She couldn't imagine her father being a good student. "My dad?"

"Yes, indeed. Now run along." Miss Keane looked up at the clock over the door. "If you hurry, you should still make your bus."

She did. Barely. Mrs. Bottoms, the bus driver, was closing the door when Maggie ran out. She opened it back up with a smile. "Cutting it close, aren't you, Mag?"

Mrs. Bottoms had been driving Maggie's bus since Maggie was in first grade. She seemed almost like a relative. Maybe Maggie could talk to her. But that was crazy. A person could barely hear herself think on the bus.

"Sorry. Miss Keane wanted to talk to me after class." Maggie slipped into the front seat.

"Oh, wow! Hope you weren't in trouble," Mrs. Bottoms said.

"She just wanted to make sure I got the assignment."

"She can make a kid shake in her boots. That's for sure. I did plenty of trembling myself when I was in her class."

"You had her when you were in school?" Maggie gave Mrs. Bottoms another look. Maybe she wasn't all that old after all.

"You bet. Miss Keane is an institution. I think she's been teaching since they built the school. Maybe since Noah built the ark." Mrs. Bottoms let out a loud laugh.

Maggie forced a little laugh too. She was glad when some kid in the back did something to make Mrs. Bottoms peer up at the mirror to call him down. She must have taken lessons from Miss Keane about how to make kids shake in their boots.

Once Maggie was sure it wasn't Jesse in trouble, she leaned back and stared out the window at the houses sliding by while the bus noise floated past her ears. When she heard Jesse laugh, Maggie peeked over her shoulder at him a couple of seats back.

He might be a pest at times, but he was still her little brother. She'd been helping her mother watch him ever since he was born. She was the one who taught him to crawl backward down the porch steps so he didn't fall. She made him peanut butter sandwiches when he was hungry. She played hide-and-seek with him back when he thought he could hide just by sticking his head under a cover. He was older now, but she hadn't stopped being his big sister. She hadn't stopped taking care of him.

Maybe the man wouldn't call again. Maybe it would be okay if she didn't talk to the police. Or anyone. She could be like Jesse when he was little and just stick her head under a cover until it all went away.

Except that she couldn't. She would have to go to Miss Fonda's house when she got home. Nothing short of the truth could get her out of doing what her mother said. That might not be all bad. If she got to Miss Fonda's house before her mother, she could climb up to the tower room and get her notebook.

She'd have to go up those stairs, but she could close her eyes and run past the place where Mrs. Harper died. Maggie shivered. She had to quit thinking about Mrs. Harper.

The bus lurched to a stop in front of Maggie's trailer. The front door was open, so that meant her father was home. That was good. Jesse wouldn't have to go to Miss Fonda's house with her. She could get her notebook, dust, and keep quiet.

Jesse ran ahead of her into the house, slamming the door behind him. Maggie flinched. She'd told him a million times not to slam the door when they got home in case Dad was taking a nap. Dad didn't usually wake up happy, and Maggie couldn't deal with him yelling at them today. She just couldn't.

She wished her mother was home. She remembered way back to before Jesse was born when she was just a kid his age coming in from school. Her mother would watch for her from the doorway. They'd go inside and eat popcorn or something while she told her mother about whatever happened that day. Maggie could tell her anything.

Her mother said she still could. Maybe that's what Maggie needed to do. Tell her mother. If she got in trouble, she just got in trouble. Her mother might not be happy with her, but she'd know what Maggie should do. She'd help her. Maggie wouldn't have to handle it alone.

That was what Pastor Karen said it was like with Jesus. That he was always right there beside you, ready to help if a person asked him to. Maggie let a little prayer slide up into the air as she headed into the house. *Don't let Dad be mad. Please don't let Jesse get hurt. Help me tell Mama about the man calling. Make me not afraid to go inside Miss Fonda's house.*

The first prayer was answered right away. Her father was wide awake and smiling as Jesse told him about running faster than all the other boys at recess. It was nice having Dad smiling. Even better, she didn't see a beer can anywhere.

"You want me to fix you something to eat before I go to Miss Fonda's? It'll be late before we get through."

A frown slid across her father's face. "I forgot about you cleaning that house today."

"I'm supposed to meet Mom there. Can Jesse stay here with you?"

"Nope. Sorry." He did look sort of sorry. "I've got somewhere I have to go."

"Can't you take him with you?" Maggie knew it was useless to argue, but if she was going to get her notebook, she needed those few minutes alone at Miss Fonda's house. Jesse would tell on her in a minute if he found out she'd been going up to the tower room.

A stony look settled on her father's face and Maggie rushed on. "I mean, Mom's afraid he'll break something with all those old antiques and everything." She wasn't making that up. Her mother was nervous about Jesse breaking something when he went with them. But he went plenty of times.

"I know." Her father rubbed his hand across his face and lost his mad look. Proof for sure he hadn't been drinking. He got mad lots easier when he was drinking. He breathed out a long sigh. "But he can't go with me today."

Maggie bit her lip. She didn't aim to cry. But all of the

sudden it was just too much. Tears slid out of her eyes and down her cheeks. She stared at the floor so her father wouldn't see them, but she wasn't quick enough. She was glad Jesse had run to the bathroom.

"Look, Maggie." Her dad put his hand on her head gently the way he used to when she was a little girl. That made Maggie cry harder. His voice sounded a little shaky too. "I'm sorry, but this is important to me."

She wanted to tell him that what she wanted to do was important too, but the tears were choking her up. She wouldn't have said it anyway.

He put his fingers under her chin and tipped up her face until she had to look at him. "I know things have been rough for you the last few months. I'm trying to make them better. Where I'm going is an AA meeting. You know what that is, don't you?"

Maggie nodded.

"I want to quit drinking and I think these meetings will help me do what I can't do by myself. But I'm not ready to tell your mother yet. It would just disappoint her if I fall off the wagon, and right now, I can't be sure I won't." He reached in his pocket for his handkerchief and handed it to her. "So if you can, I'd like you to keep our secret for another week or two. Please."

Maggie didn't know the last time her dad had said please about something he wanted her to do. She mopped off her face and nodded. She could get her notebook another time. And wasn't she already keeping secrets even bigger than what her father was asking? If her dad quit drinking, that would make everything better.

"Good girl. I don't know what your mother and I would

do without you." He pulled her close for a quick hug. "Remember, mum's the word."

He stood up and picked up his cap. He was almost to the door when he turned to look at her. "If that woman preacher has been teaching you to pray, you might say a prayer or two for me."

"Okay." Maybe that's who she should talk to. Pastor Karen. Didn't preachers have to keep what you told them secret? Or was that doctors? She didn't know. She didn't know anything.

21

Maggie sank down on the couch and blew her nose. Bertie jumped up beside her and licked her face. The dog wasn't supposed to be on the couch, but Maggie didn't push him off. Jesse crept back down the hall to the edge of the living room to stare at her.

She wanted to tell him she was all right, but even though she wasn't crying now, she still didn't trust her voice. Or trust that she might not start sobbing again. This just wasn't like her. She hadn't cried in front of anybody for years. Sometimes in bed at night she might shed a few tears when her parents were fighting, but she didn't ever break down like this. She didn't. She swallowed hard and pushed a shaky smile out on her face.

Jesse slid his feet across the carpet as though afraid to pick them up as he came closer. He hesitated a few feet from the couch. She reached toward him and he touched her hand. The static electricity popped between them and made them both jump.

"I didn't do that on purpose." He looked worried she was going to be mad. "Honest."

Maggie swallowed again and found her voice. "I know. Come here."

He cuddled beside her then, and she began to feel better with Jesse on one side and Bertie on the other.

Jesse spoke in a small voice. "I'll be real careful not to break anything at Miss Fonda's house. I can help you dust the cabinets and other stuff that won't break. Mama said I was big enough now to do that."

"She did." Maggie wasn't sure that her mother intended Jesse to help them at Miss Fonda's house today, but it couldn't be helped. "Did you hear Dad?"

Jesse nodded his head against her. "What's AA?"

"Alcoholics Anonymous. It's for people who can't quit drinking on their own. They help one another not drink."

"How?"

"I don't know."

"Does it work?" Jesse twisted around to look at Maggie's face.

"I don't know that either."

"I hope it does." Jesse looked back down at his knees.

"Yeah, me too." Maggie pushed Bertie off the couch and blew her nose again.

"Was that why you were crying, because you were afraid it wouldn't work?"

Maggie ruffled Jesse's hair. He needed a haircut. She could put her hair up in a ponytail and not worry about haircuts, but it was different for boys. The hair lapped down over his ears. "No. I was just worried about going to Miss Fonda's house. Something bad happened there last week."

"That lady with the house on her car died there, didn't she?"

"She did. But she's not there now. She's gone on up to heaven." Maggie gave Jesse a quick hug and stood up. "Come on. We need to head over there." She had to go. Her mother expected her to. It was just a house. No ghosts. Nobody hiding, watching her.

"Does everybody go to heaven?" Jesse asked. "When they die?"

"I don't know. I hope so."

"Even people who do bad things?" He sounded worried.

"Why are you asking that? Have you done something at school to get into trouble?" Maggie frowned at Jesse.

"Not yet, but I might."

"Well, don't. That will take care of that." Maggie fixed a stern look on him. "Now, stop with the questions. We've got to go to Miss Fonda's or we'll be in trouble with Mama."

Maggie scribbled a note and stuck it on the refrigerator so her mother would know Jesse was with her. She didn't say anything about where her father was and she made sure Jesse knew to keep his mouth shut too. It would be a surprise for their mother. A good surprise. At least, that was what they could hope.

They took the shortcut across the neighbors' yards. When they got to the highway, Maggie made Jesse wait until nothing was in sight. She wasn't going to take the chance that somebody might try to run them down. She'd never thought about that ever when crossing the road, but things like that happened on television shows. It was no fun thinking about somebody trying to hurt you. She wanted to go back to last week before Mrs. Harper died, when going to Miss Fonda's house had been like running out to recess in first grade.

Now she had a knot in her throat as she tried to watch

everything at once while they walked along the road. When they got to the hedge behind Miss Fonda's house, Maggie ducked through first to hold the branches back for Jesse. Miss Marble raced out to greet them as if she'd been watching for them. Maggie felt a stab of guilt. She hadn't come to feed her all weekend.

"Poor kitty." She stroked her head to tail. "I bet you're hungry."

"Can I feed her?" Jesse reached down to rub the cat too.

"I forgot to bring anything." Another stab of guilt. "But if we can find a can of food in the cabinets, you can feed her in the kitchen."

Jesse picked up the cat.

"She must like you. She'd be scratching me if I picked her up like that." Maggie laughed and fished the key to the back door out of her pocket. It was good to think about the cat instead of what she'd seen last time she was here.

But the uneasy feeling came back as soon as she stepped into the kitchen. It was too quiet, and one of the chairs was pulled out from the table as though somebody had just been sitting there and got up in a hurry to leave.

Even Jesse felt it. "I'm glad we don't live here."

"Why?" Maggie tried to hide being scared, but her voice was a little shaky.

"It's spooky."

Miss Marble must have agreed, because she suddenly yowled and squirmed free from Jesse to race out the door.

"Guess she doesn't want to eat in here," Maggie said.

"Can't I feed her on the back porch?"

Maggie hesitated, but Miss Marble was standing right outside the door, looking calm as anything now. Nobody was out there. It would be okay. Maggie found a can of cat food in the cabinet and peeled off the top. She dipped the food out into a plastic bowl and handed it to Jesse.

"You have to come back inside after she eats. I'll leave you a rag to dust the chairs and table in here. Remember you have to do the legs and not just the tops." That should keep him busy until their mother got there.

She wanted to tell him to leave the back door open, but her mother wouldn't be happy if they let in flies. But after he closed the door behind him, the house seemed even quieter. Almost like it was holding its breath.

Don't be stupid, she told herself sternly. *Houses don't breathe or not breathe. A house is a house. Bricks and wood.* She wasn't afraid of houses. She and Jesse were alone here. No one else was there.

How do you know? The question slid through her mind. She wanted to go out on the back porch with Jesse and Miss Marble, but instead she opened the broom closet to get the dust spray and rags. She left one of the rags on the chair for Jesse. He'd probably watch the cat eat every drop of food. But she needed to get started.

She took a quick look at the clock on the wall. 9:20. The battery must have run out. But it had to be close to four thirty. Her mother would be there in about an hour. She had to quit being scared and get to work. She'd start with the figurines on the shelf in the front room. She could leave the upstairs rooms and having to go up those steps where Mrs. Harper fell until after her mother got there, unless she wanted to sneak up to the tower room and get her notebook while Jesse was outside.

No, that would be too far from Jesse. She wouldn't be

able to hear him if he yelled. She'd just have to come back a different time. It might not be as scary the next time.

She peeked out the back window. Jesse was on his belly, watching Miss Marble eat. That cat was a dainty eater for a mouser.

Maggie pulled in a big breath for courage and walked through the house to the front entrance. The door was locked. She turned the knob to be sure. She stood still and listened. Nothing. Not so much as a ticking clock. They'd all run down. Everything in the house had run down.

Maggie dusted the hall tree next to the stairway. She left the stair railings in case Jesse got through with the chairs in the kitchen and needed more to do. She stepped into the front room, what Miss Fonda always called the parlor. Maybe Maggie should wind the clock on the mantel. The ticking might keep the silence from beating against her ears.

Something wasn't right about the room. Maggie stopped and looked around. The rose-colored wingback chair was shoved against the wall and the silk-fringed pillow that had a place of honor on the couch was across the room next to the fireplace. Two pictures hung askew and the third, a portrait of Miss Fonda's grandmother, was on the floor.

Somebody had been in the room. Now Maggie was glad for the silence. That had to mean whoever had been there was gone. But then she was standing there silent. Perhaps someone else was standing just as silent waiting to see what she would do.

Her heart pounded up in her ears until she couldn't hear anything. She moistened her lips and tried to look everywhere at once as she stepped away from the mantel. Nobody was there. The room was empty.

She breathed a little easier as she looked toward the open door into the library room her mother sometimes called a book closet, because in spite of its size, the only way into the room was through the sitting room. Books were every which way on the floor.

Miss Fonda loved her books. She'd be upset if the pages got torn or rumpled. Maggie picked up a book in the doorway to smooth out the pages. It would take hours to clean up this mess. Never mind the dust. And what was that peculiar odor?

New chills crawled up her back as she suddenly felt another presence in the room. She jerked around to stare toward the old rolltop desk in the corner. She blinked her eyes.

This had to be a nightmare. But no, she was awake and Miss Fonda's nephew really was in the desk chair staring at her without seeing a thing. The same as Mrs. Harper. Or not the same. Blood was caked in the corner of the man's mouth and red stained his shirt.

A scream gathered in Maggie's throat. She clamped her hand over her mouth to stop it, but it was either scream or faint. She couldn't faint. She had to get Jesse away from here. The scream burst out of her mouth as she ran back through the house.

At the kitchen door, arms grabbed her. Not Jesse's little-boy arms. A man's arms.

22

She jerked away from the man and fell against the wall.

"What's wrong, Maggie?" Anthony's voice pushed through her panic.

Maggie stared at Anthony and tried to catch her breath. He had grabbed her. No one else was there except Jesse standing in the back door, his eyes wide.

Miss Marble scooted between Jesse's legs into the kitchen. The cat leaped on the counter and up on the refrigerator to crouch under the cabinet above it. Maggie wanted to crawl up there with her.

She clamped her lips together to keep from screaming again. She was scaring Jesse. She was scaring everybody. Even Miss Marble.

"Anthony?" She gave her head a shake, not sure she could trust her eyes. But hadn't she just seen Mr. Elwood dead and bloody? A shudder made her teeth chatter. She hadn't dreamed that up. She wasn't dreaming Anthony either. He was right in front of her, those gorgeous blue eyes staring at her as if she might have lost her mind.

"Yeah. Sorry I scared you." He shifted back and forth on his feet. "But your little brother said it was okay for me to come inside."

"Oh." Maggie swallowed and pushed away from the wall. She took a quick look over her shoulder toward the front rooms. The hallway was empty, but the house was big. Lots of places for someone to hide.

"What's wrong?" Anthony asked again. He reached toward her, but then dropped his hand back down, as if unsure whether to touch her or not. "You're shaking all over. Did you see a mouse or something in there?"

She stepped closer to him. If only he'd put his arms around her again. That might make her feel safer. "I'm not afraid of mice."

"Maggie." Jesse sounded as shaky as she felt.

Jesse's voice brought it all back to her. The dead man. The man's voice on the phone. The man who could be watching her. Watching Jesse. Right now.

She turned away from Anthony. "We've got to get out of here!"

Anthony grabbed her arm to keep her from running toward the door. "Why?"

"He didn't fall down the stairs." Panic surged up in her voice again. "Somebody killed him."

"Slow down." Anthony frowned and pulled her around to face him. "You're not making sense."

"You don't understand." Maggie stared at Anthony. "Whoever did it could still be here. In the house."

Jesse raced across the kitchen to grab Maggie and hide his face against her shirt. He didn't have to be convinced to be afraid.

"Okay. Show me what scared you."

Anthony sounded like he was trying to humor her the way she sometimes did with Jesse. Maggie could tell he hadn't really heard what she said about Miss Fonda's nephew being dead. Either that or he didn't believe her.

She might not believe it either if she hadn't seen it with her own eyes. The sight of the dead man flashed through her head again. A lot worse than Mrs. Harper. Because of the blood. Maggie felt sick as she pulled Jesse close against her. She pointed toward the front of the house.

"He's in there, but please don't go look." Tears popped into her eyes. "Please."

"Don't worry." He let go of her arm and stared toward the hallway. "Nobody's here."

"How do you know?" She wanted to grab him and make him stay with them. He didn't understand.

"Well then, I'll make sure nobody's here." His face was set. "You two stay put."

He started up the hall toward the front of the house. She wanted to trail after him, but she was too scared to move. She started shaking again and Jesse hugged her tighter.

She took a shuddering breath and unwrapped one of his arms from around her waist. "Come on. We're going outside."

"Shouldn't we wait for your boyfriend?" Jesse peered past her toward the hall.

That froze her in place again. Jesse was right. She couldn't leave with Anthony in there. She gripped Jesse's hand so tightly he winced, but he didn't pull away. She dropped down in the chair beside the table before her shaky legs gave out on her. Jesse leaned against her. She had the feeling he might climb into her lap, big as he was, if she gave him the least encouragement.

"Who was dead?" he asked.

"Miss Fonda's nephew."

"Did somebody shoot him?"

"I don't know."

"Maybe he shot himself. Sometimes that happens, doesn't it?"

"Sometimes." She put an arm around Jesse. Maybe that was what had happened. Mr. Elwood shot himself. That would be bad but not nearly as bad as thinking the man on the phone had killed him and was now watching them. She hadn't seen a gun, but she hadn't looked for one. She was too busy screaming.

A scream still lingered in her throat as the seconds crept by. She listened, but she couldn't hear anything but Jesse breathing beside her. Not Anthony moving around in the front of the house. Not the cat hiding up under the cabinets. The refrigerator tried to start running, then wheezed back into silence.

The back door stood open. A way to escape, but what if the man was out there? Waiting. A blue jay shrieked outside and Maggie jumped.

Jesse patted her shoulder. She took a breath to calm down. She was supposed to be the one taking care of Jesse. Keeping him safe. If only Anthony would come back to the kitchen so they could get away from here.

She stood up and went to the hall. Jesse scooted along with her, not turning loose of her shirt.

"Anthony?" The awful silence swallowed up the sound of his name.

But then he was coming toward them. His face pale but he was safe.

"You're right," he said. "I need to call Michael."

"Michael?" Her heart started pounding too hard again. "You can't call Michael."

Anthony already had his phone in his hand. He frowned at Maggie. "Why not?"

"He told me not to call the police." Maggie could barely push out the words. "He said if I did, he'd know and that he'd . . ." She let her voice die away. She couldn't tell how the man had threatened Jesse. That would just scare Jesse more.

"You saw the murderer?" Anthony stared at her. "Now?"

"No. He called the house."

"He told you that guy was dead in there?"

"No. He called Saturday. After Mrs. Harper died."

Anthony frowned. "You're not making sense, Maggie. But I have to call Michael." He punched in some numbers.

Maggie heard the phone ringing before Anthony put it up to his ear, and for the second time that afternoon, she burst into tears.

The things a man had to do as deputy sheriff of Keane County. Michael cleaned his shoes on a big tuft of grass before he climbed back into his patrol car. But he couldn't just stand there and watch while Ezra McMurtry tried to herd his cows back in the field. Ezra was getting up in years and had to stop every few minutes to lean with his hands on his knees to catch his breath. The man looked that close to a heart attack.

It didn't help that Ezra was mad as a wet hen. As soon as Michael got there, Ezra lit in on him. "Dad-blamed speeders. Run clear through my fence. Knocked that middle post to tomorrow. Then just backed themselves up on the road and went on off for an RC Cola like nothing happened."

Ezra waved his hand at the field and then at the two heifers behind him that refused to go back through the hole in the fence. He shook his finger at Michael. "Let me tell you. If they'd a come to the house asking me to pull them out of the ditch, I'd have brought my shotgun and stood there till they fixed the fence, and don't you tell me anything would be wrong with that."

Michael held up his hands in surrender. "I don't blame you a bit, Ezra." And he didn't blame the old farmer, but he was glad that hadn't happened. He didn't want anybody shot because of a wrecked fence. But he didn't want the old farmer to have a heart attack either. So Michael parked his car sideways in the road and stationed Ezra beside it while he eased around behind the heifers. The cows eyed him with ears at attention and hooves dancing on the road, ready to run.

It took a couple of tries, but finally Ezra smacked the lead heifer's nose with a stick when she tried to run past him. That must have convinced her the fun was over and she sedately stepped back through the hole in the fence to join the rest of the herd in the pasture. The other cow followed without a backward glance.

Michael left the old farmer stringing barbed wire to fix his fence while muttering about people having no respect for a man's property these days. After Michael turned his cruiser around, he checked his phone. Sure enough, Alex had finally

called him. Well, not called him. Texted him. Not the way
Michael liked to communicate. What could a man tell about
letters typed on a screen?

> We need to talk. Can u come by later?

Maybe too much. He punched in Alex's cell number and
got her polite "so sorry, busy" message. He pulled over in a
driveway. Nothing for it but to send a text back.

> Sure. I'll bring Cindy's finest for dinner.

He hadn't even pulled back out on the road when an answer pinged back to prove she could have picked up his call.

> Remember Uncle Reece needs to eat hlthy. But
> if Cindy has choc pie…

The pie request brought a smile. Alex had a sweet tooth.
Maybe he was simply imagining her hesitancy to talk to him.
But Alex was always a step or two ahead of him. She may
have sensed his determination to finally make her give him
a yes or a no. But what if it was no?

He blew out his breath and pulled back onto the road.
He couldn't think about that. Not yet. He stopped at the
Grill and gave Cindy his order and asked her to put aside
a whole chocolate pie. His phone buzzed awake again as
he parked in the sheriff's spot beside the courthouse. He
fished the phone out of his pocket as he got out of the
car and didn't bother looking at the caller ID. Betty Jean
would be calling to tell him she was closing down the office for the day.

But it wasn't Betty Jean.

"Michael." Anthony didn't sound like himself.

"What's wrong?" Michael gripped the phone tighter, as though to squeeze the news out of it. He could hear somebody crying in the background.

"We're okay, but something bad's happened." The kid's voice sounded quivery.

Relief washed through Michael, even as every inch of him was on alert. At least Anthony wasn't hurt. "All right. Take it slow and tell me what's happened."

Anthony pulled in a deep breath and let it out, the air swooshing through the phone line. "I'm at that big old house on the edge of town. Where that woman fell last week. Somebody's dead in one of the front rooms."

"Dead? Who?"

"I don't know. But I can ask if Maggie knows."

"Maggie?" Michael got back in his car.

"Yeah. Her and her little brother are here. Maggie's real upset. Scared and everything."

"Scared?"

"Yeah. She's afraid whoever shot the guy might still be here."

"Stay on the phone, Anthony. I'll be there in three minutes." The bad feeling he'd had about Geraldine Harper bounded back full force.

Michael rarely used both his lights and siren, but today he did.

———— ❖ ————

Hidden Springs took notice. Betty Jean hung up on Vernon Trent in midsentence to key on her radio. Hank Leland ran for his old van behind the newspaper office. Storeowners and their customers rushed to the doors to see what was happening. Justin Thatcher looked up from writing Geraldine Harper's obituary for the *Eagleton News* and fervently hoped his phone wouldn't ring.

23

At the Chandler house, Michael screeched to a halt behind Sonny Elwood's BMW and Anthony's old Chevy. If anything happened to those kids, Michael wouldn't be able to live with himself.

He knew something wasn't right about Geraldine Harper's death, but he'd brushed away his suspicions. He had wanted it to be nothing more than an accident. Plus, he let Alex being in Hidden Springs distract him. He couldn't afford to do that now.

Michael drew his gun and moved as quietly as possible across the yard. The hedges and trees muffled the sound of cars passing by out on the street. He should have turned off his emergency lights. They would draw the curious. Hank Leland was probably already pulling into the driveway.

No time to worry about that now. The lights were flashing, signaling something wrong. It was his job to make sure nothing more went wrong. Anthony said they were in the kitchen, so Michael went around the house. No sign of anybody in the graveyard. Nothing out of the ordinary behind the house either. The garden shed door was closed with the wooden bar down in the locked position. Somebody could be hiding behind the shed or in the bushes, but the yard felt empty. A man got a feel for that kind of thing after a while.

He shoved his gun back in the holster and climbed the porch steps where the day before he'd caught Lana Waverly peering in the window. The back door was wide open.

He pulled his phone out of his pocket and spoke into it for the first time since he got out of his cruiser. "I'm on the porch, Anthony. Coming in." He didn't want the boy to bash him over the head with a soup kettle or something.

Inside, the three kids formed a little island of fear beside the kitchen table. Maggie sat in the chair Miss Fonda had collapsed into on Friday. The girl's face was as white as the old kitchen cabinets behind her. She'd obviously been crying, but she wasn't crying now. She had her arm around her little brother, clutching him close to her. The boy, maybe six or seven, looked more confused than frightened.

Anthony stood behind Maggie, one hand on her shoulder, the other hand gripping his phone. He was trying hard not to look scared, but everything about him was stiff. He looked afraid to blink. Anthony had come a long way from being the kid in town always in trouble. But here he was in trouble again. Not trouble of his own making, but trouble nevertheless.

A thump sounded behind Michael, and he spun around, his hand going to his gun. The cat stared at him from the counter, almost as wide-eyed as the kids. But then she sat down and began to lick her paws to wash her face. Her tail swished back and forth, brushing the canisters behind her.

Michael turned back to the kids. "Okay, guys. What's going on here?"

Both Maggie and Anthony started talking.

Michael held up his hand. "Maggie first."

"It's Mr. Elwood." Maggie licked her lips and her chin quivered. "He's in there." She pointed toward the front of the house with a trembling hand.

"You found him?" It wasn't really a question. The answer was obvious in her terrified eyes.

She nodded. "He's dead. Not like Mrs. Harper. He's got blood on his shirt. That man must have killed him."

"What man?" Michael looked away from Maggie up through the hallway. He felt the itch to go check out the house, but he needed to take care of the kids first.

"The one that killed him. He . . ." She looked at her little brother and pulled him even closer to her. After a couple of seconds, she went on. "He must have."

"Did you see someone?"

She shook her head. She blinked, obviously fighting back tears. "I'm not going to cry. I'm not."

Anthony tightened his hand on her shoulder and dropped the phone in his pocket to free his other hand to stroke her hair. "Cry if you want to," he told her.

"No. Not again." She pressed her lips firmly together and swallowed hard. "I won't."

"Take your time, Maggie." Michael stepped a little nearer to her, but stayed where he had a view of the hallway. "Start at the beginning and tell everything that happened."

Maggie took a shaky breath. "He, Mr. Elwood, wanted my mother to clean the house today." She let her gaze slide toward the front of the house and then brought it swiftly back to Michael. "Mom told me to come on over after school to get started on the dusting. Dad had to go somewhere, so

Jesse came with me. Miss Marble started meowing when she saw us. We figured she was hungry since I hadn't been over to feed her for a few days. I found a can of food in the cabinet here and told Jesse he could feed her on the back porch. I thought he'd be okay."

Her arm tightened around the little boy again and he made a face. But he didn't squirm away from her.

Her eyes got a little watery, but again she blinked the tears away. "I mean, I've been watching Jesse really close. Making sure he's never by himself. And I could hear him if he yelled."

"I'm right here, Maggie." The kid did try to pull away from her then. "You don't have to squeeze me so hard."

She relaxed her hold a little, but she didn't turn him loose. Or answer him. She kept her eyes on Michael. "He's my responsibility, you see. When Mom isn't home. I couldn't let anything happen to him."

"You didn't." Michael understood her big sister concern, but plenty of other things were far from understood. The radio buzzed on his belt and he heard Betty Jean's voice. He clicked in a code to let her know he was all right and would call her momentarily, but he needed to get Maggie's story first. "All right. You came over to start dusting. Then what?"

"I went into the room Miss Fonda calls a parlor. One of the pictures was off the wall and the couch pillows were on the floor. Then I looked over at the library room and books were thrown on the floor. I started to pick them up. That's when I saw him staring at me."

"He?"

"Mr. Elwood."

"He saw you?" Michael asked.

"No." Her face went even whiter. "He was dead, but his

eyes were open. Just like Mrs. Harper's." Her eyes flared wider then and she slapped her hand over her mouth.

Michael kept his eyes directly on her. "So you were here when Mrs. Harper fell last Friday."

"No." The denial burst from her.

"Maggie," Michael said. "You have to tell me the truth."

Her head drooped. "Okay. I was here, but I didn't see anything. I mean, I heard her fall, but I didn't see it." She looked back up at Michael and her words tumbled out super fast. "And I didn't want anybody to know I was here. Miss Fonda said I could go up to her tower room whenever I wanted, but I didn't think she would remember telling me that and I'd get in trouble. Maybe even arrested for trespassing. So I left."

Anthony started to say something, but Michael held up a hand to stop him. "But you called first."

Maggie pulled in a shuddering breath. "It didn't seem right to just leave Mrs. Harper all alone in here without telling somebody."

"So you called 911. You didn't see anybody else here that day?"

She hesitated and blew out another breath. "I didn't see anybody. I was up in the tower room. But somebody else was here. They knocked a lamp off one of the tables and it broke. Mrs. Harper ran up the stairs and said she was calling the sheriff. The other person sounded sort of panicked and asked her not to. Then I heard all this noise when I guess Mrs. Harper fell down the stairs."

"What happened to the other person?"

"They left. I heard the back door open and close. At least I thought I did. So I climbed down out of the tower room and found Mrs. Harper. I would have helped her if she hadn't been dead. Honest, I would have." She stared at Michael, her eyes begging him to believe her. "Even if I did get in trouble or arrested. But she was dead. Me sticking around wasn't going to change that."

"Michael wouldn't arrest you." Anthony reached and took Maggie's hand. "Would you, Michael?"

"We're way past that now," Michael said. "So you saw Mrs. Harper, called 911 on her phone, and left. By the back door too?"

"Yes. I had Mom's key. I had to lock the door."

"You didn't see anybody?"

"No, but—" She looked at her little brother and stopped.

"But what?" Michael pushed her.

"I guess I have to tell you. After this." She took a quick glance toward the front of the house again. "He called me. Not Mr. Elwood. Well, I don't think it was him anyway. Some man. It was after we went fishing Saturday. I thought it was Anthony calling." Color bloomed in her cheeks. "But it wasn't. The man said I better not say anything to anybody about whatever I saw on Friday. Or he'd do stuff to make me sorry."

"What stuff?"

"I don't know." She tightened her hold on her little brother again. Her voice went down to almost a whisper. "But he knew I had a little brother."

"How'd he know that?" Anthony said.

"I don't know."

"I guess he saw me," the little boy said. "Out in the yard or something."

"Yeah." Maggie barely breathed the word.

"Was it the same person you heard in the house before Mrs. Harper fell?" Michael asked.

"I don't think so. The man on the phone sounded weird. Like he was disguising his voice or something."

A board creaked outside on the porch and a shadow fell across the window. Anthony moved in front of Maggie to shield her. Michael pulled his gun out of his holster and spun toward the door. The cat hissed and leaped back up on the refrigerator.

Hank Leland stepped up to the open door, saw Michael's gun, and raised his hands. "Whoa, Mike. It's just me."

"You know better than to sneak around in somebody's backyard." Michael shoved his gun back in his holster. He didn't bother to hide his irritation. "I could have shot you."

"Kinda jumpy, aren't you?" Hank lowered his hands and let his gaze settle on the kids as he fingered the camera hanging around his neck. "You catch these kids pilfering in here or something?"

"Or something."

"He's the newspaperman, isn't he?" Maggie didn't wait for anybody to answer as she pulled her hand away from Anthony and tried to cover her face. She kept her hold on her little brother. "I can't have my picture in the paper. He might see it and know I talked to you."

Michael wanted to tell Maggie she didn't have any reason to worry, but two people were already dead. He hadn't stopped that. But he could stop the picture taking. He looked from Maggie to Hank. "No pictures of the kids, Hank. None. Zero. Zilch. Got that?"

"Whatever you say, boss." Hank stepped back, his hands halfway up again. "But why do I get the feeling I'm going to want to take some pictures?"

"Later." Michael pulled his gun out again. "Right now you stand there and don't let anybody in. Got that?"

"Got it." Hank took up position just inside the door.

Michael looked straight at Anthony. "And you stay here too. All of you. Until I check things out."

"Check out what?" Hank Leland pulled his little notebook out of his pocket, but Michael didn't answer him.

Michael stepped into the hallway. The blue from his lights out front flashed through the windows and again he wished he'd killed them.

The house had that same silent feel it had on Friday. Death was much too common in this house.

24

Things in the front room were just the way Maggie said. Pillows scattered. Pictures crooked or on the floor. But it was an island of serenity compared to the adjoining room. Books had been raked off the shelves and dumped every which way on the floor. Somebody must have been desperately searching for something.

Was that before or after they shot Sonny Elwood? Because Maggie was right about that too. Sonny slumped in the chair with blood staining his white dress shirt. Michael might have said the man didn't even own a dress shirt, but here he was. Dressed for death.

At least two bullet wounds. One in his arm that must have hit a vein. The other truer that surely killed him at once. The man's skin was cool to touch, so the murder had happened some time ago. And murder it was. No way to consider this anything but.

Michael went back into the sitting room and got the crocheted throw off the couch to drape over Sonny. Just days ago, it was Sonny who had been relieved when Justin covered Geraldine's body. What was it that made it so necessary to hide the face of death? But Michael felt better with Sonny's meeting-eternity stare out of his sight, even if the blanket was a ludicrous green and orange.

He pulled out his phone and called Betty Jean.

"You're driving me crazy, Michael." Betty Jean's voice exploded out of the phone. "You have to quit cutting me off."

He held the phone away from his ear. "Sorry, Betty Jean, but I had to make sure the kids were all right first."

Betty Jean blew out a breath. "What kids? And are they okay?"

"Maggie Greene and her little brother and Anthony Blake. They're okay. But Sonny Elwood isn't."

"Sonny? What's wrong with Sonny?"

"Somebody shot him. He's dead. You'll have to call out the troops. Buck and Justin." Michael paused. "You don't have to worry about Hank chasing after them. He's already here."

"He didn't shoot Sonny, did he?" She sounded a little worried.

"Why would he do that?" Michael frowned.

"I don't know. Why would anybody shoot Sonny?"

"I guess that's something I've got to find out, but Hank just heard my sirens and followed me here."

"Everybody in town heard your sirens. You about scared me to death." Her voice rose again. "If things like this keep happening, I'm going to hunt a new job. I don't care what Uncle Al says."

"You can't desert us, Betty Jean. We need you."

"I need people to quit getting shot." Another long sigh. "But okay, I'll call Justin and radio Buck. He probably won't answer if he's off duty. You know Buck."

"Send the right code on the radio and he'll call in. We need to have the state police in on this."

"I hate that I know the homicide code without looking it up." She hesitated for a second. "You're sure it's homicide?"

"No doubt on that one."

"Then what about Geraldine?"

"Not sure. Definitely some new questions there." That was all he seemed to have right now. Questions without answers. "Need to handle this with Sonny first."

"So you don't want to talk to Grant about his mother yet?" Something about Betty Jean's voice was too tight.

"He's not there hearing you, is he?" Michael asked.

"No, but I'm supposed to meet him later. Dinner for old times' sake, you know." She sounded a little too casual.

Seemed romance was flowering all around Betty Jean. "What about Vernon?"

"What about him?"

"Nothing." Michael didn't have time to think about romance. Betty Jean's or his. "Look, just make the calls. And try to get hold of Mary Greene at the Fast Serve if she hasn't left yet. Tell her what's going on. Maggie found the body. She's in a shape."

"Right." Betty Jean was all business as she disconnected. She'd get things rolling.

Michael went back to the kitchen where Anthony was holding Maggie's hand again and the little brother stayed frozen by her side. Hank stood in the door, trying to look in every direction at once. The lens cap was on his camera. For once, he seemed to have listened to Michael.

But as soon as he saw Michael, he deserted his post at the door and pulled out his notebook. "Okay, Mike. What's happening here? These kids look like they've seen a ghost or something." Hank pointed his stub of a pencil at them.

"No ghosts." Michael wished he could order the editor back to his newspaper office on Main Street.

"Then what? Cut to the chase and tell me what's going on."

"All right. Here's an official statement for you." He might as well tell Hank. Murder couldn't be kept secret in a little town like Hidden Springs or in any town. "It appears Sonny Elwood may have surprised an intruder here. All indications suggest said intruder shot Mr. Elwood."

Hank looked up from his scribbling. "Dead?"

"Dead." Michael kept his face expressionless and his voice level. Hank whistled under his breath as Michael went on. "The body was discovered at approximately 4:00 p.m. by someone hired to clean the house. No need for names. She's underage."

"Odd cleaning crew," Hank muttered.

"I couldn't leave my brother alone," Maggie spoke up in a shaky voice.

"One of them isn't your brother." Hank looked from the little brother to Anthony.

"Back off, Hank." Michael shot him a hard look. "They're kids."

"Whatever you say, Mike. Any suspects? Motives?" Hank peered over at him, then back at the kids. "Witnesses to the crime?"

"The incident will be fully investigated and the public kept informed as necessary."

"In other words, you don't know squat." Hank stuck the notebook back in his pocket and fingered his camera. "You gonna let me take pictures?"

"Not now. You need to step outside until the crime scene is secured." Michael pointed at the door.

"A few minutes ago you were ready to make me a deputy and now you're kicking me outside with the cat." Hank made a face.

"No, the cat can stay." Michael glanced at the calico cat staring at Hank from the top of the refrigerator.

"Very funny." Hank wasn't smiling.

"Nothing funny about any of this." Michael dropped his official tone. "You know I have to secure the area."

"Just a peek?"

"No." Michael stared at Hank. "I can escort you outside if necessary."

"I'm going." Hank held up his hands in surrender and backed out onto the porch. He even had the good sense and grace to step away from the windows. Michael stepped across the room to shut the door.

"You want us to go outside too?" Anthony asked.

"Not yet." Michael settled his eyes on Anthony. "Tell me why you're here."

"I wanted to meet Maggie's mother. I was going to ask if she'd let me come over to their house to help Maggie with her algebra homework. Maggie's having trouble with it."

That wasn't the only trouble Maggie was having. Michael shifted his gaze to her. She looked ready to fall apart. "It's going to be all right, Maggie."

"But now he'll know I told you." Maggie's voice was barely above a whisper. "He said he'd be watching me." She tightened her arm around the little brother.

"We'll catch whoever did this." He did his best to sound very sure. It was a promise he intended to keep. He couldn't imagine who in Hidden Springs would threaten a child, but then he couldn't imagine who would shoot Sonny Elwood. What in the house could be reason for murder?

Sirens sounded as the troops came toward the house. Somebody knocked on the front door. Probably Justin with his gurney for the body. Then Maggie's mother burst through the back door. Hank peered inside but didn't follow her.

The little brother jerked away from Maggie and ran to his mother, who hugged him close and then scooted him along with her toward Maggie. Both of them started talking at once. Anthony, displaced as Maggie's protector, looked a little lost as he stepped back. The cat jumped down from the refrigerator and wound around Mrs. Greene's legs the way she had around Lana Waverly's the day before.

Lana had told him that morning Sonny was going to show her the house today. Had she been there and left before Sonny was killed? He couldn't imagine her shooting Sonny, but somebody had.

Michael ordered Anthony to stay put when he went past him to open the front door to let in Justin. He had more questions to ask.

It was going to be a long day. Michael thought of his planned dinner with Alex. No time to worry about that now. Murder investigations trumped marriage proposals.

The rooms upstairs were in the same shambles as the downstairs rooms. Vases upended. Some broken. More pictures off the walls. Drawers dumped on the floor. Mattresses slit open. Once he was sure the house was secure, he asked Mary Greene to walk through it with him to see if she could tell what, if anything, was missing.

The destruction distressed Mary. "I hope Miss Fonda

doesn't see this. She always took such pride in keeping everything neat and orderly. Just the way it was when she was a child."

"Her sister lived here for a while. Wonder if she felt the same way."

"Oh no." Mary carefully righted a large Chinese vase. "Miss Fonda said her sister didn't care about the family antiques. That when she moved in, she bought all modern furniture. But Miss Fonda convinced her to store the old things in the garage instead of selling them. Then after her sister died, she brought it all back to the way it was when she was growing up. The poor woman found her greatest happiness living in the past. Of course, I didn't know her husband. She might have been different before he passed."

"How long have you been cleaning for her?"

Mary considered her answer for a moment. "Maybe nine, ten years. Maggie was just a little girl when I started. Miss Fonda would tell her stories while I worked. They were great buddies."

"Then Miss Fonda probably did give Maggie permission to come into the house."

"I don't doubt that, but she still shouldn't have come over here without telling me. She knew better." Mary frowned and then rubbed her hand across her forehead. She blew out a breath. "And look at the trouble it's gotten her into. Being where she shouldn't be."

"She didn't do any of this."

"I know. Do you think she's really in danger?" The woman's frown was back. A worried one now.

"I wish I could tell you there was nothing to worry about, Mrs. Greene, but somebody killed Sonny Elwood. Someone

218

may have caused Geraldine Harper to fall down those steps. Someone threatened Maggie. You can't ignore that. I can't ignore that."

"You're scaring me." Her face went stiff.

She was right to be scared, he thought now as he drove away from the Chandler house. Murder should scare people. It was his job to protect people and keep murders from happening. He had worked out a schedule of patrols around the Greenes' trailer park with Buck. Whoever had threatened Maggie would know they were protecting her.

Mary Greene had noted several things gone. Two of Miss Fonda's favorite figurines. A painting. Some decorative plates. Maybe more. But it was hard to tell for sure what was or wasn't missing in all the mess.

The things she noted hardly seemed reason for murder. But then people got killed over less all the time. Sometimes nothing more serious than an argument over a fence. Or a cat.

The cat, Miss Marble, had disappeared when Maggie and the others left. Anthony had offered to go feed Jasper. Michael let him with some trepidation. Not that Anthony was in danger. Nobody had threatened him. But Michael wanted to hover over them all to keep them safe.

The people in the houses across the road hadn't noticed anything out of the ordinary. One neighbor saw Sonny's car in the driveway, but Sonny had a right to be there.

Lana Waverly was visibly shocked when Michael went by to question her. She said a group of women had come in at lunchtime and lingered as they discussed forming a book club. She tried to reach Sonny to tell him she would have to come another time, but he hadn't answered his phone. Michael would have no problem checking out her story.

He called Mrs. Gibson. She gave him Sonny's sister's number in Arizona. Not a call Michael wanted to make, but it had to be done. The one person in the world who truly loved Sonny was his mother. That is, if you didn't count Felicia Peterson. Betty Jean had tried to track her down, but with no luck.

Nothing for it but to swing by Felicia's place in a small four-unit apartment building behind Main Street. He knocked on the door with no response. A new wiggle of worry woke inside Michael. He was ready to find the building's landlord to open the door for him, when the woman who lived in the apartment adjoining Felicia's stuck her head out her door.

"Felicia's not home. I saw her leave before noon. Figured she was going to see Miss Fonda. You know Ellen pays her to sit with the old lady." Carla Larson peered over the top of her glasses at Michael, curiosity mixed with annoyance. A game show sounded in the background and he was probably causing her to miss the best parts. "Is something wrong?"

Michael didn't tell her that Felicia wasn't at Mrs. Gibson's. He didn't tell her Sonny Elwood was dead. Not that she wouldn't know five minutes after he left. He was surprised she didn't already know. "You wouldn't happen to have Felicia's cell number?"

Curiosity won over whatever was happening on her television show. Mrs. Larson stepped out on the landing in front of her apartment. Michael guessed her to be in her sixties, in spite of her still-brown hair. She wore loose sweats and jogging shoes, but he doubted she'd ever jogged farther than the refrigerator.

She made a little face. "Felicia's never seen fit to share that with me. The girl keeps to herself when she's here. That's not much. In and out all the time. Can't imagine what she might be doing."

"Oh?" It didn't take much to keep somebody like Carla Larson talking.

"Well, like I said, Felicia doesn't confide in me, but let me tell you, the girl stays busy. I hear she's keeping company with that Sonny Elwood. Somebody told me they were the next thing to engaged."

"Is that right?"

"So I've heard. Not that he's around here much. You'd think he'd come by now and again, wouldn't you? Makes a person wonder if this engagement talk is all just that. Nothing but talk." Mrs. Larson paused and raised her eyebrows a bit. "Now, I'm not one to gossip but living right next door like this, a person can't help but notice things."

"Sounds like you're very observant," Michael said.

"Oh, I see things, but I don't always talk about them. But seeing as how you're a policeman, I figure you're investigating the girl for some reason. I hear tell she's been in trouble with the law before. And you know how you read in the paper about drug dealers being right in the middle of the best neighborhoods."

"I'm not here to arrest her, Mrs. Larson. Just to give her some news."

"Oh dear, is it bad?" Mrs. Larson looked genuinely distressed. "And here I have been going on and on about her."

Michael pulled out one of Sheriff Potter's old campaign cards and wrote his cell number on the back. "I'll stick this in her door, but if you see her, would you ask her to call in case she doesn't notice the card?" He wrote his number on another card for her.

"I'll be glad to, unless I've already gone to bed before she comes in."

Wouldn't be much chance of that. Not once Mrs. Larson heard about Sonny. The woman would be glued to the window.

Back in his car, Michael checked in with Betty Jean to report Felicia wasn't at her apartment. "I'll check with Justin to see if he can find her number on Sonny's phone. I should have kept that anyway as evidence."

"I tried that already," Betty Jean said. "Justin doesn't have Sonny's phone. He thought you had it."

"Nope."

"Okay then." Michael could hear her tapping her pen on her desk. She did that when she was thinking. "I guess I need to start the process to get Sonny's phone records."

"You're a gem. But I thought you had a date." Michael checked the time. It was past seven.

"Not a date. Dinner with an old friend." Her voice sounded carefully casual. "I'm leaving in a few minutes."

"The best kind of date." The kind Michael had hoped to have before somebody shot Sonny Elwood.

Instead of turning toward Keane Street and Alex the way he wanted to, he drove by Maggie's house again. The trailer was all buttoned up. Doors and windows closed. Maybe barricaded. Curt Greene's truck wasn't in the driveway. Mary Greene must not have been able to reach him or surely he'd be there to watch over his family.

Anthony's old car wasn't there either. Not that Michael expected it to be. By now, Anthony would be settled on Michael's couch with Jasper on the floor beside him.

After another loop through the trailer park, Michael eased

past Maggie's house one more time before he headed back to the main road. The state patrol would make another drive-through in a few minutes and keep a watch through the night. But Michael needed to relieve Lester at the Chandler house. The crime scene had to be secured until Buck brought in the crime technicians in the morning. Lester would be anxious to get home for supper.

Michael's stomach complained a bit too as he pulled up behind Lester's patrol car, glad to see Lester hadn't left his dome lights flashing. He'd be even gladder to see the state patrolman Buck was sending out to relieve Michael. He hoped that would be soon. He intended to see Alex before the night was over. He didn't care if all the lights were off at Reece's house when he got there. He would bang on the door anyway.

25

Mondays sometimes felt like the longest day of the week. Too many of her students came back to school after the weekend with fuzzy brains. This Monday, Malinda had been the same. Teaching by rote instead of enthusiasm.

She just couldn't stop worrying. Something she knew did absolutely no good. Something the Scripture warned against. Have faith, not worries. Not in those exact words, but the thought was there. But some worries were nearly impossible to dismiss. Worries about Michael and Alexandria. Worries about Reece. Worries about the children in her classes. Like that Maggie Greene. The girl had been a thousand miles away during algebra class.

The child might be letting her brain get clouded with young love. Malinda had seen Anthony with her in the hall that morning. They hadn't seen her. They didn't have eyes for anybody but each other. But in class, Maggie had looked like something more than that was bothering her. No doubt, problems at home.

Some thought teen years should be carefree with no problems, but being young didn't negate life challenges. Malinda knew that firsthand. Hadn't she carried Michael through the worst thing to happen to a young teen? The loss of his parents.

Maggie had her parents, but it was no secret they were struggling since Curt Greene lost his job. Through no fault of his. Layoffs and factory closings were far too common. That was no excuse for his drinking, but people had a way of messing up. She saw that every day at school, and there were plenty of things she couldn't fix. But she could help Maggie keep from messing up in algebra.

She wished she had as good a chance of keeping Michael and Alexandria from messing up in love. Funny how things worked. She'd been so sure Alexandria being here to take care of Reece was exactly what the two needed. That would give them time together to figure things out and finally embrace love.

But instead they appeared to be pushing each other away. Or perhaps not they. Michael was obviously besotted by the girl. Alexandria was the problem. Not that she wasn't besotted too. She loved Michael. Malinda knew that hadn't changed, but something had. The girl was stepping back, away from Michael. She must be sensing he was ready to risk everything to ask her to share his life. Malinda supposed she'd pushed him into that.

Malinda sighed as she peered out the window toward Reece's house. No sign of Michael's patrol car. He should be there. Fighting for love. Had he completely lost courage?

Well, she wouldn't let that happen. Even if people did decide she was a meddling old woman. Some things needed meddling to make them come out right. And a lot of prayer. She was capable of both.

She had her jacket on and was heading across the yards when Betty Jean Atkins pulled up in front of Reece's house. A man Malinda didn't recognize climbed out of the passenger seat. He was tall, and even from across the yard she could see he was nice looking. Certainly not that Vernon Trent Malinda had heard Betty Jean was dating. Thank goodness. Malinda wouldn't wish that man on anybody.

Betty Jean and the stranger lifted something out of the backseat. Takeout boxes from the Grill. And that had to be a pie the man was balancing on top of the Styrofoam boxes. Michael must have ordered the food, but where was he? Something must be wrong. That seemed way too common lately in Hidden Springs.

Malinda called to Betty Jean and picked up her pace across the yard. Not exactly running. Women her age didn't run, but she wanted to when she got a good look at Betty Jean's face.

Without so much as a hello, Malinda asked, "What's happened? Is Michael all right?"

"Michael's fine, Miss Keane," Betty Jean said. "You know you'd be the first to know if something was wrong with Michael."

Betty Jean's placating tone grated on Malinda's nerves, made her practically bark out her next questions. "Then where is he? And I asked you what happened. Spit it out."

Betty Jean shifted the food boxes in her hands and did as she was told. "Sonny Elwood got shot."

"By Michael?" Malinda was sorry for the words as soon as she uttered them. It wasn't like her to jump to conclusions. Better to let Betty Jean tell her what happened, but the girl did seem to want to drag out the news.

"No." Betty Jean gave a shake of her head. "The responsible person has yet to be apprehended."

"And Sonny?"

"Dead." Betty Jean glanced over at the man beside her who hadn't said a word.

"Are you saying Sonny was murdered? Here in Hidden Springs?" Malinda didn't want to believe her ears. Not more crime in Hidden Springs.

"I'm afraid so. His body was found this afternoon." Another uneasy look over at her friend. "At the Chandler house."

"Oh dear." Malinda's relief that Michael was safe was tempered by her sympathy for Sonny's mother. "Poor Ellen. This will be a hard blow for her. Did you have to call her, Betty Jean?"

"No, thank goodness. Michael did that. Look, we need to get this food inside before we drop something."

When she turned toward the door without introducing the man beside her, he carefully freed a hand from under the carryout boxes to stretch out toward Malinda. "You probably don't recognize me, Miss Keane, but you haven't changed a bit since you introduced me to algebra. I'm Grant Harper."

"Grant. Of course. Geraldine's son." Malinda touched his hand without letting him squeeze hers. That pesky arthritis. While Grant wasn't the same awkward boy in black-rimmed glasses Malinda remembered from high school, she did recognize him now that she looked closer. "You were an excellent student. Good math skills."

"Oh gosh, I should have introduced you." Betty Jean's face flashed red as she glanced back at them. "I'm sorry."

"No problem." Grant smiled at Betty Jean.

Betty Jean looked ready to melt down on the spot. The

man did have a charming smile. Sincere. Friendly. A Hidden Springs kind of smile. And why not? He spent a lot of his childhood years here. Those important formative years.

"Grant's right." Malinda let Betty Jean off the hook as well. "Murders have a way of distracting a person."

Betty Jean flinched at the word "murder" but didn't contradict Malinda.

"Yes." Grant jerked his hand back to grab at the pie that was sliding off the food boxes.

Malinda reached to rescue it. "I am sorry about your mother. Such a dreadful accident."

Betty Jean turned quickly back toward the house but not before Malinda noted the look on her face. So there were questions now about Geraldine's death as well. Two people found dead in the same house three days apart had to give rise to all sorts of suppositions. And eliminate the chance for romance to blossom. At least between Michael and Alexandria. It appeared to be a vehicle for romance for Betty Jean.

Inside, Reece looked better. He set his cat, Two Bits, out of his lap and stood to greet them. Smiling. Alexandria didn't look nearly as happy. Perhaps her lawyer radar sensed something out of the way or Malinda could wish it was simply because Michael wasn't there.

Betty Jean introduced Grant and explained why she was bringing the food instead of Michael.

"At the Chandler house you say." Reece felt behind him for the chair and sank back down in it.

Alexandria hovered over him. "Are you all right, Uncle Reece? The doctor said you shouldn't get upset."

"It appears time to be upset. Poor Grant here losing his

mother on Friday and now this." The cat jumped back up in his lap and he stroked it head to tail. "Sit down, everybody."

"We can't stay," Betty Jean spoke up quickly while easing toward the door. "Grant's anxious to give Cindy's finest a try. He remembers hanging out at the Grill back when he was a kid."

"I do. Should be a great place for us to reminisce about our high school days." Grant smiled at Betty Jean, but then the smile slid off his face. "It'll be food to get my mind off losing Mother for a little while. Her death was so unexpected."

"I'm sorry about your mother." Alexandria gave him a sympathetic look. "Life can sometimes be uncertain."

"Seems that way in Hidden Springs lately." Reece looked up from stroking Two Bits. "Why would anybody want to kill Sonny Elwood? He was harmless enough." He settled his gaze on Betty Jean.

"I can't talk about an ongoing investigation." Betty Jean took on an official tone, but then her voice softened. "I don't know much anyway. Michael is investigating. He'll figure it out. He always does."

"But at what cost?" Reece looked back down at the cat. "To him. To Hidden Springs. We used to be such a peaceful little town and now murder is becoming commonplace."

"Murder should never be commonplace," Malinda said. "Especially in our town."

"People are people everywhere. Some good. Some bad," Alexandria said. "I deal with both every week."

"Alex is an attorney in Washington, DC." Betty Jean turned toward Grant, then back to Alexandria. "I'm sure Grant has had his share of encounters with all sorts of people in his business world."

"Not at all. At least not anymore." Grant smiled. "Now, it's all flowers and celebration. And sometimes panic when guys forget their anniversaries. I do flowers by mail that can be ordered on the internet," he explained. "Men sometimes want to send my company flowers, they are so grateful for last-minute solutions."

Malinda gave Grant another look. He wasn't much like his mother, with her in-your-face personality. He was a man easy with his success and who in turn knew how to make those around him comfortable. Like Michael. Except Michael wouldn't be feeling comfortable about anything right now with another murder to solve. He had come back to Hidden Springs to get away from big-city crime, but it seemed to have followed him.

Then again, sometimes the Lord had a way of putting a person right where he was needed to make good come out of the worst happenings. That was what she had hoped for after Reece's stroke. Good for Michael and Alexandria to come from that, but things weren't happening as she thought they might. She'd never seen Alexandria so uncertain. She generally appeared to have the world by the tail and ready to make life happen to suit her fancy. But now under the polite façade she was showing Grant and Betty Jean was something else. Something almost fragile looking. *Fragile* was not a word Malinda would have ever used to describe Alexandria, but then perhaps everyone was fragile when it came to love.

After seeing Betty Jean and Grant to the door, Alexandria came back to the sitting room and stared straight at Malinda. "Aren't you worried about Michael?"

When Malinda hesitated, Reece spoke up. "Michael's good

at what he does. He'll be fine. If I know him, he'll stop by here before he goes home. He'll be hungry."

Malinda hadn't intended to stay. She had papers to grade. But when Alexandria asked her, she didn't refuse. The papers could wait. Reece was right. Michael would come see Alexandria. And Malinda needed to see Michael. Not only see him, but see Alexandria with him. Maybe then she could figure out a way to fix whatever was wrong between them.

26

At the supper table, Maggie's mother kept frowning over at her and telling her it didn't help anything to not eat. So Maggie dipped some potatoes onto her plate and took her time cutting her hot dog into little circles.

She tried not to look at Jesse's plate. He liked lots of ketchup with his potatoes. They didn't talk about Mr. Elwood. Her mother told her she could if she wanted to, but she didn't want to. She simply wanted none of it to have happened. None of it. Not Mrs. Harper. Not Mr. Elwood. She wanted to go back in time to when Miss Fonda was still at her house and sitting out on the porch petting Miss Marble.

Miss Fonda liked listening to Maggie's stories. Nobody else ever had time, but Miss Fonda did. It wouldn't even matter if Maggie never got to climb up to the tower room. While she did love being high in the little room, writing about the imaginary characters dancing around her, she'd give all that up to have never seen Mrs. Harper dead at the bottom of the stairs and Mr. Elwood staring at her from that chair in Miss Fonda's library. The sight of them had pushed all her made-up characters out of her head.

If she had her notebook, she could read what she'd written and maybe they'd come to life in her imagination again. But the notebook was in the tower room. Right now, Maggie couldn't think about going back to Miss Fonda's house for any reason.

Not even to feed Miss Marble. The cat would have to eat mice. Or maybe Maggie could ask Anthony to feed the cat. He hadn't acted that scared. At least not as scared as Maggie. He'd gone in, taken one look at Mr. Elwood, and then called Michael. He knew what to do.

She should have done that after she found Mrs. Harper. She shouldn't have just called 911 and run away. It could be that if she hadn't been so worried about getting in trouble, Mr. Elwood might still be alive. If she'd told about the person in the house. If she'd told about the man on the phone. If.

She pushed the neat circles of hot dog to the edge of her plate and speared one of the potato squares. When the phone rang, she dropped her fork with a loud clatter. She and her mother both stared at the phone. Jesse stared at them.

It rang three times before her mother pushed back from the table. "It could be your father."

Maggie sucked in her breath as her mother picked up the receiver. She didn't breathe out until her mother held the phone toward her with a little smile. "It's your friend. Anthony."

"You mean boyfriend," Jesse piped up.

Maggie ignored him as she got up from the table. How could she go from shaky scared to shaky excited in two seconds? She moistened her lips and stared at her mother without reaching for the phone.

Her mother whispered, "Just say hello."

But what if she did something dumb? Like bursting into tears again, or worse, stuttering. Or even worse, not being able to say a word. She pulled in a deep breath. She'd talked to Anthony at the lake Saturday and that morning face-to-face. Her heart had done some racing then the same as it was now, but she'd managed to talk. But that was before this afternoon when she'd fallen apart right in front of his eyes.

Her mother gave her a quick hug, pushed the receiver into her hand, and turned Maggie so she was looking at the phone on the wall instead of the table.

Maggie put the receiver to her ear. "Hello."

"Hi, Maggie. Are you all right?"

He sounded so concerned that a smile tugged up the corners of her lips. She shut her eyes and pictured him on the other end of the line. "Yes." She bit the inside of her lip. Surely she could say more than one word.

"Are you sure? That man hasn't called again, has he?"

"No." One word again.

"Can't you talk? Is your father listening in or something?"

"No." He was going to think she didn't want to talk to him, but she did. She really did. She pushed out more words. "He hasn't come home yet."

"Oh." Now it was his turn to only say one word.

Silence hummed in the phone she pressed tight against her ear while she tried to think of what to say. He started talking again first. "Don't you think you ought to call him?"

"Mom already did, but he didn't answer. He had something important to do." She kept her voice low. She peeked over at her mother at the sink washing the dishes and hoped she wasn't listening. Maggie didn't want to break her promise to her dad, but she did wish he would get home.

"So, he doesn't even know about you finding Mr. Elwood then or the phone call or anything."

"No." Again the monosyllable answer.

"You're going to tell him, aren't you?"

"I'll have to. When he gets home. He should be here soon." If he hadn't given up on the not drinking and fallen off the wagon. But no way could she tell Anthony that.

"You have Michael's number. Or you can dial 911 if something happens." He rushed on. "You probably won't need to or anything, but just in case."

"I know."

Again silence hummed between them for a few seconds before he said, "Your mother was nice. Pretty like you."

"Thanks." Maggie's heart beat a little faster. "People say I look like her."

"Did she like me all right? Everything was a little crazy over there. Not exactly the best way to meet somebody."

"No. I mean yes, she did." That sounded weird even to her. "Like you, I mean."

"Great. Now I just have to win over your dad. Then I can come over and help you with that algebra."

"I wish you could. I haven't done my homework yet."

"It's not that late. You can still get it done."

"If I can figure it out." Maggie didn't think she'd be able to figure anything out tonight.

"Miss Keane will give you a pass tomorrow if you don't get it done. Especially if Michael tells her about everything. Miss Keane's his aunt, you know."

"He's a lot easier to talk to than she is." At least he was before she started finding dead people. "Will you talk to him again today?"

"Probably. I'm down here at his house, but he's not home yet."

"Are you all right down there?" Michael's house way out on the lake with nobody else around had to be lonesome.

"Jasper's curled up beside me and Michael had leftover pizza in the fridge. Beats Aunt Vera's anytime. Besides, it's you we have to worry about. Not me."

"I'm okay."

"You're better than okay." His voice was soft in her ear.

Maggie's cheeks flashed warm. For a minute, she felt better than okay. Almost floating in spite of everything even though she had no idea what to say. He spoke first.

"See you tomorrow at school."

"Yeah. Tomorrow."

She hung the receiver back on the phone. They had a cordless phone in the living room, but this one was attached to the wall. She remembered the last time she'd hung up the phone after the man called and told her to keep quiet about what she'd seen at Miss Fonda's house. And now she hadn't kept quiet. She slid her eyes past the dark window over the sink to Jesse, who was making trails through the ketchup on his plate with his potatoes. And just like that, the good trembles from talking to Anthony were shoved aside by the scared trembles.

Her mother looked around from the sink. "Nice kid." She smiled at Maggie. "I'm glad he was there with you."

"Yeah, he had a phone."

"But you tried to get him not to call the police." Jesse looked up from playing with his potatoes.

"He did anyway," Maggie said.

"He did the right thing." Her mother gave Maggie a concerned look. "What had to be done."

"Yeah." Maggie didn't want to talk about it. She didn't want to think about it. She simply wanted to hide somewhere for a while. She thought of the tower room. Hiding up there was what had her all mixed up in this. In murder. A shiver crawled through her and stayed. "I better go do my homework."

In her room, she pulled her curtains closed. For the first time ever, she was glad the window was small. Nobody could crawl through it. But it wasn't just her in trouble. The man had threatened Jesse too. Out in the hall, her mother was telling him to go to bed. He was fussing and trying to put it off the same as any other night.

Nobody would bother him here. The doors were locked and Michael had told her mother a policeman would be watching the neighborhood. But she'd feel better when her father got home. He might be going through a rough time trying to find a job and everything, but he wouldn't let anybody hurt Jesse.

Maggie finished her biology and was looking at the first algebra problem when she heard her father's truck pull into the driveway. Her mother must have met him at the door because Maggie heard them talking right away. She sat very still in the middle of her bed with her books spread out around her. She didn't so much as rustle a paper, but she couldn't hear what they were saying. She didn't need to hear the words. She knew what her mother was telling him. At least they didn't sound like they were arguing.

She stared at her paper without really seeing the numbers on it and waited, not sure what to expect next. Her father might be mad that she hadn't told him about, well, about everything. He should be mad. She'd gotten herself into a mess.

The tap on her bedroom door made her jump, even though she'd been waiting for it. Her father pushed open the door and came over to sit on the edge of her bed. Maggie stuck her paper in her algebra book and closed it. She knew her father was looking at her, but she kept her eyes on her book.

"You should have told me." He didn't sound mad exactly.

"I wanted to." Maggie peeked up at him and then stared back down at her book. She smoothed her hand over the slick cover.

"Then why didn't you?"

"I was afraid."

"Not of me?" His voice was low, worried.

"No." The word burst out of her as she looked up and met his eyes. He just kept looking at her without saying anything more and waited, as if he knew she hadn't told him the complete truth. "Well, maybe a little. I didn't want to get in trouble with you and Mom."

Her father blew out a little breath. "There are all kinds of ways to get in trouble. I know. I've found plenty of them, but not owning up to doing something wrong doesn't do anything but get you in more trouble."

"I'm sorry." She started to look down at her book again, but her father reached over and put his hand under her chin so she'd have to keep looking at him.

"I am too. That I haven't been the kind of father you could trust when you were in trouble."

Maggie didn't know what to say to that, but when he kept looking at her, she had to say something. "That wasn't it. I just didn't know what to do. And then that man called and I was really afraid. Not just for me but for Jesse too. He told me not to tell anybody and so I didn't." She pulled in a ragged breath. "But now I have."

"Come here, Maggie." Her father put his hand on her shoulder and pulled her toward him. Maggie moved aside her books and scooted over to lean against him. He rubbed his hand up and down her back and held her close. "The police will catch whoever did that. Whoever called you. Then it'll all be over and you can go back to worrying about homework and boys and things a girl your age is supposed to worry about."

Maggie nodded against her father's chest.

"And I promise you I won't be drinking and being somebody you have to be afraid of. Not you or Jesse."

"Did you tell Mom where you went tonight?" She leaned back a little to look up at her father. "About the AA meetings?"

"Not yet."

"You should. Take it from me. Hiding things isn't good."

That made her dad smile. "Okay. I'll tell her. That should help me stick with the program." He looked over at her books. "So what about you? You need some help with your homework?"

"I can't figure it out." Maggie sighed as she opened her algebra book.

"It's been a while. A long while, but hand me that book. Let me see if I can remember any of my algebra."

She pointed out the problem she was working on. Maggie didn't know what the morning would bring, but for this moment with her dad beside her with no smell of alcohol on his breath, she could almost forget about what had happened and what might happen. Almost.

27

Michael sat on the back porch watching the sun go down and night creep across the cemetery toward the Chandler house. The calico cat came out of hiding to wrap her body in and out around Michael's legs. When Michael stroked the cat, he was rewarded with a rumbling purr.

"You could probably tell me a few things, couldn't you, Miss Marble?" The cat pushed her head against his hand for another rub. "Like who shot Sonny Elwood."

After he sent Lester home, Michael had turned on lights and walked through the house without noting anything new. In the library, Michael stood without moving a long time. Just looking. Hoping to see some clue as to why Sonny Elwood ended up dead there. But the house kept its secrets.

He could only hope the crime scene investigators would find something to reveal the killer. Quickly. Now he looked toward the trees and shrubs along the property line that hid the road from sight. The trailer park was not very far away down that road. Buck had sent somebody to watch the area, but Michael would drive by Maggie's trailer again too as soon as a patrolman showed up here for the next shift of watching the house.

Michael stood and stretched his back. The cat slipped away, vanishing almost at once in the shadows. What else might be invisible out past the light that spilled through the kitchen windows? Or who? Michael played his flashlight beam around the yard. Nothing there except Miss Marble glaring back at him.

He clicked off the light and darkness settled around the house again. Behind him the house practically glowed with lights on in every room. Except the tower room. No lights up there. People who hadn't heard the news about the murder might think the Chandler ghosts were having a party.

Michael shook his head. He was so tired he was getting silly. He was ready to be home. To hang up his gun and get something to eat. His planned dinner with Alex was a bust. He turned his thoughts away from what else might be a bust between them.

At least he didn't have to worry about Jasper. Anthony would take care of him. The kid would want to talk, but the way things were going, it might have to be over breakfast. Anthony reported he'd talked to Maggie and that she sounded sort of scared but okay.

Scared might be good. It would make her careful. But he had to feel sorry for the poor kid. He hoped she'd be able to sleep without nightmares. Michael yawned. He needed sleep too. A man couldn't think straight without sleep and he needed to think straight. Not just to figure out who shot Sonny Elwood but to know what to do about Alex.

He looked at his watch. Almost nine o'clock already.

A few minutes later, lights flashed in front of the house.

Michael went in the back door and straight through the house to meet the patrolman there to relieve him.

———◆◆◆———

At Reece's house, Alex opened the door. "You look tired."

"So do you. Gorgeous but tired." Michael took her hands in his. He wanted to pull her close, feel her hair against his cheek, breathe in her fragrance, but she freed her hands from his and stepped away.

"Come on out to the kitchen. We saved you a plate. I guess you knew Betty Jean brought over the food you ordered." She motioned down the hall. "We were waiting to cut the pie until you got here, although it's crazy to eat calories like that this late." She smiled back at him as she led the way. "Malinda promises me pie calories don't count. She and Uncle Reece are drinking tea, but I made some coffee. You look like you could use it."

"Aunt Lindy is here? She's usually in bed by this hour." Michael followed her.

"It's not your usual day."

"True." He watched her walk, her dark hair swinging loose down her back. If only he could come home to her after work every day of his life. The very thought of that made his heart beat faster. He wanted to reach out and put his hand on her shoulder. Stop her right there in the middle of the hallway and tell her how they had wasted too many years apart. But she kept walking and so did he.

"What happened?" She glanced back at him again, then held up her hand. "No, just wait and tell us all at the same time."

So he did. The main details anyway. Sonny Elwood dead.

Shot. The house ransacked. Maggie Greene finding the body. It didn't take long. Had it told before the microwave binged to signal his food was warm.

"But why?" Reece asked.

"I'd think 'who' would be the more immediate question," Aunt Lindy put in.

"And I don't know the answer to either one right now."

Alex set his plate in front of him. Cindy's fried chicken, mashed potatoes, and green beans. Country cooking. He wondered if Alex had eaten any of the food. Probably not.

"But you will." Aunt Lindy sounded surer than he felt. She looked over at Reece. "As for why, that too will surface. Nothing stays hidden in Hidden Springs for long."

"At least not forever," Reece spoke up. "Now eat up, Michael, so Alex will let us cut into that pie."

Alex poured him a cup of coffee and one for herself, then sat down next to him. The kitchen was small. Barely room for the table and four chairs. The overhead fluorescent fixture was ancient and the light from the bulb had dimmed. Everything in the room was old except for the shiny black microwave Alex had bought for Reece.

It had been a while since Michael had been in the kitchen, but now memories of eating peanut butter sandwiches at this table with Alex while her aunt made cookies washed over him.

He finished off his dinner and took a bite of the pie Alex set in front of him. "That's good, but nothing like those chocolate chip cookies Adele used to make."

"She was a baking queen." Reece smiled. "Didn't much like frying fish. Left that to me, but she could bake a cake."

"Angel food. She made that for my birthday every year."

Aunt Lindy looked over at Reece. "But she made you German chocolate, didn't she?"

"She thought it was my favorite." Reece chuckled. "I actually liked her applesauce cake better, but I never told her. German chocolate was her favorite. How about you, Alex?"

"I'm with Michael on those chocolate chip cookies. They melted in your mouth." Alex got a dreamy look on her face. "She gave my mother the recipe, but Mom's were never as good as Aunt Adele's."

"Maybe it was the company you were eating them with," Aunt Lindy said. "You and Michael were inseparable during those weeks you spent here in the summer."

"We fought a lot." Alex scooted a bite of pie back and forth on her plate with her fork.

"You did that." Reece laughed again. "The door would slam and you'd stomp up the stairs. Adele always wanted to go after you, but I told her to let you be. Five minutes later you'd be running back out the door. We'd look outside and there would be Michael leaning against the maple tree waiting."

And now here he was still waiting. "She just wanted to give me a chance to admit she was right."

"That's because I was right." Alex grinned over at Michael and finally put a bite of the pie in her mouth. Then her smile disappeared as she pushed the rest of the pie away and ran her finger around the handle of her coffee mug. And that quickly the easy feeling between them limped away.

"You two always had fun together." Aunt Lindy tried to bring back the warm feeling that had been around the table a moment before, but it didn't work.

"You might as well tell them." Reece didn't wait for Alex

to speak up. "Alex is heading back to the city. She's got things to do besides babysit her old uncle. Important cases."

"Now, Uncle Reece, you know I'd stay here as long as you needed me." Alex looked over at Reece and then let her gaze slide past Michael without meeting his eyes. "But I do have cases to handle. My firm has been very understanding, but you're getting better. I found somebody to come in to do the cooking and household chores. And a nurse will stop by to check on you a couple of times a week. You'll be fine."

Michael didn't doubt she was right about Reece. He wasn't so sure about himself. "When's your flight out?"

"Day after tomorrow. I need to be here tomorrow when the helper comes the first time." She kept her eyes on her coffee cup. "I'd like to stay longer. But you know how it is. The obligations of the job."

"Right." Aunt Lindy's voice was clipped as she pushed back from the table. "And I'd better get home and take care of a few of my obligations. Always papers to grade."

"I'll walk you home." Michael stood up.

Aunt Lindy frowned at him. "I'm perfectly capable of walking back to my house."

He met her stare without giving an inch. "It's dark and there's a murderer on the loose."

"But you and Alexandria have some catching up to do before she flies away." Aunt Lindy gave Michael a meaningful look.

"I'm not letting you walk home alone in the dark. I'll call Alex and make an appointment for later." He smiled over at Alex, but she didn't smile back. It could be she didn't have any appointments open for him.

Reece looked up at Michael. "I'm ready for an appointment with some fish. You get that murderer caught so you can take me out in my boat. In a weak moment, I promised Alex I wouldn't go by myself for a few weeks."

"You know what the doctor said." Alex began gathering up their dishes. She glanced at Aunt Lindy and Michael. "Thanks for coming over, Malinda, and for stopping by, Michael."

She turned to the sink without offering to see them out. They knew the way.

Aunt Lindy waited until they were on the sidewalk in front of Reece's house. "That girl doesn't know what she wants."

Michael didn't really want to talk about Alex. Not with Aunt Lindy, but he had no way of avoiding this conversation except to let her walk home alone in the dark. He couldn't do that.

"Alex has always known what she wants." Michael looked up. The streetlights hid most of the stars, but here and there a bright one shone through.

"You could be right." Aunt Lindy's voice was thoughtful. "She does know what she wants. She's simply afraid to reach for it."

"I don't think Alex is afraid of anything." He considered holding Aunt Lindy's arm as they climbed the front steps but thought better of it.

Aunt Lindy pulled her key out of her pocket and unlocked her door. After she flicked on the inside light, she turned back to Michael. "That's where you're wrong. She is afraid and so are you. Afraid to admit your feelings."

"I'm not afraid to say how I feel about Alex."

"Perhaps not. But you are afraid to ask her how she feels

about you." Aunt Lindy's voice softened as she put her hand on Michael's cheek. "She loves you, you know."

"But does she love me enough?"

Aunt Lindy looked at him for a moment, then blew out a breath. "I don't know. And you won't know either unless you ask." She patted his cheek. "Good night, Michael. Go home and get some sleep. You're going to need your senses about you tomorrow."

"You mean to catch Sonny Elwood's killer?"

"Well, of course you need to catch the murderer. That's your job. But don't forget there's more to life than a job." Her eyes narrowed on him. "And don't let Alexandria forget that either."

Grimalkin came down the hallway to meet her. Aunt Lindy stooped to pick up the cat, then gave Michael a pointed look. "If you have to make an appointment, then make that appointment." Without another word, she closed the door.

Michael went back to his cruiser, but instead of starting it up, he pulled his phone out. He felt a little foolish dialing Alex's number when she was right there on the other side of the door he was staring at. If she didn't answer, he would go pound on that door.

But she did answer. "Something wrong, Michael?" She sounded worried.

He wanted to say that everything was wrong, but he instead he kept his tone light. "Just calling to make that appointment. You got a free hour tomorrow afternoon?"

She laughed, the sound a balm to his heart. "You don't have to make an appointment to see me."

"Then how about you come outside right now."

"Not tonight—"

"I know," he interrupted. "You're tired. I'm tired."

"Well, you are. I am."

"So reserve an hour for me around one o'clock tomorrow."

"Okay. Okay. If you have time," she said. "You do have a murderer to catch."

"I'll take time. The bad guys can wait."

"Bad guys don't wait until things are convenient. You know that."

"But even the good guys can take a few minutes for lunch. I'll eat a sandwich under the maple tree here in your yard." He paused a minute. "You want me to bring you some yogurt?"

She laughed again. "Don't bother. I'll get Uncle Reece's new helper to bake us some chocolate chip cookies."

"Who did you get?"

"Felicia Peterson."

Michael frowned, not sure he'd heard her right. "You're kidding."

"Why would I be kidding about that? Betty Jean told me to call her mother to find out who I might get. Mrs. Atkins came up with this Felicia's name right away. Said she'd been helping out an older lady here in Hidden Springs, but that woman was in a care facility now. Is something wrong with Felicia?"

"She's had her problems with jobs in the past, but right now I guess her biggest trouble is that she was Sonny Elwood's girlfriend."

"Oh no. So you think she won't show up in the morning?" Alex rushed on before he could answer. "I guess that sounds heartless but Uncle Reece needs somebody to help him."

248

He wanted to say she could be that somebody. But he kept those words to himself.

As he drove away, he thought about Felicia's empty apartment. He did sincerely hope Felicia showed up somewhere in the morning. She hadn't called him.

28

The next morning Michael made the rounds. Checked to make sure no one was skulking around the high school. He radioed Lester to watch for anything unusual at the elementary school. He figured that would have Lester patrolling around the school all day. But that was okay. Michael intended to keep Maggie and her little brother safe.

Michael drove by the Fast Serve, where Maggie's mother reported they hadn't received any new threatening calls.

"My husband wanted to keep Maggie home from school." Dark circles under Mrs. Greene's eyes showed she hadn't gotten much sleep. "But I thought that would make things worse for Maggie. With nothing to do but think about it all day. She'll be all right at school, won't she?"

"She's safe at school." Michael hesitated but then asked, "Curt all right?"

Maggie's mother actually smiled. "He doesn't want to tell everybody this yet, but he's going to AA meetings. That has to be good, doesn't it?"

Michael agreed it was good, but then made her smile disappear when he reminded her to let him know if they got any other calls. He ate the Fast Serve sausage biscuit on the way to the office.

Main Street looked the same as any other morning, except that a wreath hung on Geraldine Harper's realtor office. Her funeral was at two. Lana Waverly had a closed sign on her door. She must be content to let Cindy have the breakfast crowd. Two storefronts down, Bygone Treasures was open for business. Vernon Trent was rearranging the furniture displayed in the picture window. He threw his hand up in a wave as Michael passed in his cruiser. Maybe after Michael checked in at the office, he'd walk back up the street to have a talk with Vernon. See what his intentions were with Betty Jean.

Then again, Betty Jean appeared to have a new suitor in town. Michael hoped Betty Jean wouldn't decide to follow Grant Harper to Florida. With a little encouragement, she might do just that. With encouragement, could Michael follow Alex to Washington, DC?

Michael radioed Betty Jean and then made a slight detour by Mrs. Gibson's Gentle Care Home. He wanted to make sure Miss Fonda didn't make an escape back to her house while it was crawling with crime technicians.

"Poor dear." Mrs. Gibson paused from clearing off the breakfast table and looked at Michael. "It would upset her to no end to see her house like that." She clicked her tongue. "It's all just so hard to believe."

"Yes, it is."

She sniffed a little. "I didn't tell Miss Fonda about Sonny. I didn't see any reason to. It wasn't like she was fond of him or anything. She said he only came to see her if he wanted something. For her to die, she sometimes said. Then again, dementia can cause some patients to have delusional episodes."

"Have you known Miss Fonda to do that?"

"Not really." Mrs. Gibson began scraping and stacking dishes again. "She mostly just lives in the past. I couldn't tell you whether the stories she remembers from then are delusional or not. I'm no spring chicken, but I wasn't much more than a baby when Miss Fonda was dancing in the parlor at Chandler mansion."

"She does love that house," Michael said.

"That's for sure. I never understood why Ellen didn't hire someone to move in there with the dear old lady. She's not a difficult case except for wanting to go home all the time." Mrs. Gibson sat the dishes down and wiped her hands on her apron. "I'm glad enough for the business, but I feel sure Felicia Peterson would have taken on the job. Ellen pays her to come check on Fonda here, but Felicia says she needs more hours than that. She seemed pretty desperate for money when she asked me for a job a couple of months ago. I felt bad saying no, but I can handle things here with my daughters helping out now and then." Mrs. Gibson gave Michael a look, as though asking for understanding. "Plus, with that trouble she had at the drugstore, I really couldn't have her here with all the ladies' pills, you know."

"I guess not." He should have gone by Felicia's apartment to check on her.

"She was here this morning."

"Who? Felicia?" Michael was relieved when Mrs. Gibson nodded.

"Yes, poor girl. Quite beside herself." Mrs. Gibson

clucked her tongue again. "Understandable, considering. I let her cry on my shoulder, but I didn't let her talk to Fonda." Mrs. Gibson's mouth straightened out into a determined line. "I fudged the truth a bit and said she wasn't up to visitors. May the Lord forgive me, but Fonda is my first concern."

"So when was this?"

"You mean when Felicia was here?" Mrs. Gibson's forehead wrinkled as she thought about her answer. "Early. Very early for Felicia, but then I guess this can't be a regular day for her, what with Sonny and all. The ladies were still in their rooms waiting for me to bring them out for breakfast."

"Is Miss Fonda in her room now?"

"Oh no. This is Tuesday. Puzzle day. She likes puzzles. Go on in and see her if you want." She waved toward their activity room and then looked worried. "You won't have to question her or anything, will you?"

"I don't think that will be necessary." Michael could hear happy chatter coming from the other room. "I'll come by and see her later."

His phone jangled in his pocket on his way out to his cruiser. Betty Jean.

"Are you coming in?" No hello. Betty Jean sounded tense. "Soon?"

"I'm on the way. What's wrong? Hank in there pestering you?"

"That wouldn't be a problem. I'd just show him the door."

"So what?" Michael got in his car.

"Congressman Carlson is here." She was using her official telephone voice. "To report a crime."

"Carlson?" It took a minute for Michael to pull up the name. "Bradley Carlson? Audrey's husband?"

"Yes. He's been waiting awhile." She lowered her voice a bit. The man must be listening. "There are limits to patience."

Michael knew whose patience was being tested. "I'll be there in five minutes."

Bradley Carlson stood up when Michael came into the office. Michael knew he had to be in his seventies, but if he hadn't known, he would have never guessed him that old. The man's hair was white but thick and wavy. He looked fit, with just a little extra weight around his middle. His gray eyes were shrewd and direct as he looked Michael over. No smile touched his lips as he shook Michael's hand.

"I have been here almost an hour, Deputy Keane. Apparently your office lacks adequate personnel to handle the needs of the community."

His voice was strong and firm. His manner suggested he was accustomed to having his needs met.

"We do all right most of the time, Congressman. This is an unusual week with a critical investigation going on. Plus the sheriff is on vacation."

"Yes, Miss Atkins gave me that information." He didn't look toward Betty Jean. "She was very helpful but adamant that I must speak with you about the matter. But then she wouldn't call to tell you I was here."

"I called." Betty Jean spoke up. It was plain Congressman Carlson hadn't won any votes from Betty Jean.

"True." He did give Betty Jean a look then. "After my patience ran out and I demanded you do so."

Michael could practically see the steam rising off Betty Jean. He stepped between her and the congressman. "I'm here now. What can I do for you?"

"Arrest Lana Waverly."

29

Silence dropped over the room like a shutter. Michael kept his face expressionless as he met the congressman's stare. Betty Jean stopped typing on her keyboard. Even the phones stayed silent.

Just a couple of days ago Lana Waverly had done her best to convince Michael to pursue a murder charge against Bradley Carlson. Now Carlson was in Hidden Springs wanting Michael to arrest her. The last thing Michael needed right now was to get in the middle of a personal feud between the two. But he'd have to hear the man out.

"On what charge?"

"Extortion, blackmail, terroristic threatening." The man's voice rose a little with each word, his calm shattering. "I don't care. I just want the woman stopped."

"Are you saying Miss Waverly has threatened you in some way?"

"I think that's exactly what I said, Deputy. Is there something wrong with your hearing?" The man threw up his hands in irritation.

"I suggest you calm down, Mr. Carlson, and have a seat."

Michael motioned toward the chair in front of his desk. "Then you can explain what this is about."

Carlson glared at Michael. Apparently, he didn't like taking orders, but he did as Michael said.

"Want some coffee?" Michael stepped over to the pot behind Betty Jean's desk.

"I didn't drive five hours for coffee. I've already made that clear to your office help." The man's voice was tight. He looked ready to explode.

Michael glanced at Betty Jean to see if she was taking offense at his tone of voice, but she merely rolled her eyes. "And good morning to you too," she muttered and started typing again.

"Why did you come all the way down here, Mr. Carlson?" Michael carried his coffee over and settled at his desk. "If you needed to report a crime, you could have done that where you live."

"You're right. I could have." Carlson ran his hand down the button placket of his shirt, as though straightening a tie even though he wasn't wearing one. The gesture seemed to calm him. "But when I found out Lana had moved to Hidden Springs, I decided to expedite matters and find a way to take care of this without making such a big splash in the news back home. Better for her. Better for me."

"I'm not sure how being arrested could be better for Miss Waverly no matter where it took place." Michael studied the man across his desk.

"All right then. Better for me." Carlson's eyebrows almost met in his frown. "I'm sick to death of Lana's attempts to discredit me. But I'm sure you know how reporters are continually on the hunt to dig up stories about elected officials.

Half of what they report is hogwash, but rumors once started are hard to squash."

"What rumors are you worried about?"

"Maybe I should start at the beginning." Carlson blew out a breath and stared over Michael's head at the wall a few seconds. "My stepdaughter was not happy when I married her mother. I tried to reason with her, to win her over, but she has never been one to listen to reason. About anything."

"So she doesn't like you. That's not a crime."

"Extortion is."

"Yes. But statutes of limitations can apply." Michael kept his gaze locked on the man. "Unlike for murder."

Color flooded Carlson's face. He jerked forward in his chair and almost shouted. "I knew it. I knew she came back here to stir up trouble. What has she told you?"

Instead of answering him, Michael said, "We don't operate on a he-said, she-said basis here. We need facts."

"Yes, facts." He sank back in his chair and rubbed his hand across his face. "All right, here are the facts. I loved Audrey Chandler. Why else would I have spent over a decade in this backwater town? She was the mother of my son. The day she died was the worst day of my life." A genuine look of distress settled on his face. "All so long ago now."

"Were you in the house when she fell?" Michael didn't know why he asked. He wasn't investigating Audrey's death.

"I was." Carlson looked down at his hands, clutched in his lap now. As though realizing that revealed his tension, he pulled them apart and placed them on the chair arms. "We were all three on the upper floor. I was repairing those ladder steps up into the tower room. Why, I don't know. Nobody ever went up in there." He grimaced at the memory. "But

Fonda wouldn't rest whenever she noted something in need of repair in the house."

"But she didn't live there then, did she?"

"That didn't matter. She was always poking around, pointing out things to do, and believe me, something always needed to be done in that old house. Even after she married Gilbert, she was in and out constantly, telling Audrey how to do things or that she was doing them wrong. The worst thing she did wrong, according to Fonda, was marry me. I used to worry about her poisoning my coffee." A ghost of a smile slipped across Carlson's face. "Is the old girl still living? She has to be getting up there in years. She was at least ten or twelve years older than Audrey."

"She's still living," Michael said.

"At the house? Or the Chandler mansion, as she liked to call it."

"She's at an assisted living home now." Michael glanced over toward Betty Jean. She'd given up any pretense of working and was watching them. "She has memory problems."

"She always had memory problems." Carlson breathed out a disgusted sound. "She tried every conceivable trick to have me charged in Audrey's death. She kept saying it was my fault, but I assure you, I had nothing to do with Audrey falling. The two of them were fighting about something, but then they always were. I tuned them out. Do you have sisters or brothers, Deputy?"

"No."

"Consider yourself fortunate." Carlson made a face. "I tried to get Audrey to move. Just let Fonda have the house. But Audrey said her parents wanted her to have the house and not Fonda. That really rankled Fonda. As it turned out,

Fonda got the house, but that wasn't all she wanted. She would have done her best to take over my son too. I wasn't about to let that happen."

"So you left." Michael considered taking notes, but he didn't pick up a pen.

"The day after the funeral. I packed our clothes and Brad's toys in the car and we headed north. I wanted to get my son away from Fonda. While I suppose I never really believed Fonda would poison my coffee, I had no doubts she would attempt to poison young Brad's mind against me."

"Where did you go?" Michael took a sip of his coffee. It was already cold.

"To Indiana. We needed a fresh start. And we found it with Lorene. She was no Audrey, but she had a sweet gentleness about her. Brad liked her from the start. He needed a mother and she made her house our home. It was only after I ran for public office that she began to have nervous problems. I tried to convince her she didn't have to be the typical politician's wife. I was quite capable of campaigning on my own, but she felt she was letting me down."

"Were you married long before she died?"

"Twelve years. Things didn't really get bad for her until after Brad left for college. He went to a school out in California and didn't make it home much. Lana was busy with her publishing ventures in New York, and I was on the road a lot or in Washington. Lorene didn't want to come with me, but she missed having someone there to take care of. That's the kind of person she was. Then she hurt her back and started making the rounds of doctors. Too many doctors, I think."

"What happened?"

"It wasn't suicide." His eyes were sad as he sighed a little.

"That's what the coroner ruled. Suicide. He was wrong. Lorene didn't kill herself. Not intentionally. Lana is absolutely right about that. But Lorene had been having trouble sleeping. I suppose she didn't realize the potential danger of taking a combination of pills after having a few drinks. I got home late that night after a campaign meeting. So rather than wake her, I slept in the guest room. I found her the next morning after it was too late." His distress deepened. "If I had checked on her that night, things might have turned out differently. But I didn't. It took a long time for me to forgive myself for that, but in the end, it was a tragic accident. Just like Audrey's fall down those stairs."

Michael twirled his cup again, but didn't pick it up. "If I've got the years straight here, your second wife's death had to have been over twenty years ago."

"That's right."

"And you say Lana Waverly is just now blackmailing you about it? That doesn't seem reasonable."

"I told you right off the bat that Lana Waverly isn't reasonable. Has never been reasonable when it came to her mother and to me."

"But why would she have waited so long?"

Carlson threw up his hands. "I don't know. Nothing she ever did made much sense."

Michael kept his gaze steady on the man. "There must be something."

"All right. It could be that I am considering a run for governor and she wants to spoil that for me. I haven't even made a final decision yet. I'm not sure I want to take on the challenge at my age, but my potential opponents are already building a campaign against me just in case. I think some of their henchmen must have contacted Lana hoping to dig up dirt on me."

"Simply discrediting you with her suspicions isn't extortion."

"I know the law, Deputy Keane. You're not talking to your usual country bumpkin off the street. I wouldn't be here without proof of a crime." He reached into the inside pocket of his jacket and pulled out a folded sheet of paper. "Here's your proof." He leaned forward and flipped it down on Michael's desk. "A printout of the message she sent demanding cash for her silence."

Michael unfolded the paper. Something about it all wasn't adding up. He didn't doubt Lana Waverly was eager to discredit the man staring across the desk at him. But he did have a hard time believing her silence could be bought.

The message was short and to the point. *I know what you did. Everybody else will know too unless you send $5000 by October 30.* The message gave details on how the payment could be made online to what was surely a bogus company, Secret Books. No signature. Just another threat. *If you don't send the money by the end of the month, I'll contact the newspapers. I have proof of what you did.*

Michael looked up at Carlson. "I suppose you had your office check out the company."

"I haven't involved them. Totally unnecessary to waste taxpayer money on this. I expect you to do your job and arrest the woman. I know Lana. That will be enough to get her to stop. After a night in your jail, I'll drop the charges with a cease-and-desist warning."

"You seem to have it all figured out." Michael fingered the sheet of paper. "But this is all pretty vague. The message could have been sent from anywhere about anything. Nothing mentioned here about Hidden Springs or either of your wives. Plus, five thousand dollars is a lowball figure to keep a murder from being reported."

"I didn't murder anyone." Carlson's voice was almost a growl.

"But that is what you are assuming whoever wrote this has against you."

"Not whoever. Lana Waverly."

"Nothing here implicates Lana Waverly." Michael held up the paper. "I would need more than this for an arrest warrant. Much more. As far as I know, you could have written this and printed it out to incriminate her."

"Why would I do that?" Red crept up Carlson's neck to flood his face.

"I'm not saying you did. I'm merely saying there's nothing here to prove Lana Waverly sent it." Michael kept his voice steady with his eyes directly on the man. He hoped the man would realize the sense of what he was saying.

Carlson didn't. He sprang up from the chair and put both hands on Michael's desk to lean toward him. "I know people in this state. I can have you fired."

Michael stayed unmoved. "Are you threatening me, Congressman Carlson? In front of a witness?" Out of the corner of his eye, Michael saw Betty Jean pick up a notebook and start writing something. "Again, I suggest you sit down and look at this with a clear eye and stop letting emotion carry you."

Carlson sank back down in the chair. "You're right, of course." He took a handkerchief out of his pocket and wiped off his face. "So what do you propose I do, Deputy? Just forget this?" He waved his hand toward the paper on Michael's desk.

"Not at all. You can still report the incident to your local police or the FBI, since extortion using a communications means is a federal crime. That's what I would advise since you are a congressman."

"You could be right." The man looked defeated. "I can't force you to act, but since Lana Waverly is here in your town, I do think it's your job to talk to her. Investigate this as a serious threat."

"I will talk to her. Get her statement." Michael gave the words on the paper another look. "What proof do you think whoever wrote this has?"

"How would I know? You need to ask Lana that."

"Is this the only message you've received?"

"Yes. I got it last week and couldn't get away until today."

"You haven't answered the threat in any way? Had any contact with anybody in regard to this?" When Carlson shook his head, Michael went on. "How were you supposed to get whatever proof they supposedly had after you made the payment?"

"I suppose that would have been addressed when I responded to the threat. It could be that's what I should do." Carlson suddenly looked thoughtful. "Set up a meeting to take Lana the money and have her give me whatever proof she thinks she has. That would be proof she sent the message."

"I don't advise that, Mr. Carlson. The thing for you to do is go back to Indiana, make your report there, and leave the matter in the hands of the proper authorities."

"Yes, of course." The congressman stood up. He didn't offer Michael his hand. "I would say it's been a pleasure, but I've always found it better to be truthful when I can. It's apparent that nothing has changed here in Hidden Springs since I had the misfortune to live here."

Without another word, he turned and left.

"Well, that was interesting." Betty Jean stared at the door. "Do you think he'll scoot on back up to Indiana and do what you told him?"

"No."

Betty Jean looked over at Michael. "Looks like he forgot to take his proof."

Michael picked up the printed message. "He can make another copy."

"Do you think Lana Waverly is blackmailing him?" Betty Jean frowned. "That doesn't seem like her."

"I don't know. People do things you don't expect."

"True enough. Somebody shot Sonny Elwood. Who would have ever expected that?" Betty Jean got up and peered over Michael's shoulder at the note.

"Not me." Michael handed her the paper. "Why don't you write up a report on this? Since you heard it all."

"Sure. I took notes while he was talking. I should have turned on the recorder. I can't believe he threatened to have you fired. He doesn't know Uncle Al, does he?" Betty Jean made a sound of disgust.

"I'm not worried about that, but I better go talk to Lana Waverly." He pushed away from his desk. "If Buck calls in, tell him to send us a copy of the report on whatever they found at the house." Michael looked at the clock. The morning was almost gone, but he should have time to do what he needed to do and still make it to see Alex at one.

"I'm going to Geraldine's funeral," Betty Jean said. "I'll have to leave here around one at the latest."

"Tell Lester to come in and cover the office." Who knew how long it would take to propose to Alex? And he was going to propose. He had his grandmother's antique diamond ring in his pocket. Not exactly Alex's style, but it was a ring. She was going to have to give him an answer.

"Have you forgotten that Lester likes to be in position for his school crossing duty at the elementary school by two?"

Michael was not calling Alex to change the time. "Okay. Is anything going on?"

Betty Jean raised her eyebrows at him. "You mean other than people getting shot?"

"Right. Other than that."

"Not much." She shrugged. "The phones have been unnaturally quiet. Most everybody in town will be at Geraldine's funeral."

"Then put a note on the door and lock up. I'll get back here as soon as I can."

Michael was not going to let Alex fly away without talking to her. He didn't care how many murderers were on the loose. Or blackmailers. Maybe it would be good if the congressman did get him fired.

"If you say so." Betty Jean gave him a funny look. "Are you all right, Michael?"

"I've been better."

"Alex trouble?"

Betty Jean knew him too well. "Murder is trouble enough," he lied.

30

At her tearoom, Lana Waverly's smile turned wintry when Michael asked when she'd last been in contact with Bradley Carlson. She turned from him to promise her customers she'd be right back to freshen up their tea. Then she wiped her hands on her apron and led the way outside.

Once out on the street, no trace of a smile remained. "I have not seen or talked to Bradley Carlson or even had the unpleasant experience of seeing him on the news for over a year."

Michael was a little surprised at her reaction to his question. She'd been more than ready to talk about Bradley Carlson on Sunday, but now she was staring at Michael, her whole body stiff and on alert.

"Have you contacted him in any way, through any means, in the last few weeks?"

Instead of answering him, she said, "Is this an official visit, Deputy Keane? Should I call my attorney?"

"If you feel the need for representation before you answer, that is your right, Miss Waverly. But I merely asked if you had contacted Bradley Carlson via any method in the last few weeks. A simple question."

"One that reeks of accusation." She narrowed her eyes on him. "What has Congressman Carlson accused me of doing?"

"I'm the one asking the questions." Michael didn't let his gaze waver from her face, even though people were approaching them on the street. The middle of town wasn't the best place for an interrogation. "It might be best if we step back inside and sit down at one of your tables."

She stared at him without speaking. Then all at once, the harsh lines on her face vanished and she laughed. "You could be right. I'm sure the ladies inside are doing their best to peer through the window at us."

Two people stepped past them with a curious look. Lana gave them a big smile and an invitation to try out her teas, but they nodded and hurried on. Lana laughed again. "And now you're scaring away potential customers. Rumors will start floating around that I'm serving tea without a license or something. So let's make this quick. I haven't contacted Bradley Carlson for years. He must have heard I was here in Hidden Springs and his guilty conscience is bothering him. Did he dispatch his henchmen down here to discredit me?"

Michael found it interesting that Lana echoed some of Carlson's own words in his complaint about her. "No henchmen. He filed a complaint himself."

"Here?" She looked shocked. "In Hidden Springs?" When Michael nodded, she went on. "About me? For what?"

"He claims you sent him a message demanding money to keep you from revealing proof of wrongdoing on his part."

The disbelief on her face looked genuine. Then her face hardened. "Let me assure you, if I had such proof, I wouldn't be contacting him. I'd be contacting the authorities. You can tell Bradley Carlson that for me." She poked her finger at Michael's chest to emphasize her words. "Now, if you'll excuse me, I have customers."

She whirled and disappeared into her shop. Michael had the feeling he'd just lost his chance for that free cup of tea. He also believed her. She wouldn't trade her chance for public revenge on Carlson for any amount of money. None of it was making much sense, but then little had in the last few days.

He checked the time. Noon. He had time to pay his respects at the funeral home before he went to see Alex.

When he got to the funeral home, Betty Jean was already there, on the front row where family usually sat. Not that she was taking anybody's chair. Geraldine's only family besides Grant was a few cousins and an elderly aunt from Tennessee. But if family was scarce, townsfolk made up for it. While Geraldine might not have been the most popular woman in Hidden Springs, nobody had wanted her to meet such an untimely end. Then again, maybe somebody had.

Michael looked around the room. The thought of any of these familiar faces being that of a murderer defied everything he wanted to believe about the people in his town. But whether Geraldine's death was accidental or intentional, there was no doubt Sonny Elwood's was no accident.

After Michael offered his condolences to Grant, he was on the way out when he ran into Justin in the hallway. The undertaker had on his black funeral suit, but he didn't wear his usual calm funeral expression.

"Are you all right, Justin?" Michael asked.

"Hard to be all right with what's been happening. I've got

269

to talk with Ellen Elwood later today and nobody has given me any information on when Sonny's body will be released. Buck said they would do a routine autopsy in Eagleton, even though the cause of death was plainly evident." Justin lowered his voice when two people came in the door at the end of the hall. "Do you think my finding of accidental death for Geraldine was wrong?"

"You weren't wrong about the fall causing her death."

"Yes, yes, of course." His face lost some of its tenseness. "It's good to see Grant back here in Hidden Springs, isn't it? Not for this reason, of course, but he appears to be very successful. Sells flowers on the internet, they say. The internet is going to put everybody out of business."

"Not you, I wouldn't think," Michael said.

"Who knows? Online funerals may be the next big thing." Justin looked over Michael's shoulder as the door opened again. This time he lowered his voice to a near whisper. "Vernon Trent there is busy selling everything he can lay hands on that way."

"That's his business." Michael looked around at the man.

Trent's smile was subdued as he came toward them, but it was there. "Hello there, Justin. Michael. Too bad about poor Geraldine and then Sonny Elwood getting shot. Still can't get my mind around that."

"Yes," Justin said. "Quite tragic."

Trent shifted subjects without a hitch. "You ready to sell me that lamp in there, Justin?" He pointed toward the chapel. "I'll give top dollar."

"Your top dollar or the internet's top dollar?" Justin kept his face solemn. No answering smile for Trent.

"A man has to make a profit or he can't stay in business."

Trent glanced around. "I'm sure you make a tidy profit every time somebody dies."

Justin didn't answer him. "If you'll excuse me, I have duties to attend to." He gave Michael a tight smile and nodded curtly to Trent before he turned on his heel to go back into his office.

"Strange fellow, but I guess that's what it takes to be an undertaker." Trent looked toward the chapel. "You already paid your respects?"

"Yes." Michael eased toward the door.

"They say her son is rolling in dough." Trent stepped with him, still talking. "It must be nice. Me, I have to work for every dollar I make."

"I guess that's the challenge of starting up a business."

"Yes sirree. I'm the one who has to make things happen. And I can do it too." Trent's smile turned shrewd. "What do you think will happen to all that stuff in the Chandler house? They'll have to sell it, don't you think?"

"Sonny Elwood died. Not Miss Fonda. She's the one who owns the place."

"Yeah, but the old lady must be way up there. She can't live all that much longer, and believe me, that house has some treasures."

"Have you been in the house?"

"Not yet. But I've heard people talk. Must be a fortune in there."

"Sometimes people talk without knowing what they're talking about." Michael wondered if the man ever thought about anything but making money.

"You're right there, Deputy. That Betty Jean, she's a talker too. I haven't seen her for a few days. You been working her too hard at the courthouse?" His smile was back.

"Betty Jean keeps her own schedule so you'll have to ask her that. She's in there." Michael motioned toward the chapel.

"Sure enough? You see everybody at the funeral home, don't you? Guess I'd better go get the viewing over with." He went on toward the chapel.

For a second, Michael considered following him to see what Betty Jean would do with both her potential suitors in the same room, but instead, he fingered the ring box in his pocket and headed for his car.

Hank Leland was climbing out of his old van when Michael headed across the parking lot. The editor tried to flag him down, but Michael just waved back, got in his car, and drove away.

Michael checked his watch and drove past the high school. He met a state police car patrolling too. Maggie was safe inside.

After he left the school, he stopped at the store to buy a chocolate toffee bar. Alex's favorite when she was a teenager. Then he went to the flower shop for a single yellow rose. He thought about making one more stop at the church. But a man could pray anywhere.

By the time he got to Reece's house, he could barely swallow. He didn't know when he'd ever been so nervous. But he was putting everything on the line. Everything. He had reason to be nervous.

He didn't go to the door. He waited by the maple tree the way he always had when they were kids. The weather was nice. Sunshine. A little breeze. Good for Geraldine's funeral. Good for a proposal. He kept the rose in his hand, but hid the candy in his pocket with the ring box. Best not overwhelm her.

As if a candy bar and an antique ring could be overwhelming. When had he gotten so foolish? Such small, common things weren't going to convince her to give up a high-profile career for him. But who said it had to be her who gave up something?

He thought about how the organ music would be starting soon at Justin's funeral home. Geraldine expected to be selling houses this week. Not be the main player in a funeral. Then there was Reece inside. The old lawyer would be fishing on a day like this if not for a stroke changing things for him in an instant.

Life could be that way. Michael saw that often enough as a police officer. As much as he wanted everything to be good and come out right, he had witnessed plenty of times when it didn't. The way it hadn't for Sonny Elwood. While Michael still couldn't imagine why Sonny ended up dead in the library room of the Chandler house, he had.

Michael pushed all that aside. He would have to do his job and find the murderer, but right now, this moment, he was going to think of nothing but what he wanted most in life. Alexandria Sheridan to be his wife.

31

The minutes dragged by. Sometimes Michael felt as though half his life had been spent waiting. Could be it was time for the waiting to be over. Time for him to stop acting like a scared teenager and go knock on the door. Not just knock. Bang on the door. Lay his heart at her feet.

But he stayed where he was. He wasn't that great at romantic moments. He hadn't found a way to put his proposal up in lights or have an airplane write it across the sky. He didn't even have a ring made just for her.

Instead he'd stepped back in time to a place where things were easier for them. They'd solved the world's problems in the shade of this tree. They'd made up after fights countless times. Here, future success and love had dangled enticingly in front of them. The success had come for Alex and for him too, he supposed. But right now, he was more worried about love.

Ten minutes after one, the door opened and Felicia Peterson came outside. Alex stepped into the doorway behind Felicia, who had her head down as she walked across the porch and down the steps. Alex looked straight at Michael—she knew he'd be there—and held up five fingers for him to give her a few more minutes.

"Take your time," he called as she shut the door. He didn't have anything else to do. Except catch a murderer.

Felicia jerked her head up to stare at him. "Oh, I didn't see you there."

"Sorry, Felicia. I didn't mean to startle you." He put the rose down on the ground and walked across the yard toward her.

She backed up a step. "I-I was talking to Miss Sheridan about working for them. You know, since Mr. Sheridan had a stroke. I guess you knew he had a stroke. Then all this other happened and things got crazy."

"I tried to find you last night to tell you about Sonny. I left you a message to call."

"I saw it. But I already knew about Sonny and I just couldn't talk to anybody then. You know?" Felicia blinked a few times, but she wasn't crying. "Do you know who did it?"

"It's under investigation." Michael tried to sound confident. "We'll catch the responsible party."

"Responsible party." Felicia echoed his words. "I wish I was going to a party instead of a funeral."

"I'm sorry about Sonny. I know you were close."

"Yeah. Thanks." Felicia swallowed hard. "I saw police cars at the Chandler house. Nothing else happened there, did it?"

"No. The police were checking for fingerprints. Things like that." Michael wondered if the shock of Sonny's death was too much for Felicia. She didn't seem herself.

"I've been in the house. My fingerprints will be there." Her forehead wrinkled in a worried frown. "Ellen had me get things for Miss Fonda sometimes."

"You'll have to come in and leave your fingerprints for comparison."

"Oh." Felicia stuck her hands in her pockets.

"It doesn't hurt."

"I know." Felicia gave him a shaky smile. "I did fingerprints once for a job I was trying to get. You know, so they could run a background check."

"Then your fingerprints might already be on file and you won't have to worry about it."

"I'm not worried. I didn't do anything." But she looked worried.

The door opened behind her. She glanced over her shoulder at Alex coming outside. "I gotta go. But will you tell Miss Sheridan I really need the job?"

"I can tell her, but Miss Sheridan makes her own decisions." Michael looked past Felicia at Alex. She wasn't running toward him the way she had as a kid. The way he'd hoped she might.

"Yeah," Felicia said. "I wish I could make my own decisions."

Before Michael could say anything else, she hurried on down the walk to her car.

Alex stopped beside him to watch Felicia leaving. "I think the girl has problems."

"Her boyfriend just got murdered."

"Right. I told her it wasn't going to work out, but she said she needs the job. She told me that at least six times after she got here."

"She asked me to tell you the same."

"I feel sorry for her." Alex blew out a breath. "Her fiancé murdered. Yesterday. But I can't hire her."

Michael wasn't surprised, but he was curious. "Why not?"

"I don't know. Something's just not quite right." Alex made a face. "I'm not sure what, but I couldn't saddle Uncle Reece with her."

"Good decision." He wanted to ask if that meant she was staying longer, but he didn't. He had a more important question to ask.

"But what am I going to do? Uncle Reece needs somebody."

"First, you need to stop worrying about it for a few minutes." He reached over and gently smoothed away the worry lines creasing her forehead with his thumb. "Come sit in the shade with me."

She hesitated. "We can go inside. The coffeepot is still on."

He took her hand. "It's nice out here. Like old times."

She resisted when he pulled her toward the tree. "There's leftover pie."

He kept her hand in his but stopped to look directly into her eyes. "Why do I get the feeling that you don't want to talk to me? Out here alone."

"You mean here in the middle of memory lane?" She slid her glance away from him toward the tree.

"Memory lane can be a good place." He kept his eyes on her face. "Are you afraid to go there? Afraid to talk to me?"

"Afraid might be too strong a word." She looked back at him.

"Then what?"

"Concerned."

"About what?"

"Hey, I'm the lawyer. I'm supposed to ask the questions." She smiled.

He didn't let her turn the conversation. "But I asked this one. Why are you afraid? I mean, concerned."

"You're different, Michael." Her smile drained away.

"How so?"

"Like this. Looking at me like this." She waved her free hand toward him, but didn't pull her other hand away. "Before, at least since we grew up, you always pretended not to love me and I pretended not to care."

"I thought it was the other way around." He tugged on her hand and this time she let him lead her over into the shade. "But don't you think it's time to stop pretending?"

"More questions. You seem to be full of them today." Again she tried to shift the conversation. "Are you sure you don't want some pie?"

"I'm sure. I've got something for you." He picked up the rose. "For you."

She pulled her hand free then to take the rose. "Yellow roses are my favorite."

"I know."

She leaned back against the tree trunk and sniffed the rose. With her wavy dark hair falling down around her shoulders, she was so beautiful that the sight of her grabbed Michael's breath.

"I could have changed since we were kids. Started liking pink roses better," she said.

"But you didn't."

A smile played around her lips before she sniffed the rose again. "No sweet smell to this one. Does Malinda still have that rose in her garden that your great-uncle cultivated? The yellow one with that divine scent?"

"She does. We can walk up there to see if it has a late bloom." Aunt Lindy's rose garden might be the perfect place for a proposal.

"It's too late. There's already been a frost, hasn't there?"

"Sometimes roses surprise you, but we can go look later." He pulled the candy bar out of his pocket. "I've got more treats."

"Another favorite." She laughed as she reached for the toffee bar. "You always were a romantic."

"And a big spender too." He smiled back at her.

A smile lingered on her lips that he wanted desperately to lean down to kiss, but first things first. He could feel the ring box in his pocket against his leg. Then again, if the answer wasn't what he wanted to hear, he might never get that kiss. A man couldn't stay on the brink hesitating forever. Time to go for it all.

He traced his finger across her cheek. Her smoky blue eyes searched his as he leaned down to touch his lips to hers. She moved into his embrace, her hand sliding around his neck to push long fingers into his hair. Time seemed to stand still and he wanted it to as long as Alex was in his arms.

A blue jay squawked up in the tree and Alex pulled back from him. "Always a critic hiding out somewhere."

Michael paid the bird no notice and kept his eyes fastened on hers. "Alexandria Sheridan, I love you." Her eyes widened a bit and he rushed out the next words before she could say anything. "Will you marry me?" He pulled the ring box out of his pocket and held it up to her.

She glanced at it and then back at his face. Tears floated in her eyes. She blinked and a couple of drops escaped down her cheek. "Oh, Michael, I knew you were going to do this. Ever since last summer when you faced down that murderer and Malinda told us to stop wasting time, I knew you were going to ask."

He brushed her tears away with the tips of his fingers with the awful feeling they weren't tears of joy. "Is that why you stayed away from Hidden Springs?"

She didn't shy away from the truth. She never had. "It is. I didn't want to answer."

"It's not hard to say yes." His heart felt as though it were being squeezed.

"But it is. Very hard."

"Are you saying you don't love me?" The ring box in his hand suddenly weighed a hundred pounds.

"You know I can't say that." A couple more tears slid down her cheeks. "I do love you. I have always loved you, but our lives are too different."

"Not so different. We love each other. We can work the rest of it out. I'll find a job in Washington."

"You'd be miserable, Michael. You know you would and soon you'd hate me."

"Never. That could never happen. You are all I need to be happy."

"You want children." She stared straight at him.

"You don't?"

"I don't have time for children right now."

"Or time for me?" Sadness fell down on him like he'd stepped in a waterfall of it. He'd asked and she'd answered.

She blinked away her tears and stared straight at him. "No. No, I don't."

"You can't say no."

"I can't say yes." She pushed away from the tree. "I'm sorry. So very sorry." She stepped away from him, then turned toward the house.

He watched until she went through the door and shut

it behind her. She didn't look back. He stared at the door another long minute. What did a man do when he went to the brink and jumped off only to find nothing but rocks at the bottom?

The rose lay where she dropped it. He put the ring back in his pocket and walked away.

32

"But somebody needs to feed Miss Marble." Jesse had been pestering Maggie about going to feed the cat ever since they got home from school. He didn't understand why they couldn't go to Miss Fonda's house.

Maggie had done all right at school. Better than Monday when she was trying to hide everything. It wasn't all on her shoulders now. Her parents knew about her being in the house. She'd told what she heard the day Mrs. Harper died and nothing had happened. She and Jesse were okay.

Mr. Elwood wasn't. That wasn't good. She did her best to block away the sight of him slumped in the chair staring at nothing. That wasn't too hard to do at school while she concentrated on her classes. When worries did creep into her thoughts, she thought about her dad. He wouldn't let anything happen to Jesse. Or her.

That morning during study time, she looked up Alcoholics Anonymous on one of the library computers. She'd even checked out the program they had for kids of alcoholics. It helped to know about things. For sure, she didn't want to cause problems and be a reason her father might slip back into drinking.

So at school things were fine. On the bus going home with the kids chattering all around her, things were okay. At the house, things were still all right. Her mother was at work, but her father's truck was in the driveway. But then when they went inside, he had his keys in his hands. He'd gotten a call about a job.

"Your mother will be home in an hour or two." He must have seen Maggie's worry because he went on. "If anything at all feels wrong, you call 911. Anything at all, Maggie."

"Okay." Maggie managed a smile.

"That's my girl." He patted her cheek and rushed out the door.

He needed the job. She and Jesse would just stay in the house until her mother got home. Still, when her father's truck started up and backed out of the driveway, she wanted to run after him. Ask him to stay.

That was when Jesse started in about feeding Miss Marble. Maggie told him no straight out. "Miss Marble will be okay. She's a mouser."

"But what if she doesn't catch any mice? She might be hungry." Jesse pointed at a leftover sausage from breakfast. "We could take her that and some bread."

Maggie narrowed her eyes on Jesse. "I said no and I meant no. We can't go feed Miss Marble."

Jesse put his hands on his hips and glared at her. "You're not my mother."

"But I'm the boss when Mama isn't here. So go watch television or I'll make you wash the dishes." She held out a dirty plate toward him. That was enough to make him backpedal to the other room where he clicked on the television and turned the volume up loud. He gave her a look over his shoulder almost daring her to holler at him, but she ignored him. It wasn't that loud.

She was running hot water in the sink when the phone rang. She stared at it and let it ring two more times. If only they had caller ID. She thought about not answering, but it might be her mother checking on them.

She turned off the water, dried her hands, and lifted the receiver. Nobody could hurt you over the phone. "Hello."

"Hi, Maggie."

Relief swept through her. It was Anthony. She was more than happy to pick up the phone to talk to him.

"Everything all right at your house?" Anthony asked.

"Yeah. Dad had to go see about a job, and Mama's not home yet, but we're okay. Jesse's watching some silly show on television." Maggie peered through the doorway.

Jesse had grabbed the pillows off the couch to make a little fort around him and Bertie. The TV was so loud Jesse must not have heard the phone because he didn't even look around. That was fine with Maggie. She didn't want him listening to her talk to Anthony. She turned her back to the living room and leaned against the wall by the phone.

"I'm glad you're all right. You think it would be okay for me to come by later after I get off work here at the auto supply store?"

"I can ask Mama when she gets home, but that won't be for a while."

"Yeah, I guess you should ask first."

"I'm sorry." Maggie felt juvenile not being able to simply say yes.

"That's okay. I understand. Besides, the store doesn't close until six. So I couldn't come until then."

"I guess you don't have to ask permission about things like this. Being older and all."

"Things are different for me. My aunt doesn't much care what I do as long as I don't cause her any trouble," Anthony said. "Trust me. It's better to have folks that care."

"I guess. I was afraid I'd be grounded forever after my mother found out I'd been sneaking into Miss Fonda's house."

"Why did you?" Anthony hesitated. "Sneak into the house?"

Maggie's throat felt tight. She didn't like talking about her writing because she was afraid people might make fun of her wanting to be a writer. But if you were going to be friends with somebody, real friends, you had to tell them about things that were important to you. She swallowed hard while the silence hummed on the line.

"You don't have to tell me if you don't want to," Anthony said.

Maggie moistened her lips and pushed out the words. "I hid out up in the tower room to write in my journal." She'd wait until another time to confess to making up stories and even playing with the idea of writing a book.

"Have you written anything about me?" Anthony's voice whispered in her ear.

Her cheeks got warm and she was glad he couldn't see her. "Not yet. I left my notebook at Miss Fonda's."

"But when you get it back, you'll write something nice, won't you?" Anthony sounded like he might be smiling.

Maggie smiled too. "I wouldn't know anything else to write."

"Uh-oh. My phone's about to—"

The line went dead. Maggie held the receiver against her ear for another minute, then sighed and hung it up. Maybe he'd call her back. She ran her fingers down the phone, almost expecting it to jingle under her hand.

A commercial came on in the other room and the volume went up even louder. "Jesse, turn that down," she yelled.

When nothing changed, she looked around. Bertie was there, his head on one of the pillows looking toward her, but Jesse was gone. She stepped into the living room and looked down the hall. Bertie hopped up and circled around her.

"Jesse, you better answer me!" She pushed open the bathroom door. Empty. She looked in his bedroom with her heart beginning to beat faster. The room was a mess, but no Jesse.

"I'm going to tell Mama if you're hiding from me!" Still no answer.

She went back in the living room and clicked off the television. She thought sure then she'd hear him giggle. She waited for him to pop out at her from behind a door, but nothing. All she could hear was Bertie panting and the blood pounding up in her ears. Jesse must have gone outside without asking her. He knew he wasn't supposed to do that.

Then she noticed the leftover sausage was missing from the plate on the table and her heart sank. "Did he give you the sausage?" Maggie looked at Bertie, who stared back at her and wagged his tail. "Tell me he didn't go to feed Miss Marble."

The front door was slightly ajar. Since it took an extra hard pull, Jesse rarely closed it completely. Her father's words echoed in her head. *Call 911 if anything at all feels wrong.* But she couldn't call 911 because Jesse didn't do what she'd told him. She should have been watching him closer. Besides, he might be out in the yard.

Even if he was heading for Miss Fonda's house, she could catch him before he got there. She looked at the clock and tried to think how long she'd talked to Anthony, but she had no idea when he'd called.

When she found Jesse, he was going to be in so much trouble. She'd drag him back inside and make him stay in his room until her mother got home.

She left Bertie inside. He'd be no help tracking Jesse and she'd end up having to hunt the dog too if he ran off. Jesse wasn't in the yard. She looked down the row of trailers. Nobody in sight. Not even any cars. He could have gone to play with a friend, but he wouldn't have to be sneaky about that.

She considered running around the trailer park, but it would be faster to check Miss Fonda's backyard first. Then if he wasn't there, she could look for him in the neighborhood. She hesitated a minute, wondering if she should go back inside and call 911. No, that was silly. Jesse was acting up because he was mad at her. He was going to have more reason to be upset when she found him.

She ran all the way to Miss Fonda's house and slipped through the hedge into the backyard. The cat was on the back porch, licking her feet as if she'd just finished eating, but no Jesse. Maggie looked at the house. The back door was standing open. Jesse wouldn't have gone inside by himself. But what if he wasn't by himself? That man, the one who threatened them, might have grabbed him.

Maggie's heart, already racing from running to Miss Fonda's house, began pounding even harder. She should have called 911. If only she had a phone. There was a phone in the kitchen. Maggie could go inside, dial the emergency number, and be back out in an instant. That would be quicker than running back to her house.

The cat slipped through the door in front of her. Maggie stopped and listened. Maybe after they were there when Mr. Elwood died, the police went out the front door and forgot about the back door. She wished she hadn't thought about Mr. Elwood. She tiptoed across the kitchen to pick up the phone. No dial tone.

Her heart jumped up into her throat when she heard voices. Inside the house. Coming closer. In a panic, she stepped into the broom closet and shut the door.

"Did you hear something?" A man's voice. Maybe the man who had called her. Maybe not. "Out in the kitchen."

"Probably that cat."

Maggie did recognize the second voice. The person who had asked Mrs. Harper to not call the sheriff. Maggie was suddenly sure she was a woman.

"Don't tell me you left the door open."

"I think I closed it." The woman sounded nervous.

"I can't believe you." The man's voice got louder. "Do you want to get caught?"

"You know I don't. I didn't even want to come back in here. You made me." Now she sounded almost as frightened as Maggie.

"What about getting money out of that senator? You told him you'd meet him here."

"I was supposed to have some proof, but I can't find it. She said it might be in a book, but I've looked in every book here."

"You should have known better than to believe that old woman. She hardly knows her own name anymore. Of course that's good for us. She won't remember what she had in here. Nobody will miss a few paintings."

"What difference will it make what she remembers if you're going to burn the place down?"

"True, dear girl. Very true." The man made a sound that might have been a laugh. "Now get that cat out of here and shut the door. We don't need any unexpected company. Best not complicate matters by killing anybody else."

The woman protested. "I didn't kill anybody. That woman fell."

"Do you think anybody will believe you? Anybody at all? After Elwood?"

"I didn't want you to do that either."

"You didn't seem all that upset about it at the time. Now go chase out that cat."

The man sounded like he was right on the other side of the closet door. Maggie scarcely dared breathe, but her heart was hammering so hard against her rib cage, she feared he might hear it.

The woman must have moved past the closet. "I don't see the cat. It must have gone back outside."

"Then shut the door and come on. We need to get this stuff packed up before your man shows up. What time did you tell him?"

"Six."

"You told him to bring the money, right?"

Maggie heard the door click shut and the woman's hurried steps back across the kitchen. "But I told him I'd have the proof. I don't have anything."

"A gun will be enough to convince him to hand over the money and then we'll set this old place on fire and be on our way."

At least it didn't sound as though they'd seen Jesse. Now, she had to make sure they didn't see her.

33

She said no. Not maybe. Not we can talk about it. Not some-day. She didn't actually say the word "never," but Michael heard it in her voice. Felt it in his heart.

He drove through Hidden Springs, looking at the town through Alex's eyes. Small. Provincial. Old-fashioned, adjoin-ing two-story brick buildings down both blocks. People in blue jeans and tennis shoes. Not a suit in sight. And for the first time since he was a teenager, maybe forever, he wished he were somewhere else. He wanted to be someone else. Someone who could be loved by Alex.

No, that wasn't it. She did love him. She hadn't denied that. That was why she said no. The problem was she didn't trust him to love her enough to be happy wherever she was.

Don't you want children? That question echoed in his head. He'd always thought he would be a father someday, and not simply because Aunt Lindy wanted to keep the Keane name going. He liked children. Didn't he sometimes think his purpose, the higher purpose in his life, was helping young people?

He'd find plenty of troubled young people in Washington,

DC. More than he would ever encounter in Hidden Springs. But they wouldn't be his children. A little boy or girl with his name. Funny how he'd always assumed somewhere deep inside him that when he did have the courage to ask Alex, she would say yes. She would want to be his wife and the mother of his children.

He was delusional. That was the only way to explain his thinking. He'd wanted to believe it, so he had. He still wanted to believe it. It was all he could do to not slam on the brakes, turn around and go back to Reece's house. Make another plea. Promise anything. Offer everything.

He was almost to the courthouse when cars began pulling to the side of the road in front of him. With lights flashing, a city patrol car led the way for the hearse carrying Geraldine Harper to her final resting place. A string of cars with head-lights burning followed along behind. The Hidden Springs people paused to pay their respects to the funeral procession. No law made them. They just did.

Aunt Lindy's car was near the end of the procession. She must have left school early. Michael didn't look directly at her. Ever since she'd practically crawled into his head and pulled him out of the coma when he was a teen, she had the uncanny ability to read his mind. He didn't want her to read his mind right now. Not until he got a lid on the heartbreak hollowing him out.

When the last car passed, he looked toward the court-house. He should stop, go inside, open up the office. But he drove on through town. He didn't have a destination. No destination at all. Not anymore.

His cell phone jangled in his shirt pocket. Hope sprang awake inside him. Maybe he'd been wrong about the never in her voice. His hand shook as he punched to answer it without looking at the screen. Not Alex. It was Buck.

"Just wanted to let you know we had to pull the patrolman watching that girl's trailer park. Something going on in Eagleton. I figured you could handle it for a while."

"Sure, Buck. Thanks for the help last night and today. We'll cover it now." He hit the off button. At least that would give him something to do besides think about Alex.

His phone jangled again right away. This time Anthony.

The kid's words spilled out in a rush. "I was talking to Maggie and the battery on my phone died. After I found my charger, I called her back. She didn't answer."

"Maybe she just went outside." Michael flicked on his lights and did a U-turn.

"I guess she might have, but I don't think so. She was there alone with her little brother. I can't leave. Mr. Deaton left me in charge while he went to Mrs. Harper's funeral. They gave me an excuse to leave school early and everything."

"Don't worry, Anthony. I'm sure everything's fine, but I'll go check." He tried to sound calm, but panic was rearing its head inside him too. Instead of wallowing in self-pity, he needed to remember his job. Protecting the citizens of Hidden Springs. Especially Maggie and her little brother.

He sped past the cemetery as the last car in the procession turned in. He reached for his siren, then pulled his hand away, but he didn't slow down until he spotted the boy on the bike not far from the Greenes' trailer.

When he eased over beside him, Maggie's little brother stared at him with big eyes. Michael killed his lights and got out of the cruiser. For a minute, the kid looked ready to pedal away from him.

Michael stepped in front of him. "Hold up, Jesse."

The boy put his foot down to balance his bike. His lips trembled. "Did Maggie send you to arrest me?"

"Why would she do that?"

He stared down at the road. "I didn't tell her I was going to ride my bike. I'm not supposed to go outside without telling her." He peeked up at Michael and then back down at the ground again and continued his confession. "I was mad at her. I wanted to go feed Miss Marble and she said we couldn't."

"How long ago?" Michael looked down the road toward their trailer.

"I don't know. A couple of hours." The little boy frowned.

Michael would have smiled if he hadn't been so concerned. It couldn't be two hours. The kid had still been at school an hour ago. Maybe guilt made the time seem longer to the boy.

"I think you'd better go home and apologize to your sister, don't you?"

"Yes sir." He put his feet back on the pedals and wobbled a few feet before he got the bike going.

At the trailer, the kid ran inside, yelling for Maggie, but the only answer was their dog barking. Michael followed him in and waited while Jesse ran back to the bedrooms. But the place felt empty. The girl must be out looking for Jesse. She might have gone to the Chandler house if she thought the kid had slipped away to feed the cat.

He had no reason to really worry about that. Nobody was at the house. A murderer wouldn't hang around the scene of the crime. But Michael had a bad feeling. He wanted Maggie in front of his eyes. Safe.

He flicked on his radio to call Lester. Michael couldn't wait

294

for the kid's parents to show up or leave the boy by himself while he looked for Maggie.

Lester's siren signaled his progress through town, but that was good. Michael wanted him there fast. Michael went outside to peer up the road. No girl in sight. He stood still to wait for Lester, but he felt like ants were crawling around inside his socks biting him.

When Lester braked beside Michael, he turned off the siren but left his lights rotating. People peered out of the nearby trailers. A few took one look, then shut their doors. If trouble had found their neighborhood, they wanted no part of it.

"Turn your lights off, Lester. You've got the neighbors thinking we're doing a drug bust or something."

Lester switched off his lights. "Are we? Doing a drug bust?" He looked eager as he climbed out of his car and reached for the snap on his holster. "Or have you found Sonny Elwood's murderer?"

"Ease down." Michael held his hand out to stop Lester. "We're not arresting anybody right now. I want you to watch this kid for a little while." Michael pointed toward the front stoop where the boy sat, his chin in his hands and tears on his cheeks. The little dog leaned against his knees.

Lester narrowed his eyes on the kid. "What's he done?"

"Nothing. Just make sure nobody bothers him while I look for his sister. Got it?"

"Protective custody." Lester dipped his head in the affirmative, almost pitching his hat off in the process. "You can count on me." He marched up the walk to sit down by Jesse.

No sign of the girl on the road or when Michael pulled into the circular drive in front of the Chandler house. The place looked peaceful enough. The only noise was the cars leaving the cemetery beside it. The graveside service must be over. Michael glanced up at the tower room. Maggie surely wouldn't be there. Not after finding Sonny Elwood's body yesterday. She'd been terrified. The only thing that could possibly make her venture back to the house was worry about her little brother.

Michael didn't disturb the yellow police tape strung across the door and around the posts at the top of the porch steps. Instead he headed for the backyard.

As he went around the house, he could see the tent over Geraldine's gravesite on the far side of the cemetery where the workers would be preparing to fill in her grave. Across the fence closer to the Chandler house were older graves, including the stone spire that marked the grave of his ancestor, Jasper Keane. Michael's roots in Keane County went deep.

He couldn't think about how those roots might be what made Alex say no. Not now. He needed to find Maggie.

34

Malinda caught sight of the police car's flashing lights in her rearview mirror after she turned into the cemetery. She frowned and hoped it wasn't Michael with some new emergency.

Malinda shook her head. She couldn't be borrowing trouble every time she saw police lights. She hadn't been able to see who was driving. It could have been Lester chasing somebody going five miles over the speed limit. No reason to be concerned at all.

Of course, she had just passed Michael in his cruiser as she followed the hearse to the cemetery. And he hadn't looked at her. That could have simply been in respect of the dead. A person couldn't very well wave at people in a funeral procession. But he could have looked at her. A new worry scratched awake inside her as she gathered with the other mourners around Geraldine's grave.

She made herself listen as the preacher read the Twenty-third Psalm and prayed yet again nearly the same prayer he'd prayed at the funeral parlor. Justin Thatcher pulled a few of the red roses from the spray on Geraldine's casket and handed one to Geraldine's son and then to Betty Jean, who had obviously taken it upon herself to be Grant's best friend. The young man seemed comfortable with that. Good. The thought of Betty Jean getting involved with that Vernon Trent had been a concern.

Malinda didn't wait to speak to Grant again. She'd done right by Geraldine, attended her funeral and burial, but now she'd give in to her fears and call Michael on her cell phone. She didn't like using the thing, but no sense getting ulcers from worrying unnecessarily.

Back in her car she dug the phone out of her purse to punch in Michael's number when the fetched thing rang in her hand.

Reece Sheridan. Why would he be calling her? Worry exploded inside her.

"I'm sorry to bother you." Reece sounded worried too. "But I don't know what to do. Alexandria and Michael must have had some sort of disagreement. They were talking outside under their tree and then she came inside and ran upstairs."

"Did you ask her what was wrong?" Malinda's heart sank. She knew without Reese telling her what was wrong.

"She says she doesn't want to talk about it. That she did the right thing. The only thing." Reece hesitated. "But she won't stop crying."

"She turned Michael down, didn't she?"

"That's what I surmise. She's always been ready to listen to you. I can't stand seeing her like this. You know Alex never cries."

"I'll come." Malinda punched off her phone and stared at it a long moment. But it would be better to talk to Alexandria before she talked to Michael.

At Reece's house, she spotted the yellow rose under the maple tree the second she got out of her car. The sight of it stabbed her heart. Discarded. Left there to wither. She stepped off the walk to pick it up. Reece opened the door before she got to the porch.

"Is she still upstairs?" They had no need of greetings. Their concern was united and focused solely on the two children they loved. Perhaps not their normal parents, but parents just the same.

"No. She came down. Went in the kitchen." A frown furrowed Reece's forehead. He looked too pale. "She's sitting there staring at the wall."

"Maybe she'll talk to me." Malinda touched Reece's arm and stared straight into his eyes. "I suppose whatever she decides, whatever they decide, we'll have to accept it."

"I know." Reece blew out a little breath. "But I had hoped they would end up together."

"Same here, but we can't live their lives for them." Those words were hard for Malinda to say. She had so long dreamed of Michael and Alexandria marrying.

She left him in the hall and went toward the kitchen. Alexandria was at the table staring at the wall, just as Reece said. A notepad lay in front of her and she held a pen that she had yet to use to write the first word on the page.

Malinda laid the rose in the middle of the table and sat down across from Alexandria. The girl looked at the rose and then at Malinda.

"Uncle Reece shouldn't have called you." Alexandria's eyes were red. "He should have let Michael tell you whatever he wanted to tell you himself."

"What would he tell me, dear?"

"I don't know. Maybe nothing." She stared at the blank pad as though wishing words onto it.

"Then it's good I came so you can tell me what's wrong."

Alexandria looked up and a tear slid out of her eye and down her cheek. She didn't brush it away. "I told him no."

"I see." Malinda didn't need Alexandria to tell her what the question was.

"No, you don't see." Alexandria leaned across the table toward Malinda. "I had to say no. I had to."

"Why did you have to?" Malinda tried to keep her voice casual. If she let her emotions match Alexandria's, they wouldn't get anywhere.

"Because he's your nephew. He belongs in Hidden Springs. He wants to have children. He deserves to have children." Alexandria looked defeated as she slumped back in her chair.

"I see," Malinda said again. "Then perhaps you did the right thing, but don't say it's because of me. Say it's because you don't love him enough or he doesn't love you enough."

Another tear escaped from Alexandria's eye and followed the same trail down her cheek. She stared at the blank pad of paper, as though hoping to see answers there. "I don't think I can give him up forever. Even if it's the right thing. I feel as though half of me is being ripped away."

"You don't have to give him up." Malinda moistened her lips and pushed out words she didn't want to say, but she had to think of Michael and not herself. "He'll go wherever you go. He loves you more than Hidden Springs."

"But what am I going to do, Malinda? I sent him away."

"Call him. Tell him you were wrong." Malinda reached across the table to squeeze Alexandria's hand. "The two of you need to give love a chance."

Alexandria pulled her phone out of her pocket and stared at it as though she'd forgotten how to make it work. "I can't do this. I have to see his face. To see if he really wants me to change my answer."

"He will want you to change your answer." Malinda had no doubt of that.

"But what about the children?" A note of panic crept into Alexandria's voice.

"What children?"

"The ones he wants to have." Alexandria's voice was barely over a whisper.

"And you don't?"

"I would be a terrible mother. You know I would."

She looked so worried that Malinda almost smiled. "I know nothing of the sort, but my dear Alexandria, this isn't a trial where you have to know all the answers before you start. This is life where love gives you a beginning. You hold the hand of the man you love and move toward the future with trust that within that love, you will find answers that work for the two of you."

"I do love him, Malinda. I don't think I can live without him."

"Then go find him."

"But how? He could be anywhere."

"Call Betty Jean. She'll know where he is."

Malinda waited until Alexandria disappeared down the hall. The front door opened and closed. For another minute she sat where she was, her eyes closed while a prayer without words rose within her. A bit of Scripture came to mind.

Casting all your care upon him; for he careth for you.

She stood up and found a vase for the yellow rose.

35

The backyard was empty. No Maggie. Michael didn't even see the cat. The back door was closed. Nothing looked out of the ordinary.

He radioed Lester, but Maggie hadn't come back to the trailer. Of course Michael couldn't be sure she had come to the Chandler house to look for Jesse. She could be searching for the kid in the trailer park. It would take her a while to make it around the neighborhood.

He was headed back to his car, when a noise stopped him. Miss Marble stared out the kitchen window at him. The cat must have slipped inside without being noticed while the detectives were there earlier.

The cat wasn't hurting anything. He could come back to let her out later after he found Maggie. Buck had left the house key at the office. But when he started to turn away, the cat frantically scratched her claws against the windowpane.

"All right. I'll give the window a try." Michael stepped up on the porch and lifted on the window, but it didn't budge. Either locked or frozen shut by years of paint. The cat butted her head against the glass and mewed piteously.

"Sorry, cat." Michael muttered. "You'll just have to wait."

He started to turn away when a new sound caught his attention. Not a meow, but a thud. Like something fell or was dropped. Inside. Where nobody was supposed to be. Maybe Maggie wasn't as frightened as he thought. She could have brought her mother's key to go back inside.

That didn't seem reasonable, but when he tried the door, the knob turned easily. He pushed it open and stepped inside. Miss Marble jumped down from the window and raced past him to freedom.

The kitchen table was shoved to the side. On top of it were a couple of boxes stuffed with newspaper-wrapped items, as though somebody was packing to move. A framed painting leaned against the wall near the door.

Michael stood still to listen. Outside a bird sang a cheerful song and cars passed on the road, but the house was silent. Then he heard what might be a footstep on the stairs. Maybe Maggie. Maybe not. He slipped his gun out of his holster and reached for his radio. Before he could key it on, a board in the doorway creaked behind him. He whirled around as something crashed into his head. His knees buckled and everything went black.

Maggie had her hand on the inside doorknob of the broom closet, ready to peek out to see if the coast was clear. The man had gone out the back door earlier while the woman climbed back up the stairs, her steps light compared to the man's heavy footsteps out the door. It was amazing what a person could hear when every inch of her strained to catch the slightest noise.

She had counted to one hundred while she listened to be sure it was safe to step out of the closet. Then the cat meowed and the back door opened again. The cat's paws skittered across the floor as she wasted no time getting outside. If only Maggie could escape with her. Maggie's heart began pounding up in her ears as she waited for the man to go outside again or up the hall toward the front of the house.

But the man didn't move across the floor. Instead he must be standing still to listen, the same as Maggie. Why would he do that? Unless he suspected she was there. She held her breath and dropped her hand away from the knob. She stayed frozen where she was, afraid to move and maybe knock against a broom or mop that would give her away.

A floorboard creaked, followed by a thump. A grunt of pain and then a crash that shook the floor. She stuffed her fist in her mouth to keep from screaming.

Someone came running down the steps and past the closet. "What have you done?" The woman's voice was tight, panicked.

"You rather I invited him in to arrest us?" The man sounded irritated.

"I can't go to jail. I can't."

"You may not want to, but you definitely can."

"What are you doing?" The woman's voice rose again. "Don't shoot him!"

The man laughed. "You weren't that concerned about me shooting Sonny Elwood."

"I didn't want you to shoot Sonny."

"You could have fooled me, but that's neither here nor there. Sonny got greedy. Greed brings its own punishment."

"To us too?" She sounded ready to cry now.

"Only if you are dumb like Sonny. Brace up, girl. We don't have time for tears. We need to get out of here."

"Please don't shoot him. Please. Michael's such a nice guy."

Michael. Maggie pulled in her breath. If only she'd peeked out of the closet a few seconds before the man came back to the house. She could have warned Michael.

"A nice guy policeman."

"Can't we just tie him up or something?" She was pleading now.

Michael's radio chattered awake. "Michael, Mrs. Gibson called. Miss Fonda got out the door again. Can you track her down?"

After a pause, the man said, "Ten four." He didn't sound much like Michael, but with the static on the radio, the dispatcher might not notice.

"Good thing there's an off button on these things." The radio chatter went silent. "They'll think he went offline."

"What if Miss Fonda shows up here?"

"You better hope, for her sake, she forgets the way."

"You can't shoot everybody."

"Only those I have to. But it could be since I knocked out our nice deputy before he got a look at me, we can spare him. Get that packing tape off the table."

The sound of tape stripping off the roll made Maggie shiver.

"Tape his eyes shut," the man said. "That way if he comes to before we get out of here, he can't see us and I won't have to shoot him."

"I don't know why I ever got mixed up with you." The woman sounded disgusted.

The man laughed again. "Don't you remember? You needed money. To buy your little pills."

The woman began sobbing. Maggie wanted to do the same.

"Don't worry, girl. He'll probably scoot his way out of here and escape the fire."

"I thought you wanted to get more stuff out first."

"Circumstances have changed. It's time to leave this burg behind. You can go with me or stick around and play innocent. Maybe the deputy here won't figure things out and nicely arrest you."

"But what about the senator? He's supposed to meet me here, remember?"

"Call him. Tell him you're changing the meeting place to the Stop and Go out by the interstate. A good place for a little exchange of cash. His pocket to ours. Now get those boxes out to the truck while I set some books on fire."

He was going to burn down the house. Maggie thought of her notebook full of stories and poems hidden in the tower room. But she couldn't worry about lost stories right now. She had to figure a way out of this mess. If that man saw her, he'd shoot her. Simple as that. Her knees felt weak.

The thing to do was make sure he didn't see her. The two would leave the house and then she could either wake up Michael or drag him outside. All she had to do was wait until they left. She'd have time before the fire spread.

The woman went out the door. Maggie counted to a hundred. Then somebody was coming inside again. Not the woman. Maggie knew the sound of her steps by now.

Maggie cracked open the closet. Miss Fonda. That changed everything. The man would kill the old lady in a second.

Maggie had to do something. Her mind was racing almost as fast as her heart was pounding.

The man said he was going to set books on fire. That must mean in the library. No door out of that room except the one into the sitting room. If she could block that door. But how? *Think, Maggie, think.*

Once when the lock on their trailer door was broken, her mother had fastened the door by propping a straight-back chair under the knob. She'd dusted the spindles on a chair like that in the entrance hallway dozens of times. She pulled in a deep breath for courage and stepped out of the closet directly in front of Miss Fonda.

Miss Fonda looked surprised. "Audrey?"

Maggie put her finger over her lips to shush the old woman. Then she raced up the hallway, grabbed the chair, and tiptoed into the sitting room. Through the doorway into the library, she glimpsed the man tearing pages out of books and piling them on the floor under the table. His back was to her. That was lucky. But she smelled smoke. He must have already lit some of the paper.

She slammed the door shut and shoved the top chair slat under the knob. With strength she didn't know she had, she shoved the couch over against that.

The man yelled and then a gun went off. The bullet thudded into the heavy oak door. Maggie ran as fast as she could back to the kitchen where Miss Fonda was still standing in the same place, a puzzled look on her face.

"We have to get out of here, Miss Fonda." She put her arm around her and turned her toward the door. But she couldn't leave without Michael. The man would get out of the room. The woman would be back.

"Whatever is wrong with you, Audrey?" Miss Fonda refused to budge when Maggie tried to move her toward the door.

"Only everything." Another gunshot sounded from the front of the house. "We've got to help Michael."

"Where is he?"

Maggie pointed toward Michael slumped against the refrigerator and then ran to shut the back door. She turned the lock. Then she knelt by Michael and shook him. No response, but he was breathing. That was good.

"Michael, wake up. Please." Maggie looked for his radio, but it was gone. The man must have taken it. And Michael's gun. A tremble swept through her at the thought of the gun. He'd shoot them all if he got out of the library.

Miss Fonda tottered over to look down at Michael. "Don't you think you should pull that off his face?"

Maggie looked up at her. "Do you remember how to pray, Miss Fonda?"

"Well, of course I remember how to pray. Our Father who art in heaven. My mother taught me the Lord's Prayer when I was a little child."

"Deliver us from evil." That was part of the prayer too. At the sound of broken glass from the front of the house, Maggie gave a little shriek. "Oh, dear Lord, please."

Miss Fonda said amen as Maggie jerked the tape off Michael's eyes and mouth.

36

Michael had been in this place before. Dark, but somehow familiar. A voice was calling him back, but not Aunt Lindy's voice the way it had been before. This was a young voice. Maybe Alex when she was fifteen. *Wake up, Michael.*

But it wouldn't be Alex. She had sent him away. He gave in to the dark again, but the voice chased after him. A panicked voice. He tried to open his eyes and couldn't. Maybe it was all a dream. What if he had never come out of the coma when he was fifteen and his whole life was only one lived here in the darkness?

No. He must have hit his head. He felt the ache. He tried to open his eyes again. They were glued shut. Was that someone praying? Aunt Lindy had prayed him out of the coma before. But this wasn't Aunt Lindy. He knew the voice. If his head wasn't pounding so hard. If he could open his eyes.

It was a girl. He tried to reach out and touch her, but he couldn't move his hands. Couldn't open his eyes. Maybe he was paralyzed.

Not paralyzed. Bound with something. Not rope. Maybe tape. A minute later tape was confirmed when it was ripped off his face. He blinked open his eyes. Maggie was kneeling beside him looking terrified as she ripped the tape off his mouth. Miss Fonda was standing behind her.

He shook his head and set it to pounding even harder. Nothing was making sense. "What's going on?"

"We've got to get out of here. He'll kill us." Maggie looked ready to weep. "He has your gun."

At the word "gun," Michael tried to jerk his hands free, but the tape held tight. "We need a knife."

Maggie started to stand up, but before she could, Miss Fonda stepped around her to open a drawer and pull out a butcher knife. "Will this do?" she asked.

Michael twisted around so Maggie could slice through the layers of tape binding his hands. Her hands were shaking so much, he took the knife from her and freed his ankles. "Where is he?"

"In the library. I pushed a chair and the couch against the door, but I heard glass breaking. He might get out the window." Maggie took a quick look at Miss Fonda and lowered her voice to a whisper. "He was starting a fire. To burn the house down."

Miss Fonda didn't appear to hear her. She was getting plates out of the cabinet. "You will all stay for dinner, won't you?" She smiled over at them. "We can have pie."

Michael managed a smile her way. That seemed to satisfy her as she began humming and turned back to the cabinet. Michael pushed himself up to his feet and then had to grab hold of the table when his head started spinning. Maggie's face faded away from him, as though she were falling into a tunnel, and for a second the blackness tried to grab him again. He fought it off.

"Who is it?" he asked.

"I don't know. I just heard them. I didn't see anybody."

"Them?"

"A man and a woman. She's the one I heard when Mrs. Harper fell down the steps."

Miss Fonda dropped a dish on the floor and it shattered. "Audrey's name was Carlson. Not Harper. She did fall, but it was Bradley's fault. That she fell. All his fault." She sank down in one of the kitchen chairs and stared at the glass shards at her feet. "And now I've broken her favorite dish."

Michael pulled in a breath. He had to forget the way his head was pounding and find something to use as a weapon. He had the knife, but it would do little good against a gun. The smell of smoke drifted back to the kitchen. He could almost hear the house crying along with Miss Fonda.

He spotted a rolling pin on the cabinet. Again, not much help against an armed man, but all he had.

"Time to get out of here." He put a hand under Miss Fonda's arm to pull her up.

She refused to move. "I have to fix dinner."

He tried to think. "We have to go to the store. We're out of eggs."

Miss Fonda sighed and got to her feet. "I can't make a pie without eggs."

Somebody was trying to open the back door. Michael pointed Maggie toward the front. "Take Miss Fonda out that way. It's closer to the grocery store."

Maggie looked in a panic, but she nodded and tried to get Miss Fonda to go with her. Miss Fonda refused to move. "That's not the way." She headed for the back door just as somebody began pushing on the knob.

"Run, Maggie. I'll take care of Miss Fonda."

The girl looked hesitant, but then a gunshot splintered the lock. Maggie took off toward the front door. Michael wanted to follow her, make sure she got out safely, but he couldn't leave Miss Fonda, and the way his head was spinning he couldn't carry her out. Michael pushed Miss Fonda over in front of the refrigerator.

"Stay there," he ordered. She looked upset but stayed put.

He took up a position beside the door. Michael raised the rolling pin up and felt like an idiot. This wasn't going to work.

He needed to grab Miss Fonda and get out the front too. Get his rifle out of his car. Call for backup. Too late now. The door crashed open.

Vernon Trent came through the door, Michael's gun in hand. He ducked just as Michael brought down the rolling pin. Trent grunted as the blow glanced off his shoulder, but he didn't go down. Michael grabbed for Trent's arm that had the gun and knocked it away, but Trent was quick on his feet and whirled around to shove Michael against the wall. Another bump to the head. Dazed, Michael staggered toward the man, but Trent kicked him and Michael went down. Miss Fonda screamed. Michael scrambled for his gun and grasped it, but again, Trent was faster.

He pulled a snub-nosed revolver out of his pocket and jerked Miss Fonda over in front of him. "Drop the gun."

Michael stared at Trent. "You're in enough trouble without adding to it."

"In for one, in for a dozen. Little difference now." The man put his hand on Miss Fonda's neck. "I probably can take you both out at once. A little jerk here. A bullet there. All before you can get a shot off." He tightened his hold and Miss Fonda whimpered.

Michael dropped his gun.

"Now if you'll be so good as to stand up and pick up that painting behind you and carry it outside before the fire gets too advanced. It would be a shame for a van Gogh to perish in the flames. It could bring millions at auction."

"Where is it?" Michael pretended not to see the painting leaned against the wall.

"I could just shoot you both and carry the painting out myself." Trent's voice was dry.

Michael picked the painting up and held it in front of him. It wasn't quite large enough to use as a shield, but he could hold it up to at least make Trent worry he might hit his million-dollar painting if he tried to shoot Michael. But that wouldn't protect Miss Fonda. "This it? Doesn't look like a million dollars to me."

"That's because you're a hayseed from Hidden Springs."

Trent must have loosened his hold on Miss Fonda, because she stepped away from him to peer at the painting of fishing boats. "That was Father's favorite, but Mother hated it. I haven't seen it for years. I thought it was in the attic."

"So it was." Trent kept the gun pointed at the old lady. "Too bad I didn't have more time to explore the other castoffs up there, but I kept getting interrupted. Time to go now. I seem to smell smoke." He took Miss Fonda's arm.

She frowned at him and tried to jerk free. "I don't think I want to go with you."

"Makes no difference to me." Trent raised the gun up.

Michael shifted the painting to take Miss Fonda's hand. "Come on, Miss Fonda. We need to take the painting outside where the light is better."

Michael was relieved when Miss Fonda moved toward the

door. Outside he'd have more room to somehow get her out of the way and find a way to disarm Trent. Perhaps a million-dollar painting would make a good weapon. But where was the woman Maggie said was with Trent?

Maggie hesitated as she went by the stairs. Smoke was drifting out into the hallway, burning her eyes. She choked back a cough and thought of her stories up in the tower room. She could run up there and get them before the fire spread. The thought of her notebook pages curling in the flames and turning black made her heart hurt. She shook her head and moved on to the front door. Her heart would hurt worse if the man shot Michael and Miss Fonda. She needed to get help.

A dark-haired woman stood beside Michael's cruiser. It had to be the other person. Maggie hesitated, but she couldn't go back into the burning house.

The woman ran toward her. "Where's Michael?"

She didn't sound like the woman in the house, but who else could she be? Maggie tried to run past her, but the woman caught her.

"Is he inside?" The woman looked as scared as Maggie felt.

"You should know. You helped tie him up." Maggie didn't want the woman to know that Michael was free now. Maybe that would help Michael.

The woman frowned and shook Maggie. "What are you talking about?" Her blue eyes looked toward the house. "Are you saying Michael is in there? Tied up?"

The woman didn't wait for an answer. She let go of Maggie and turned toward the house. Sirens sounded in town.

"Wait." Maggie grabbed the woman's arm. Her voice wasn't the same as the woman in the house. "Who are you?"

The woman jerked away from her. "Stay here. I reported the fire. Help is on the way."

"Michael's not tied up now. We cut him loose." Maggie rushed out the words. "But don't go in there. The man has a gun."

The woman looked back at Maggie, taking in her words. "I have to," she said, then ran on up the steps to disappear into the house.

Maggie stared after her. Then she sank down to the ground beside Michael's cruiser and put her head in her hands. Miss Marble came from nowhere to climb in her lap and push her head against Maggie's chin.

37

Michael looked around when he went out of the house, but no other person was in sight. Just Miss Fonda between him and Trent, who still had the gun trained on her as he backed down the porch steps. Michael considered throwing the painting at him, but every time he shifted to get a clearer path toward Trent, Miss Fonda stepped with him.

Sirens were sounding. Maggie must have gotten to a neighbor's house. Michael stared at Trent. "You might as well give up, Trent. No way for you to get away now."

"I make my own ways." Trent pointed toward a tree next to the gate into the cemetery. "Set the painting down over there."

"I don't think so." Michael held the painting up in front of him. "I think I'll just hold it right here."

The sirens were getting closer.

"Do as I say or I'll shoot the old lady."

Miss Fonda peered over at Michael, a lost look on her face.

"All right." Michael slowly moved toward the tree. Time was on his side. The sirens were getting closer.

"Drop the gun!"

Michael thought he had to be seeing things. Alex on the

porch. With his gun pointed at Trent. A beautiful, terrifying sight.

"I don't know who you are." Trent shifted his gun toward Alex. "But we can see which of us is the better shot."

Alex held the gun with both hands in a shooter's stance, but would she pull the trigger soon enough? It wasn't an easy thing to shoot a person point-blank without hesitation if you'd never done it before. Trent had done it before. Michael's head was still spinning as he calculated how long it would take him to cover the distance between him and Trent. Too long. But the sirens ripping through the air were close now. That had to be making Trent uneasy, even if he showed no sign of that as he kept his gun steady, pointed at Alex.

"Watch out!" Michael shouted at Alex when he saw movement in the door behind her. Too late. The woman rammed her shoulder into Alex like a football blocker. Alex went down hard. The gun bounced on the steps and into the grass. She scrambled after it, but the woman leaped in front of her to pick it up and hand it to Trent. Alex sat up, looking as dazed as Michael felt.

"Timely, Felicia." Trent put his gun back in his pocket and pointed Michael's gun at Miss Fonda again. "Now grab that painting and let's get out of here."

"Felicia?" Michael stared at her, not wanting to believe she was mixed up with Trent.

She kept her gaze downcast as she took the painting from him. "I'm sorry, Michael."

"You don't have to do this." He reached to touch her arm. "It'll go better for you if you give yourself up."

"Don't listen to him, girl. All the nice deputy has for you is a ticket to prison," Trent said. "Now, hurry it up. Company's coming and I'd just as soon not be here to greet them."

Miss Fonda picked then to have a moment of clarity. "Felicia. Thank you for bringing Father's picture down from the attic. There's a perfect place for it in the hallway." She stepped over and reached for the painting. "You are such a blessing to me."

Tears welled up in Felicia's eyes. "I can't give it back to you, Miss Fonda."

Miss Fonda frowned and clutched the top of the painting. "Of course you can. It's mine."

"Enough is enough," Trent said. "Get out of the way, Felicia. Time to end this nonsense."

Michael lunged for Trent as he leveled the gun at Miss Fonda.

"No!" Felicia jumped between the old lady and Trent. The gun went off and Felicia screamed and fell.

The next second, Michael hit Trent and wrestled the gun away from him. He knocked the man to the ground and kept a knee on his back as he pulled his arms behind him. The man roared and fought against him, but Michael pressed down harder to immobilize him.

Out front the fire truck sirens went silent, replaced by water hitting the house. The red-and-white flicker of emergency lights lit up the surroundings. Then more sirens were sounding. Lester or maybe Buck or city policeman, Paul Osgood. Michael didn't care who. He needed backup.

"Vernon Trent, you're under arrest for murder, theft, and arson. That'll get us started." Michael read Trent his rights with one eye on Felicia huddled on the ground beside them. She groaned as red spread across her shirt.

Then Alex was beside Felicia, carefully easing back Felicia's shirt to look at the wound.

"It hurts," Felicia moaned. "Am I going to die?"

"Not if you stay still and do as you're told." Alex yanked off her sweater and folded it to press against Felicia's shoulder.

Michael kept his hold on Trent as he stared over at Alex. "What are you doing here?"

"Not glad to see me?" Her eyes met his.

"Not with a gun pointed at you." At the thought of Trent threatening to shoot Alex, Michael tightened his hold on the man, who let out a yell. Michael paid no attention to Trent's protests and kept his eyes on Alex.

"Later," Alex said, "Right now a woman is bleeding. A man needs arresting, and a house is burning down."

"And an old lady is heading back into that house." Michael spotted Miss Fonda tottering toward the house, carrying the painting. "Miss Fonda, wait."

Before Alex could stand up to go after her, Maggie came around the house with one of the firemen on her heels.

"Stop her." Alex pointed toward Miss Fonda.

The fireman went after Miss Fonda, but the old lady dug in her heels. "Let go of me. I have to hang Father's painting in the front room."

Maggie ran over to her. "Here, Miss Fonda. Let me carry that for you." She took the painting from Miss Fonda. "You need to tell me about this painting. Are these fishing boats?"

As she and the fireman led the old woman away from the house, Lester showed up, panting a little. "What do you want me to do, Michael?"

"Give me your handcuffs." Lester would have his with

him. He never went out unprepared, even if he rarely met crime firsthand. "Where's the kid?"

"I got him." Lester unhooked his cuffs and handed them to Michael who snapped them on Trent's wrists and pulled him up off the ground. "He's out in the car with his dog. Is that Mr. Trent, Betty Jean's boyfriend?"

"Yes and no. Trent. Not Betty Jean's boyfriend."

Felicia spoke up. "He's my boyfriend."

Lester gave her a funny look. "But what about Sonny?"

"He's dead," Felicia said.

Alex looked at Lester and then Felicia. "This place is a circus."

But Alex was smiling and breathing. They were all breathing.

⁂

Maggie held Bertie and dared Jesse to move away from her side as they watched the firemen put out the fire. She didn't say them aloud, but she thought a lot of prayers. Some of it still felt like her fault. If she hadn't come looking for Jesse. If she had called somebody instead. Why did she always think she could do things herself?

She didn't want the house to burn down. And not just because that meant she'd lose her stories. Miss Fonda would lose so much more. All her things. Her memories. While she didn't remember things happening now, she did remember times in her house. Mrs. Gibson had come after Miss Fonda and taken her back to the home. She'd taken the painting with her. The one that man said was worth millions. Just some boats, but Mrs. Gibson said it might be a van Gogh. Maggie had read about him.

Maggie looked up at the tower room. The perfect place to

come up with her stories. All lost to her now. Even if the fire-men did save the house. She could never hide out there again.

Michael kept coming over to make sure Maggie was all right. And she was. All right. Not great, but all right.

"They think the fire is out," he told her when the firemen came out of the house. "Mostly water damage except for the library. Probably ruined a lot of things."

"Do you think the tower room is okay?" Maggie knew she shouldn't keep worrying about her stories, but she did. "I won't hide out there anymore, but I need to go back up there one more time."

"Why?"

"I left something up there."

"Something important?" Michael looked from the house to her.

"Not to anybody but me. A notebook. It has my stories in it." She had to push out those last words. She hoped Michael wouldn't laugh at her.

He didn't. "Sounds important, but I didn't see anything like that when I climbed up there last week."

"I hid it. Between the wallboards."

"Oh." He stared up at the tower room. "You can't go up there, but let me talk to the fire chief. I'll see if I can get them for you. I think you deserve that much."

"But you being here and everything is my fault."

"None of it is your fault, Maggie. None of it." He leaned down to look her in the face and Bertie tried to lick him. Michael pushed the dog's head to the side and kept looking at Maggie. "You helped Miss Fonda. You helped me. You were very brave."

"I didn't feel brave."

"I know. But you were." Michael squeezed her shoulder. "Your parents will be here soon and Anthony. He called me, you know."

"She likes him," Jesse looked up to poke into their conversation.

"You hush," Maggie said.

Michael laughed. "That's okay, Maggie. He likes you too. It's good to have somebody like you."

Michael looked away from her then at the dark-haired woman who was leaning against a tree, watching everything like she might be some kind of reporter. Maggie didn't know if she was or not, but she did know Mr. Leland was. He'd tried to ask her questions earlier about why she was there, but Michael told him to leave her alone. It was all too scary to talk about anyway, but when Michael moved away from her, Mr. Leland raised his camera up and pointed it at her and Jesse and Bertie.

Maggie shifted Bertie in her arms. The dog was heavy but she didn't dare put him down. Or let Jesse step away from her. She wished her mother or father would get there so she could quit being the responsible one.

The dark-haired woman pushed away from her tree and came over to them. "Hi, my name is Alex. And Michael told me you are Maggie and Jesse, but he didn't tell me your dog's name."

Jesse spoke up. "Bertie. Maggie named him. Said he looked like a Bertie."

"He does." The woman ruffled Bertie's ears. "I like dogs. You think he'd let me hold him?"

"He stinks a little," Maggie said. "I've been aiming to give him a bath."

"I'm not smelling too good right now myself." The woman

laughed and reached for Bertie. "As long as he doesn't bite me."

"He doesn't bite. He licks," Jesse said.

Maggie was glad to hand off the dog. Bertie did immediately lick the woman's face, but she just laughed again.

"Thank you," Maggie said.

"Thank you," the woman said back.

"For what?" Maggie couldn't imagine what the woman would be thanking her for.

"For helping Michael."

"Michael's great. I like him."

"He is. Great." The woman's eyes went away from Maggie to search through the people milling about in front of the house. "I've loved him forever." She looked back at Maggie, her eyes sparkling in the flashing lights.

"Maggie has a boyfriend too," Jesse piped up. "She's in lo-uve." He drew the word out.

"Watch it, kid. Someday you might get bitten by the love bug too." The woman grinned down at Jesse as she dodged Bertie's tongue.

In spite of everything that had happened, Maggie felt a smile spilling out on her face. It was good to be alive and in love. Especially when she saw Anthony running up from the road toward her.

38

The booted feet of B.J. Bland, the fire chief, sounded loud as he led the way up the stairs. "It's good to check out the upper floors again anyway to make sure nothing is smoldering in the walls."

"You think it might be?" Michael looked around. Daylight was ebbing outside and it was even darker inside except for the flicker of the emergency lights through the windows.

"Unlikely. The fire appeared to be contained in that one room, but we'll keep an eye on it. It would be a shame for the old house to burn down." B.J. looked back at Michael. "I've always heard some kind of treasure is hidden in here somewhere. Is that what you're after?"

"A different kind of treasure." Michael smiled. "Only worth something to a kid out there."

"Guess you better get it then." B.J. laid his hands on the wall at the top of the stairs and then again when they went through the door that led to the tower room. "Feels cool. That's good. But are you sure that ladder will hold you?" He motioned toward the steps up the wall.

"It did last week." Michael grabbed one of the slats and pulled himself up.

He clicked on his flashlight and played it around the small room. The space was unchanged since he checked it out last Friday, but now Michael saw it through Maggie's eyes. A dream room where her imagination could take flight. Until nightmares had intruded.

Her hiding place wasn't hard to find, but his hand was too big to reach down between the boards. Nothing for it but to prize the top board off. He wasn't about to go back to Maggie empty-handed.

A little tug pulled the board off easily. It must have been removed in the past and shoved back in place. Michael lifted out a purple notebook with a pen stuck down in the spiral. Maggie's name in loopy letters was across the front. Michael flashed his light down into the dusty recess and spotted something else stashed there.

He pulled out a small brown book. Not new. The cloth-covered back and spine were frayed and bent and the pages yellowed with age. The tower room must have been the hideaway for more than one young writer. Michael flipped open the book. More pages were empty than filled, but the front page showed who had hidden the diary there years ago.

Fonda Chandler's Diary – 1949

"Find it?" B.J. called to him.

"I got it." Michael shut the diary. He started to shove the old book back into its hiding place, but Miss Fonda might get pleasure reading it, since the old days were what she remembered best.

At the trapdoor, when Michael dropped the books down to B.J., a folded sheet of paper fell out of the diary. B.J.

picked it up and stuck it back before he handed the books to Michael after he climbed down.

Out in the hall at the top of the stairs, B.J. said, "This is where Geraldine Harper fell, isn't it?" He didn't wait for Michael to answer. "I can see why. Dangerous-looking steps. And they say Geraldine wasn't the first to die here."

"True." Michael followed B.J. down the stairs. "Audrey Carlson, Miss Fonda's sister, died here years ago."

"Audrey, you say. I just saw that name. It was on the letter that fell out of those books you handed me. Funny how sometimes things circle around."

"It is. Audrey's husband is out there in the crowd. Just came down from Indiana today. His son stands to inherit the house from Miss Fonda."

"He didn't have anything to do with the guy setting it on fire, did he?"

"No. Just coincidence that he's here." No need talking about Carlson being blackmailed. Maggie had told Michael she'd overheard Felicia talking about getting money out of a senator. That Felicia was upset about not finding some kind of proof and the man, Trent, saying a gun was all the proof they would need. Michael and the fireman went outside where the crowd had grown, as people gathered to see if the Chandler mansion would survive. Lester was in his element keeping everyone away from the house. Hank Leland was scribbling in his little notebook and pointing his camera at anything and everything.

Anthony had shown up while Michael was inside. He had the dog now, but it was easy to tell he'd rather be holding Maggie. Michael knew how he felt. He'd give a lot to have his arms around Alex, who was standing with the kids, probably dazzling Anthony with her smile. Then again, Anthony might not be as dazzled as when he first met Alex a couple of years ago. Now Maggie had moved into the center of his vision.

Michael on the other hand was as dazzled as ever. His chest felt too full and not simply because of the acrid smoke hanging in the air. He wanted to forget everything else and pull Alex aside. Find out why she was there, but duty first. A thankful prayer rose inside him as he walked toward Maggie. Safe. Alive.

Vernon Trent was locked away. Buck took him in. Michael had called Betty Jean so she would know before Vernon showed up in handcuffs. Turned out she was more worried about being involved in perhaps listing stolen property on Vernon's website than the loss of a suitor. A new man in town had already shoved Vernon out of the picture.

Felicia was on the way to the hospital. Michael might not be alive if not for Felicia. Maggie said Felicia talked Trent out of shooting him straight away. That and stepping between Trent and Miss Fonda should help her when she went to trial. The jury might even believe Geraldine Harper's fall down the steps was an accident. But whether Felicia was directly responsible for Geraldine's death or not, she had plenty of other charges hanging over her head. Accessory to murder. Theft. Breaking and entering. Extortion.

Michael remembered the letter B.J. said had Audrey's name on it. Could that be the proof Felicia had wanted to find?

First things first. Maggie was waiting for her notebook. A smile broke out on the girl's face as she hugged her notebook to her chest. "Thank you."

"You're welcome, but I'm afraid you'll have to find another

place to write this story down." Michael smiled at her and waved up toward the tower room.

She laughed. A good sound. Anthony must have thought so too the way he joined in. They moved away with Maggie's parents. Anthony was still carrying the dog. Maybe that would help him get on the good side of Maggie's parents. He'd already won over Maggie. Young love was fun to watch.

Young love had been fun to experience. With Alex. But young love had turned into forever love for him. Had Alex followed him to tell him the same? Or merely to part with him on better terms?

"You didn't give Maggie the other book." Alex pointed to the old diary.

"It's not hers. It's Miss Fonda's. Her diary from 1949."

"Wow. That might be interesting to read."

"I flipped through it. A lot of pages were blank."

"Everybody has slow days." Alex looked up at him. The red lights reflected off her face. "Or days when all the wrong things happen and you don't want to remember them."

"But writing it down the way it happened keeps the memory straight." Michael fingered the edge of the letter sticking out of the book and looked across the yard at Bradley Carlson. Lana Waverly had joined the crowd and was watching the man too.

Would the words on the letter incriminate Carlson in Audrey's death all those years ago? One way to find out. He pulled the letter out of the diary and unfolded it. The paper was old and stiff.

"What's that?" Alex asked.

"I'm not sure. Maybe something that will clear up a mystery from years ago. Audrey Chandler Carlson's death."

Alex frowned. "Do you think her death is connected to the other deaths here this week?"

"Perhaps in a roundabout way. Felicia was looking for some sort of proof of what happened to Audrey when Geraldine must have discovered her in the house. Maggie says Geraldine threatened to call the sheriff. She heard them running down the hall, and then Geraldine fell."

"Maggie didn't see it?" Alex's attorney brain was kicking in.

"No. She only heard what was happening from her hiding place in the tower room up there." Michael pointed toward the room.

"So what about Audrey? Was somebody accused of pushing her down the steps?"

"Miss Fonda claimed the fault lay with Audrey's husband, Bradley Carlson."

"Right. You and Uncle Reece talked about him at the hospital. The congressman from Indiana."

"Oddly enough, that's him over there talking to the fire chief, perhaps protecting the interest of his son who might inherit the house someday. Felicia was trying to blackmail the congressman by implying she had proof of his wrongdoing, when all she really had were Miss Fonda's accusations."

Alex pointed toward the letter in Michael's hand. "You think that might be the proof Felicia hoped to find?"

"It might."

"So are you going to read it or just hold it and wonder?" She stepped closer to him. "Next question. Are you going to let me peer over your shoulder while you read it?"

"You don't even know the people."

"But I love a mystery. Especially one with the cobwebs of age on it."

Michael didn't see what it could hurt and he liked her standing so close to him. "Here." He handed her the letter. "I'll hold the flashlight and you read it aloud."

She was tantalizingly close, but he restrained his impulse to take her into his arms. Instead he directed his flashlight beam over her shoulder onto the letter. "Can you see a name to tell who wrote it?"

"It's signed Fonda Chandler Elwood and dated December 1, 1980."

They had stepped into the shadows next to the house away from the noise of the crowd. Alex cleared her throat and began to read.

Dearest Audrey. I am so very sorry. My heart hurts every time I think of you. While we never saw things alike, you were my sister. We shared Chandler blood. That's why I could never understand you not loving this house. I blame Bradley for that. His ambitions poisoned your mind against our heritage. And in so doing, destroyed you.

He caused it all. Without his demands to strip the house of everything of value, we would have had no reason to argue. I only wanted to protect our family treasures for young Brad. You, his mother, should have wanted him to receive his rightful inheritance. That was what I was trying to get you to see that day. But you refused to hear me. I grabbed you to make you listen, but you jerked away and lost your balance. You screamed and Bradley ran down the hall toward us. I was reaching to save you when he shoved me aside. He stood and watched you fall. I would have caught you. If not for him.

Too late he went after you. Too late. You lay broken at the foot of the stairs. I stood broken at the top of the stairs.

He is the reason you fell and he should pay. But now he's gone. Taken young Brad and sneaked away in the night. Left the house keys in an envelope taped to my door. Nobody will listen. They say I am distraught and not thinking clearly. Even Gilbert, pitiful man that he is, says the same.

Alex looked up from the letter. "Who's Gilbert?"

"Miss Fonda's husband."

"Oh." Alex shook her head. "This is all so very sad."

Michael peered at the letter. "Is that all?"

"One more line." Alex stared down at the letter again. Tears sounded in her voice as she read. *"All I have left now is this house—a shrine to what has been lost forever."*

Alex folded the letter and handed it to Michael. "She ended up with nothing but things."

She sounded so sad that he did put his arms around her then to pull her close. She rested her head against his shoulder a moment before asking, "What are you going to do with the letter?"

"I don't know. I could give it to Miss Fonda."

"If she has dementia like you say, that would do little except bring her pain."

Michael remembered Miss Fonda's keening cry when she found Geraldine's body. Alex was right. It would be cruel to push her toward that pain again. "Maybe I should take it back and put it in its hiding place in the tower room."

"Or give it to Bradley Carlson. So he'll know Felicia had nothing that showed any real wrongdoing on his part. Only in Fonda's mind."

That made sense. If Carlson wanted to share it with Lana Waverly, it might even lay her suspicions to rest too. The man had tragically lost two wives, but Carlson had told the truth about Audrey. Michael had no reason to doubt he told the truth about his second wife too.

He reluctantly let Alex pull away from him and left her there in the shadows to walk across the yard to Carlson. When he looked back, she was gone.

39

As much as he wanted to, Michael didn't go after Alex. It was her move. He had to wait for her to take it.

He stayed at the Chandler house after everyone else left. It was a relief to have the emergency lights gone and let the night fall down around him. Since the firemen were wet, tired, and hungry, he took the first watch at the house in case a pocket of fire sprang up. Michael was tired too, but he felt responsible for the house. He should have prevented the fire from being set.

He could almost see Betty Jean shaking her head at him. She was always telling him he couldn't be responsible for everybody in Keane County. Or keep them all safe and happy. Maybe not, but he could manage a few hours until the fire chief sent someone else out to check on the house.

Anthony was headed to Michael's house to feed Jasper. He reported that Maggie was fine, and from the tone of his voice, Michael could tell Anthony thought she was extra fine.

The October night was warm, so Michael sat on the porch and watched the lightning bugs twinkle in the night. Nature going about her business while the lingering smoke hung like a pall over the house. Life had happened in the house, but so had death. When he went inside to check the house, he paused to stare up at the graceful stairway. Would a family ever run up and down it again?

Lights flashed in the front windows when someone pulled into the driveway, so he wasn't surprised by a voice behind him a few minutes later.

"What are you thinking, Michael Keane?"

He wasn't even surprised that it was Alex. Just grateful. Very grateful she had come back. He turned to look at her in the doorway. Moonlight lay softly behind her, but her face was in shadow.

When he didn't answer her right away, she went on. "You can't make up an answer. You know the rules. You have to tell exactly what you were thinking no matter what it was."

They'd played this game when they were kids, but he'd never been sure she played fair, since her thoughts always seemed to be deep and meaningful while his were usually simply about how much he liked being with her no matter what game they were playing.

He started not to play fair himself, but then he did. "I was wondering if this place would ever be home to a happy family again. And then I turned around to see you and my only thought is how beautiful you are."

She laughed softly. "Same old line every time."

"But true every time." He reached toward her and she let him take her hand. "And never truer than right now, this minute."

"Come on." She tugged on his hand. "Let's get out of here before I start smelling like smoke again. I brought you some coffee. Betty Jean told me you'd still be here. Protecting the world."

Her hair, still damp from her shower, swung against his arm as he stepped up beside her. "You're my world."

She ducked her head to hide the smile that slipped across her face. Hope bounded higher inside him, but he didn't rush out more words. It was her turn.

"Here's your coffee and Malinda made you a sandwich. She says you never remember to eat." She handed him the food she'd left on the porch railing.

Michael took a bite of the sandwich. Pimento cheese as always. He gulped down the coffee and then put both the thermos cup and the sandwich back on the railing. "I'll eat the rest later."

She climbed down the steps and then glanced at him and away quickly. "Aren't you going to ask me what I'm thinking?" She looked out at the yard.

"Okay. What are you thinking, Alexandria Elaine Sheridan?"

Alex whirled back toward him. "I can't believe you remember my middle name. I was hoping that would be one of your lost memories."

"I never want to lose any memories of you." He drank in the sight of her, standing in the traces of moonlight that filtered down through the trees. A moment to store in his heart no matter what happened. "But you can't forget the rules of the game. I asked you what you were thinking."

She reached for his hand. "I was thinking how lovely it would be to take a walk in the moonlight. Away from the streetlights."

"Where did you have in mind? Down by the lake?" Wherever

she wanted to go, he was ready. Somebody would be back to check on the house soon.

"That would be lovely, but I was thinking somewhere closer." She motioned toward the cemetery. "Let's go stroll among the silent citizens of Hidden Springs."

The gate in the side yard screeched when he pushed it open and the cat appeared out of the shadows to trail along after them.

"She must think you have a mouse in your pocket," Alex said.

"Could be I smell like I do. Maybe we should put off our walk until I take a shower." With smoke and worse odors clinging to him, he wasn't at his best to entice the woman he loved into his arms.

"We've put off too much between us too many times." Alex slipped her hand under his elbow and leaned against him as they walked between the stone monuments. "Besides, you smell like life. And danger. Who would have ever imagined being a deputy sheriff in Hidden Springs would be so perilous?"

"Not me. I was happy directing traffic on high school ball game nights."

"But that wasn't meant to be."

"What was meant to be?"

"Perhaps that you would be here in Hidden Springs when you were most needed. To protect the innocent. Like Maggie. Like Anthony." She stopped in front of a tall spire and stepped away from Michael to trace the name on it with her finger. "Keane. Your roots are all around us, from Jasper right on down to your father, James."

Michael didn't take his eyes off Alex to look around. He

didn't need to. He knew the graves of the Keanes around him.

"But I'm not buried here." Relief swept through him at that thought after the events of the day. Alex was there in front of him breathing the same air he was. "Why are we here, Alex?"

"Is that a philosophical question?"

"No." He kept his eyes on her face. "Did we come out here to simply play out the goodbye scene again?"

"Is that what you want?" Her voice was low, almost timid.

"You know it isn't." The distance yawned wider between them. Two steps and he could have her in his arms, but he stayed where he was. Perhaps rooted too deeply, as she claimed.

"What do you want?"

"You know that too. You've always known that." He felt almost like he was swallowing her with his eyes. "You."

"But what about your roots?"

"We can grow new roots together wherever we are."

She was silent for a moment, but she didn't slide her gaze away from his. "I never really thought I had roots. You know how my parents were always moving when I was a kid. I used to wonder how it would feel to have your kind of roots. The type of roots people here in Hidden Springs have. But I always thought I floated above that. Free to go wherever I wanted. To land for a brief interlude or zoom off if I decided."

"Like a balloon without an anchor."

"Yes, that's what I thought. But then you asked and I answered."

"I never believed in my heart you would say no and then you did."

"I didn't think I could give any other answer. Not if I truly loved you. Not if I wanted to stay free to float wherever I willed."

He didn't say anything then, not sure if he wanted to hear her next words. He couldn't bear another knife stab to the heart.

"But I was wrong about not having an anchor. And the anchor isn't my work." Her eyes glittered in the moonlight, but she didn't move toward him. "It's you. Without you, I'll float off into outer space. Lost forever."

"A cemetery isn't the most romantic place for a proposal."

"I don't want you to propose."

"You don't?" Michael's heart was getting sore from all the rises and falls.

"No. It's my turn." She pushed away from the gravestone and stood up straight. "Michael Keane, will you marry me?"

The word yes wanted to explode out of him, but he held it back. She wasn't ready for his answer.

She took a tiny step nearer him. "I don't know if I can live in Hidden Springs. I don't know about children."

"What do you know?" His voice sounded husky in his ears.

"That I can't live without you and that I'm trembling like I just went before the judge in my first case waiting for the only answer I need right now. So what are you thinking, Michael James Keane?"

"That you are the most beautiful woman I have ever seen."

"Same old line." Her eyes glistened in the moonlight as she stared at him. "But did I win my case? Yes or no?"

"You knew the verdict before you presented your case. I will marry you, Alexandria Sheridan. Right now if you want me to wake up the county clerk to get our license. I can pull strings here in Hidden Springs."

She laughed then, the sound sweeping through the air to wrap around him. "Tomorrow will do."

"Any tomorrow you say." He held his arms out to her and she stepped into his embrace. She tilted her head up, offering him her lips. An offer he was more than willing to accept.

And then it was as if he were floating with her. Love was the only anchor they needed.

Acknowledgments

I am so blessed to be able to do what I've wanted to do ever since I was ten years old and that is to write stories. I started out, way back then, writing a wish-I-could-be-a-Hardy-Boy mystery and now many books later, I've circled back to mysteries. I thank each and every reader who has given my stories a try. I especially appreciate those of you who have trailed along with me through my Shaker books, Hollyhill and Rosey Corner family stories, a side trip back in time to 1855 Louisville, and now to Hidden Springs to solve some mysteries. You're the best.

I've also been blessed by many helping hands to turn my stories into books. Many thanks go to Lonnie Hull DuPont for liking my first Hollyhill book enough to open the door for me into the Christian publishing world. It's been great working with Lonnie on every book since then. She always sees ways to make the story better.

I appreciate Barb Barnes, whose careful editing makes my stories the best they can be. Cheryl VanAndel and her team came up with yet another outstanding cover. I love the cats on the covers of these Hidden Springs mysteries. I thank Karen Steele and Michele Misiak who are ever ready to help in so many different ways. I appreciate all the Revell and Baker people behind the scenes who get my books out to readers.

I have more blessings to count with my agent, Wendy Lawton. She's not only always ready to help with whatever I need, she's a prayer warrior for me and for all her clients.

And of course, I have to count the blessing of having a family who supports me as a writer and loves me as a wife, mother, grandmother, and sister.

Last but certainly not least, I thank the Lord for giving me stories and for letting me share those stories with you, my reading friends.

A. H. Gabhart is a pseudonym for Ann H. Gabhart, the bestselling author of more than thirty novels for adults and young adults. *Angel Sister*, Ann's first Rosey Corner book, was a nominee for inspirational novel of 2011 by *RT Book Reviews* magazine. Her Shaker novel, *The Outsider*, was a Christian Book Awards finalist in the fiction category. She lives on a farm not far from where she was born in rural Kentucky. She and her husband are blessed with three children, three in-law children, and nine grandchildren. Ann loves reading books, watching her grandkids grow up, and walking with her dog, Oscar.

Ann likes to connect with readers on her Facebook page, www.facebook.com/anngabhart, where you can peek over her shoulder for her "Sunday mornings coming down," or walk along to see what she might spot on her walks, or laugh with her on Friday smiles day. Find out more about Ann's books and check out her blog posts at www.annhgabhart.com.

Meet A. H. Gabhart at
www.AnnHGabhart.com

Be the First to Learn about New Releases,
Read Her Blog, and Sign Up for Her Newsletter

Connect with Ann at

 Ann H Gabhart
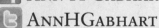 AnnHGabhart

Don't Miss the Other
HIDDEN SPRINGS MYSTERIES!

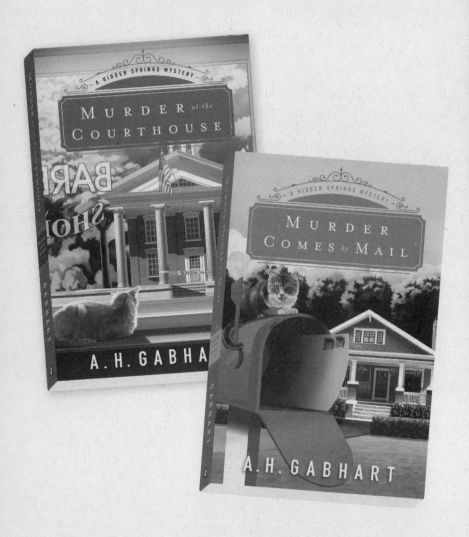

If You Liked **Murder at the Courthouse**,
You May Also Like **The Cate Kinkaid Files**

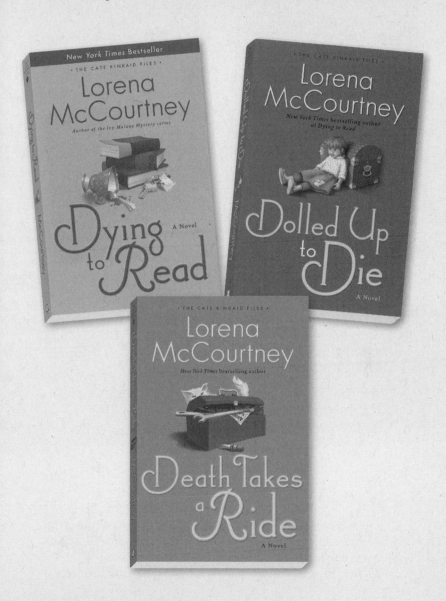

Nothing Will Be the Same
after the Summer of 1964...

Hollyhill, Kentucky, seems to be well insulated from the turbulent world beyond its quiet streets. Life-changing events rarely happen here, and when they do, they are few and far between. But for Jocie Brooke and her family, they happen all at once.